Jack Out of the Box

By

Timothy Vincent

W & B Publishers
USA

W & B Publishers

For information:
W & B Publishers
9001 Ridge Hill Street
Kernersville, NC 27284

www.a-argusbooks.com

ISBN: 9781942981909

This is a work of *fiction*. All of the characters, organizations and events portrayed in this novel are either products of the author's imagination or used fictitiously.

Cover Art and Photography by Blue Harvest Photography: blueharvestphotography.com

Printed in the United States of America

Dedication:

For my Mother.

I

"Idle Hands"

I knew better. Rule number three of the LongPost's handbook: *never deviate from your designated route....*

It was just a blip, a flicker of light on the scanner. It could have been one of a hundred things, even a mistake.

The same rule book will tell you a responsible LongPost captain keeps to his or her route at all times. But I like to think somewhere between the lines of the expressed LongPost ethos is an unspoken, unfettered adventurous spirit waiting to be released. In that light, a decision to act against every accepted protocol could be seen as a cry for independence, a small gesture to the unconquerable human spirit fighting against the heartless system.

And well, I was losing again. To Mic. That may have been part of it.

I looked from the scanner to the gameboard. My thumb-sized, three-dimensional lieutenant was signaling for support, struggling between the logical step of retreat and his personal ambition for victory. Looking across the way at Mic's encroaching army, I thought retreat a pretty good idea. But that would mean losing my hold on the hill, and that meant the battle, and that meant the war. *That* meant forty-three and zero. As in, construct of human intelligence and design, forty-three wins; representative of said intelligence, me, zero. I don't like zero.

That's when I decided to take one for the unconquerable human spirit.

"Mic," I said, turning away from the game board, "About that blip."

Mic, who was busily adjusting her flanking blue army, replied with a slightly distracted air. "What blip?"

I looked back to the board to find my lieutenant making frantic gestures toward our approaching doom, and glaring at me for help.

"The one we are going to investigate," I answered, and flipped off the game board.

As the geography and pieces began to fade to the nether world, I watched Mic's angry horde shake their fists in frustration and derision. I noted with pride that some of my men (now well accustomed to this divine and improbable intervention) dropped their drawers, turned, and offered an equally enthusiastic response. I ignored my lieutenant. Disapproval is not a quality I look for in an avatar.

"Hey!" said Mic, turning a bright crimson. "I was about to..." There followed the slightest of dry pauses. "Oh, I see."

Mobile Integrated Computer units, like the floating bowling balls they resemble, do not normally possess the ability for sarcastic irony. Somewhere in her many travels, Mic picked it up in spades. I ignored her too of course.

"Ship, take a left," I ordered.

Mic floated over to the console. "I presume you mean to follow the optical delusion?"

"No delusion, my little floating number ten. There's something out there. What's more, it's something neither you nor the ship comp is willing to recognize. That makes it worth pursuing."

"You know the ship's computer has to report this deviation from our course directory to LongPost, and why."

"Spare me the idle threats. What are they going to do, fire me?"

Mic whirled around on her axis, her internal colors revolving from deep sea blues to bright red sunsets.

"At this point, that's a distinct possibility," she reflected.

I ignored that as well, and watched her spin. She could be very pretty at times, especially when she's angry.

"A left it is then," I said with a smile.

Why left, and not right, or up, or down? Creative triangulation. What some might call flying by the seat of my pants. Both Mic and the ship's computer found this completely irresponsible and illogical, so I knew I was on the right track. Unconquerable human spirit, and all that.

Of course, to take my left I first had to pull us out of auto-pilot. The ship computer flat out refused to participate in any deviation from our appointed rounds. But I was reveling in my new dictatorial fever, and assumed the wheel without a second thought. Manual control was another strict no-no for LongPosts in deep space, except in emergency situations. All kinds of bells and alarms went off. I manually turned these off as well. I decided I liked manual control. Mic made more threatening noises, but it was just for show at this point. She knew I wasn't about to change my mind.

And that's how we turned left. I offered a silent rebel yell for liberated humanity and steered the *Pelagius* toward what I thought was the general direction of the mysterious signal's origin. Then I kicked my feet up, and gave the old girl her head. I felt much better. Time to relax.

Forty-two, and holding.

…Relaxation forms the core of my personal philosophy. Hence, my occupation as a LongPost. Nothing is more relaxing than pre-plotted, pre-programmed space travel. Crossing space, any space, is a lengthy process, no matter how fast or powerful the ship. It's a journey of decades to travel from Earth to Colony I. A LongPost might make that roundtrip three, maybe four times before retiring. Most LongPost pilots cryo through both legs, so actual up-time is more like three months, give or take. Doing cryogenic time has its risks, but it beats hell out of sitting around in a tin can for twenty or thirty years.

But why take the risk at all? It's all about the money. A LongPost pilot earns a professional salary (adjusted annually to cost of living expenses back on Earth) for the time served, not the distance. That adds up over a century or so. With a sound investment policy (and LongPost has one of the best), a pilot can comfortably retire after those three or four trips.

Seems a bit unfair? It's one of those high risks, high reward situations. First of all, the Civil Service Test and Background screening are intense, and most applicants don't make it through the initial psychological evaluation (they make you sign a waiver freeing them of legal responsibility before you get in the isolation chamber). Then there are the hard numbers: 1 in 3 LongPost suffers a debilitating or fatal accident sometime in their employment. That number goes up considerably if you do more than 3 trips.

The big-ticket item, though—the one keeps our applicant numbers down, and wages up—is the time cost. It became obvious with the first batch of retired LongPosts. It's hard to adjust to everyday living when everything you know is considered ancient, or just plain gone. Families and friends are particularly difficult. They've aged (or passed); you haven't. After the first group, they got smart. Retirees were settled away from their original homes and had to take extensive reorientation counseling. Recruiting focused on single men and women, preferably without living relatives.

I was on my fifth run. A dinosaur; a legend; an eclectic ass; a political burden—depending on who you talked to. Time had measured more than a hundred years since my first mail run. Thanks to careful cryo maintenance, and some lucky genetics, my body showed twenty of those years, and I was twitch free. With care, I reasoned I could do one more run, and retire. Then it was hello sun and sand.

But I was in no hurry. I liked the experience of deep space. I liked the solitude, the endless silence. I liked lying around with nothing but a blur of sparkle and night outside the port window. I liked the unlimited time to think, and to read. After my first run, I bought some antique books. The real thing, not the electronic versions. Leather binding, dog-ears, ink, paper, the whole tactile mess. They cost a fortune, but they provided an unexpected (and necessary) counterpoint to my otherwise modern context.

Not that I am a technophobe. Far from it. I enjoy my scientifically engineered world as much as the next person. I particularly like playing computer games. Another perk of being in space: no one bothers you about how use your time. I've honed my skills on the ship's game board in between bouts of exercise, reading, and the occasional general ship maintenance. The computer offers plenty of challenge, but is a bit flat when it comes to communication.

Mic, a Mobile Integrated Computer I'd picked up at a yard sale, was supposed to provide a more entertaining gaming partner. And she did, bringing some spark and color to the games and the *Pelagius* in general. That is, until she started winning all the time, and got an attitude. Little things, like an extra spin after a particularly clever maneuver, or a shift in color when I quit in frustration (to me, her purple always held a hint of smugness).

I suppose I should have suspected something earlier. The woman who sold her to me, a retired professor of some sort, said there was something special about the unit. I thought she was just trying to sell high.

The professor was a tiny thing, with lots of energy. She seemed amused to find me hanging around the old games section at the yard sale, and started a long, one-way conversation. She asked a lot of questions, about me. I wasn't paying much attention, because suddenly she was shaking my hand and giving me "final instructions."

That's when I realized I'd bought something. A small unit MIC floated up, shy and pensive in spinning baby blue. I remember the professor brushing something from her eye, and then taking my arm and escorting me off the yard with a big smile. I remember sitting in the car and noting the debit for the MIC on my virtual bank statement. Not cheap, I thought about returning it but didn't have the time. Frankly, I was still a little confused by the entire process. I put the MIC in my luggage for the next LongPost haul, and forgot all about it.

About two weeks later, I opened the bag, and out she came. I wasn't prepared for the change. Somewhere over the two weeks, tucked between my socks and underwear, she had lost her color—and her reserve. She informed me, in very angry tones (matched by the deepest shade of red I've ever seen) that this would be the last time she submitted to such degradation. She then proceeded to make herself at home on board my ship without so much as a by-your-leave. She's been spinning free ever since.

Of course, I did a little background check later, when she wasn't looking. Turns out the retired professor had been a specialist in theoretical computer science initiatives at MIT. Well, do tell. I'm no rocket-scientist (I just pilot them), but after a month of losing, and some ill-disguised smugness, I got suspicious. I accused Mic of tapping the ship's computer for illegal upgrades. She got so worked up over the accusation, I doubled down and asked her to submit to a full scan. To my surprise, she did. When the results indicated no anomalies, Mic was practically insufferable. For two days she stayed an iridescent white, and if she had a nose it would have been hard north.

It did occur to me that accurate diagnostics would only work if the ship's computer programming were more sophisticated than Mic. But a floating game console shouldn't come anywhere near a LongPost state of the art, fifteenth generation computer system. Maybe I was just getting beat, and should take my lumps.

And yet, there were times where I wondered just what the good professor had pawned off on me…

Like now.

We had been flying for about an hour after my blip, looking for what I didn't know, and where I had no clue. I began to suspect my little diversion had just about run its course, when Mic started humming a tune.

"What are you doing?" I asked.

"Passing the time," answered Mic. "You have your

diversions, I have mine."

I ignored that. I did a lot of ignoring around Mic.

"What's that tune?" I asked.

"It's a popular piece from the twentieth century. It is from *The Man of La Mancha*. There are lyrics. Would you like to hear them?"

"No, and stop humming. It's very rude and I'm trying to concentrate."

"Okay."

We flew in silence for a time.

"Is that the adaptation of Cervantes' novel?" I asked.

"What?"

"*The Man of La Mancha*?"

"Why, yes, it is. Want to hear the line about the hopeless quest? It might remind you of someone."

"I told you to be still."

We flew again in silence. I tried to look like I knew where I was going. Mic just sat there, hovering in haughty disapproval.

"This is important," I said, finally. "There was something on the screen."

"I understand," she answered.

"No, really," I explained. "I had to stop the game. We were getting farther and farther away."

"Of course."

"Why are you turning that shade of brown? Are you implying something?"

"My internal coloring is a random selection process," she said, "designed to be aesthetically pleasing, so as to enhance human/artifice relations."

"Oh, shut up."

"By the way," she said, in a voice I swear dripped with irony. "Are we there yet?"

"No! And listen here, if I had twenty yards of waxed flooring, some white paint and ten good pieces of wood, I'd...."

BANG!   Alarms and whistles; blinking lights and

warning flashes.
    We had arrived.

II

Pandora Knocks

Arrived where? A good question.

"Mic, could you please tell me again what this thing is, which you say isn't there, but that we're so obviously in?"

Mic consulted the ship comp for a moment before answering.

"I don't know," she said, "because it still isn't there." I noted with some satisfaction that her color had changed to a puzzled taupe.

"Or at least, it shouldn't be," she added a moment later.

"It's doing a pretty good damn job of pretending then," I retorted. "I can't get around it."

The '*it*' we were talking about was a dark nothing, and I mean pitch-dark nothing. Think of your darkest black paint, pour it on black canvas set in a black frame, then dip the whole thing in tar and throw it down a deep well, close your eyes, and try to see it. That's about how dark it was.

And it was everywhere. It filled the ship screens, all of them, backwards and forwards. I checked the console. Nothing was wrong with the external camera system as far as I could tell. What we saw on the screen was what was out there—or not there, as it were.

"Mic?" I prompted.

"I'm having the ship comp search the database, but preliminary findings indicate there is no known record of this phenomenon, apart from a black hole. Of course, this is definitely not a black hole, or we wouldn't be talking right now."

As I took that cheery detail in, a number of other

possible explanations came to mind, none of them particularly happy. The rebel yell was becoming a bit shrill. Suddenly, normal, official, somewhat boring postal route protocol didn't look so bad.

It was time for another cautionary retreat.

"Mic, how about telling the ship's computer to get us out of here?"

"Now he says."

"Just do it."

"Right."

I waited.

Nothing happened. I looked over to Mic, who was turning multiple shades of crimson and spinning like crazy.

"Well?"

"The problem is," she answered, slowing down. "I can't. Neither the ship comp, nor I, can get a reading of any kind outside the *Pelagius*. It's as if we were no longer in physical space. And without a spatial relation point, the ship refuses to move. It's a failsafe program."

"Come again?"

"Since we are no longer located in space," she said carefully, "I cannot have the ship move us out of *here* or *there*, or for that matter anywhere."

"Just put it in reverse and press the pedal," I offered helpfully.

"First, are you sure reverse is the way to go? Second, the pedal, as you call it, is offline. The ship can't or won't move at any speed or direction."

"How about firing the guns?"

"At what?"

"Anything. Everything." I said in exaggerated authority. "Whatever the hell is holding us back. Hit a broadside, by God! Damn the torpedoes, and all that."

"I would caution against using what limited projectiles we have until we know what the nature of our captivity includes," she replied. "Otherwise, we run the risk of damaging ourselves."

This was, of course, a reasonable caution.

But I wasn't feeling very reasonable. "Okay. What would you suggest? Send up the white flag? Flush the commode?"

"Oh, you're taking my suggestions now? If you recall, just an hour ago I suggested we don't deviate from our flight plan."

Apparently, Mic wasn't feeling all that reasonable, either.

"All right," I said. "Let it go."

"Go! That's just what you said you had to do, and look where that's got us."

"Enough already."

She stopped, but not because I told her to.

The black abyss around us had grown a crack. Or to be more accurate, a slice of light had opened like a rift down the center of the view screens, cutting it in half. As we watched, the light slowly expanded to either side until it eventually filled the screen. Where before everything was black, now it was white: gleaming, pristine polished, white; a white so white that your eyes ached to look at it.

I panned the cameras and discovered perfect white-out in every direction—every direction but one. The starboard camera was showing what looked suspiciously like an etched door frame.

"That looks promising," noted Mic.

"Maybe," I answered.

"We probably should investigate, don't you think?"

I sighed. "Probably."

The atmosphere was in my favor (that much, at least, the ship could tell me), so no suit was necessary. But I had decided to obey the rules again, so I took a few moments to put on my standard-issue LongPost All-purpose Personal Decompression Suit. The deflated version of the suit was quite comfortable, and had the added advantage of being self-cleaning. It also functioned as a personal hygiene system, but the less said on that the better. The helmet-hood had a pliable front visor which could be fashionably tucked in the neck collar when not in use. It didn't look too bad, if you like high collars. And, of course, the whole thing could inflate into a full-bodied spacesuit in less than 7 seconds, capable of withstanding deep space conditions and providing forty-eight hours of oxygen via its micro-density O2 cell packs. That's a nice feature to have around you when you walk into the unknown.

We left the *Pelagius*, and I stood on the bottom of the ramp with Mic tucked in my official LongPost satchel. I had decided Mic should go incognito and out of sight, which simply involved her retracting her outer shell to core status (i.e., bowling ball to cue ball), and carrying her in the satchel. She wasn't exactly thrilled with this arrangement, but recognized the tactical advantages and went along.

"No signs of life," said Mic over my ear port. "But then again, I can't pick up anything on my scanners anyway."

"Shh," I muttered, trying not to move my lips. "Incognito means no frivolous talk."

"How is that frivolous?"

"Be still."

There was a floor, so to speak. It was like walking on a bowl of marbleized milk. My feet kept telling my brain that we were on solid ground, but my eyes couldn't seem to agree. It helped to keep my eyes almost closed, and let my feet determine reality.

The door proved to be just that, or at least a sketch of one. The frame was a simple vertical rectangle of etched black lines, about eight feet high and three across. There was no apparent handle.

"Now what?" I asked.

"Try to open it," said Mic over the port.

I waved my hand, stepped back, then forth, then side to side, said "open sesame," barked, made funny faces— everything I could think of, short of actually touching the funny white material. From up close, the surface looked to be glowing, making it near the top of my personal *Do Not Touch* list. After about a minute of performance art, I gave up.

"Okay, Mic. I'm open for suggestions again."

"Knock."

I frowned, rolled my eyes, and then remembered she couldn't see my face.

"That would mean touching it," I said.

"Of course." That dry tone again.

I thought about it, and then had an inspiration. I took Mic out.

"Hey," she started, "what are you doing?"

I tapped her hard cue-ball form against the surface somewhere close to the middle of the frame.

Nothing.

"That was extremely dangerous," said Mic, her color now a pale winter's snow.

"And fruitless," I agreed.

"Which means it's your turn."

I shoved her back in the satchel. "Be still. Hide. Incommunicado."

But she was right; there was only one thing left to do. I reached out to touch the frame with the tip of my gloved finger. One, two, three…okay, four, five….

Eventually, I did touch it. Things happened, as they are bound to do. First, the "door" disappeared. In its place was a framed view of a long hallway. It was like one of those hologram windows you see sometimes in an art museum or fancy hotel lobby, the kind that hangs there like a window to another dimension. I stepped in, of course. What else could I do? I had the odd sensation of walking into a giant rolling barrel, one that suddenly stops just before your foot touches the bottom. I reached out a hand to catch myself, but drew it back again as my feet found their balance, and my inner ears reoriented.

I looked around. To either side were dark wood paneling walls. The ceiling, which was low, was a spackle of dull plaster, and the floor was covered with a thin burgundy carpet. The space where I stepped through was now a similarly solid wall of wood paneling, complete with a framed painting hanging in the center. The painting was of a rather melancholy cliff overlooking a beach. I reached out, tapped the wall. Nothing happened.

I turned back to the hallway.

Immediate first impressions: Edgar Allen Poe, creepy Victorian mansions, and the sense of not wanting to be here. The air was musty and heavy with the rich, oily smell of polished furniture. There was a lone table-clock ticking away on a nightstand next to me, but otherwise the hall was eerily still. More landscape paintings lined the walls, all dark, all austere: scenes of cliffs and sheep, cliffs and ships, cliffs and people. Somebody liked cliffs.

Glass oil lamps were mounted periodically on the walls, their dim, smoky panels making as many shadows as they drove away. Halfway down the corridor was an ornate end table with an ancient fountain pen and ledger. The hall ended in a cross section, with more shadowy halls to the right and left.

Frankly, it was not at all what I expected.

"Life forms," said Mic in my ear. "At least one."

Pause to let my heart start again. "One of them isn't by chance a big dog," I asked, "or some kind of axe wielding butler, is it?"

"What do you mean by big dog?"

I pulled Mic out again and showed her the hallway. "What do you make of all this?" I asked. "Because I feel like I just walked into the Baskervilles' summer home." I turned around, still holding Mic. "And where's the door back?"

A thin metal rod extended from Mic's center and touched the paneled wood wall next to me. This surprised me almost as much as my surroundings. I didn't know she could do that.

Mic retracted her probe. "There appears to be something

beyond the wall, but it's a real wall."

Before I could reply, I heard the unmistakable sound of a human cry from somewhere down the hall.

"Did you hear that?" I asked.

"Yes."

I put Mic back in the satchel and pulled out my other critical supply, a gift from my sister for the long treks far from home: a 9-shot, large caliber, antique pistol. The fact that it was a bit old helped me get it by LongPost regulations (I claimed it as an heirloom). Heavy and still highly lethal, the weight made me feel better just holding it. I took a deep breath. This wasn't going to make the boys and girls back in LongPost central happy. Rule number 42: *Never, under any circumstances, engage in private affairs while running your designated route.*

I checked the safety, and started down the hallway, stopping for a quick peek at the book on the table. It was obviously a ledger of some kind. A header with *Guests* and *Date,* ran across the top. There were a number of listings underneath. The signatures below were written by various hands, some legible, others barely. I didn't have time to do a quick study, but didn't see any names I immediately recognized. They were all dated 1888.

I started off again.

The sounds of struggle grew clearer as I reached the end of the hallway. I took the left-hand passage, as that seemed to be where they were coming from. I was now in a short passage, similar to the one I just left. The cries were coming from an open door to my right. Peeking around the corner, I saw a study-sized room with more dark wood walls and plush burgundy carpet—and a man dressed in odd clothes, struggling to close a giant vault door in the back wall. It was clear that someone on the other side of the vault was working toward the opposite end.

The man in view had his shoulder to the door, and his face was red with exertion. He made no noise, but from the other side came a string of grunts, curses, and what sounded like human imprecation.

"Never!" hissed the man on my side of the vault, and with renewed force he dug his heels into the floor. I watched as the vault began slowly to close. Just as success looked inevitable, the vault door stopped its progress and I saw what looked to be a metal pipe sticking out from the other side. The man on my side yelled in frustration, grabbed the pipe and tried to pull it through. As he released his grip on the vault, however, it started slowly opening again. He quickly let go of the pipe and stopped the vault's progress once more.

At this point the man on my side turned his head and saw me in the doorway. His look of astonishment changed quickly to one of hope and supplication.

"Hurry, for God's sakes!" he shouted. "Help me!"

I don't know why, perhaps it was some ancient instinct against the unknown, or maybe it was the complete desperation in his voice, but I found myself wanting to stop that door from opening. I tucked the pistol in my satchel, and raced across the room to put a shoulder next to his. With my aid it was easy to stop the vault's progress, but a shoed-foot now accompanied the pipe in the opening and our struggle came to another temporary impasse.

"Hold it!" ordered the man next to me. He then let go of the vault and stomped upon the obstructing foot, at the same time jerking the pipe from whomever, or whatever, held it on the other side. The foot was quickly withdrawn with a gasp of pain. My companion slammed his full weight against the vault, and this time it swung shut with an audible click. He then pressed a button in a panel set in the center of the vault door. Immediately the gunmetal gray was replaced by the same glowing white substance that held the *Pelagius*.

Without looking at me, the man then turned and ran to an odd, but very modern console in another corner of the room. He seemed to be searching for something.

"Ah ha!" he cried, pressing a series of keys. I heard a deep metallic grind, and when I turned around the mysterious white wall was gone, replaced by wood paneling. The only reminder of the vault's presence was the button panel in the middle of the otherwise solid wooden wall.

The man grinned at me in excited triumph. "Yes!" he cried. "Finally."

He looked me up and down. "Who are you?"

Then he slumped to the floor of the dais in exhausted relief.

III

Victorian Space

I helped him climb to his feet again. He was short, somewhere well below six feet. His complexion was waxy and very pale, as if he had not seen the sun for some time. He wore a dark moustache and full beard, but was balding on top, and was dressed in a long, formal smoking jacket, starched white shirt, pleated pants, and hard leather shoes. Behind the facial hair he had a relatively simple face, but for the eyes. These were of the darkest black, the kind of eyes you remember long after you lose the face. I found those eyes searching my own and felt oddly naked.

"Thank you," he said, breaking the silence.

"You're welcome."

"You are not from this ship, are you?" he asked.

"No. I just arrived."

"You are from Earth?"

"I've been there, was born there in fact. But this time I'm coming from the other end: Colony I."

"Colony I," he repeated. Those black eyes lost some of their focus, but none of their hypnotic appeal. "You have a ship?"

"Yes."

The eyes held fire for a moment. I didn't like the direction the conversation was heading.

"Who are you?" I asked, trying to turn the direction. I nodded to the vault-now-turned-wall. "And what was that about?"

He looked to the wall, his eyes focusing again and drawing to tight lines. "Ah, yes. That." He looked to the floor, then back to me. "That's a long tale. Which you are entitled to," he added quickly. "But first, I must beg your patience a little longer. There are things I must check on. He was out, you see? He may have done things. I won't be long. When I get back we can talk more. Will you wait here?"

"Do you want some help?"

"No," he said. Then, more slowly and with a smile, "No. It is kind of you to offer, but no. I will not be long."

"I'll wait then."

He started away, but before he reached the door I called after him. "By the way, if you come upon my ship in one of your checks, please be careful. The security systems are fully automated."

He stood in the doorway for a moment, the black eyes measuring mine. Then, with an abrupt laugh, he nodded and left.

I wasn't too worried about the *Pelagius*. It was true about the security systems. The veiled threat was just for added insurance. I looked around the room, and got my first real impression. It was an odd mix of old and new. The lighting was provided again by boxed gas lights mounted to the walls. Two overstuffed chairs faced a coffee table in front of an old-fashioned brick fireplace. There appeared to be a real wood-burning fire behind its iron grating. *Neat trick that*, I thought. Along most of the walls were numerous framed paintings, some quite large. The open door I came through was one of those clever affairs made to look like part of a bookcase when closed.

Spoiling all this aesthetic was the very modern, very sleek pie-shaped dais in the corner of the room, upon which sat the black marble console the man had used to seal the vault-wall. The console was full of glowing hieroglyphs, flashing buttons, and empty video screens.

"Is he really gone? Can you track him?"

"Yes, and yes," said Mic, over my earport.

"Good. I think we should do some exploring before he gets back."

I opened the pouch, and Mic took to the air.

"Keep an eye open for his return, and don't let him see you," I said. "You've got the console. Find a way to free the *Pelagius*, if you can. I'll take the rest of the room."

Mic expanded to bowling ball size and floated to the console. She was welcome to it. I took a stroll to the vault wall, for a closer look at the more immediate problem.

The hand-sized rectangular panel the stranger used to seal the vault now sat in a slight recess in the wall. The top half of the panel had two buttons, one pale blue, the other a dark red. The red one was depressed. The bottom half of the panel was filled with a pattern of raised dots, like Braille, but I didn't recognize the pattern. As I stepped closer, I felt something slippery under my shoe. Looking down I discovered a small dark stain. I smeared it around a little with the toe of my shoe and saw the dark turn to red. I didn't remember any cuts or wounds on my recent ally, so I guessed the blood belonged to whoever was on the other side of the vault.

Finished with the panel, I moved around the rest of the room. I discovered, with a slightly burned finger, that the fire was real. I spent some time looking carefully up what I could see of the chimney, and wondering where the smoke went to.

That got me to thinking about where I was exactly. The white emptiness had been one thing, this hybrid Victorian-Sci-Fi, quiet another. Neither, however, gave me any insight as to where I'd landed. Assuming I landed anywhere. Was this a ship? A planet? Some kind of vortex? Maybe all of this was a dream? Or maybe I was dead, and this was the afterlife? I looked to Mic. She was busy hovering over one of the console's glowing sections. If this was the afterlife, why was she here?

I walked around the room, touching things, thinking, and idly checking out the art. I was particularly drawn to one of the paintings hanging on the back wall. It was hard to miss. The framed canvas was at least six feet in height. The scene was of a sullen man trapped in the branches of a tree. A woman in a long dress was in the act of turning to regard him. She had a book in her hand, as if she were reading to him. The man looked lost and angry.

"Exploring the art world?" asked a voice behind me, startling me out of my reflection. I didn't bother to turn around.

"I don't expect you to understand, Mic," I said. "This could be an important clue."

"I'm sure."

"So," I said, turning around. "What did you discover?"

"I managed to retrieve a working schematic of the general structure from the console records." She seemed to hesitate, her revolutions slowing just a bit. "I'm working on the white material that is holding the *Pelagius*—that's still proving to be a problem."

"So, we can't leave?" I asked.

"Not until we understand what is holding the ship." Her color turned a very soft white.

"Tell me more about the console technology," I said.

Mic shifted to a smoldering sunset, then to a practical light gray. "It's not actually a computer-system as we know it, though there are elements that resemble one. The schematic data was easily retrieved, but the rest is tied up with an odd coding language. I'm currently upgrading my systems to translate the coding. It will take some time to process it completely, of course."

"You can do that?" I asked, forgetting for a moment that this was a can of worms I didn't want to explore. "I thought you were limited to formal axiom systems. I've never heard of a Mobile *learning* a new language, computer or otherwise."

Mic turned a deep crimson. "Yes, never mind that now. And *no*, I didn't cheat in any of our games, so don't start that again. The point is I have processed some of the console's language—let's just call it that for now—and I have information."

I frowned. *Never mind that now*, indeed. Mic could not possibly possess that kind of programming. In fact, I wasn't aware of any system that could learn a new language. This put the can-opener to the worm tin again. Mic's recent months of insufferable confidence, her intuitive leaps, and wry rejoinders were simply beyond a personal computer companion. She knew it too, judging by her current pensive yellow-brown coloring. But she was right about the timing as well, so I put the can away again, unopened, for now.

"So, what did you learn?" I asked.

"From what I've accessed so far, it looks like our ship is held in one of the points of an immense icosahedron."

"Come again?"

"The construct—I'm not sure whether to call it an asteroid, space station, or just some strange celestial body at this time, but either way we are definitely inside it—has a very unusual shape. It is a geometric icosahedron. Think of a three-dimensional star, or a snowflake with 20 convex sides. Now extend triangular points or spikes from every angle of the core." She stopped and projected a three-dimensional image of just what she said: a many-pointed, three-dimensional star. It looked a little like a pincushion with giant blue, red, and gold extended triangles, or a giant soccer ball with blades. The whole thing was rotating slowly on axis.

"I think we are near the corner of one of the vertices here at the bottom." One of the paneled triangular points grew brighter. "Our ship is in the tip of the spike. When we traversed the white space, or door, into the hall, we moved further down the spike. We are now in the core segment." A corresponding spot near the edge of the inner globe flashed briefly.

"Not a very big ship then?" I pointed out.

"On the contrary. It is immense. About the size of a small planet."

"Planet?"

"Yes," she answered. "Very similar to Earth, in fact, apart from the fact that we are inside and not on the surface. You are breathing oxygen, gravity is generated relative to the flooring, and this room, the hall we traveled, and the ship's location are clearly pressurized. Something is working to create a livable atmosphere. I'm not certain, but I suspect the spikes and white material are somehow responsible."

"How come we couldn't see it from the *Pelagius*?" I asked.

"The outer surface of the construct," she answered, highlighting the surface and spikes, "not only repels light, but also acts like a focused vacuum of space. This is what masked the structures presence to our detection systems."

"Stealth technology," I suggested.

"Better."

"So, this thing, the size of a planet, could approach Earth or a Colony, and no one would ever know it was there?"

"Theoretically," she said. "Although it would have to stay some distance, or we would begin to see causal effects on Earth."

"Tell me more about the white material."

"It's everywhere."

"Everywhere?"

"Everywhere. It's in the objects you see around you, the flooring, and, apparently, the air you are breathing."

"But what is it?"

"When in its malleable form—the white material—it is like light, only solid."

"Solid light? Isn't that impossible?"

"That's the best I can do for now. Apparently, it can be manipulated to take on the actual form and appearance of other materials and phenomena, like the pictures in the hallways and the furniture in this room."

I looked to the fire.

"Speaking of rooms," she added a moment later, "there appears to be a tremendous amount of them in this section of the core."

"This section?" I prodded.

"Here," she answered, rotating the 3D image again, and highlighting the inner space. Two large vertical lines now segmented the snowflake core, roughly dividing it into three unequal portions, the largest section being the center space. A third line ran horizontally, almost, but not quite, a third of the way up the core. The right hand vertical segment, the smallest, was now highlighted in blue above the horizontal line.

"That's our current location," she confirmed, making the small blue section flash. "The schematic I pulled from the console suggests a complex system of rooms, corridors, flooring, stairways, elevators, roads, and open space." The image of our section expanded and began to be populated with more and more divisions, until I was looking at a complex blueprint of space and lines.

"The central core," continued Mic, the image revolving again, now highlighting in yellow the large middle vertical section, "is more topographical; full of open space and even what appear to be large bodies of water." This time the image remained relatively flat but for a few mountainous risings, and what looked to be clouds along the top.

"The final segment," she continued, highlighting the far left section in black, "is unreadable to me, as is the bottom portion." "Likely a transcription error, or some kind of firewall. I'm working on it."

"Okay," I said, just to sound like I was keeping up. The giant pincushion now looked like some kind of sick urchin.

"Something else you should know," said Mic, turning a soft white again. "I'm not getting a complete reading of any section, including this room. There are a number of dead or blank spaces, like the wall-vault over there. Either these spaces are deliberately left out of the schematics, or beyond my abilities to read. What's more interesting, is some of the rooms I *can* read appear to have no direct access."

"Hidden doors, secret entrances. Sounds like a fun house."

"Are you having fun?" she asked, revolving into a sooty puce.

"Hmm. Maybe we can approach this another way. This

looks a little familiar." I turned to the painting. "Tell me more about it."

"It should," she answered. "It's called *The Beguiling of Merlin*, by Edward Burne-Jones. Victorian era. But it's another puzzle."

"Why?"

"The problem is the reproduction. It's too good. It reproduces the original to the smallest detail. I'm comparing this one now with one I have in my files. Even the frame is the same. But it simply can't be the original, as that is currently residing on Earth in a museum." She floated a little closer, becoming a reflective green. "Yet, if it *is* a copy, it is, in a real sense, an exact copy. The carbon readings on the frame, the canvas, the actual paint strokes and signature— they are precisely the same as the original."

"I see," I said. "That is a puzzle." Frankly, I wasn't as worried about this as she appeared to be. "What about this one?" I pointed to a smaller painting further along the wall. It depicted a giant woman flanked by panthers. She was pouring something into a flask of wine. Where the first painting was moody and full of smoky blues and olives, this one was a vivid blend of yellow, scarlet, and gold, the figures more defined.

"Also by Burne-Jones" answered Mic. "It's called, *The Wine of Circe*. And yes, it too is an exact copy. By the way, Circe was a mythological figure said to be responsible for turning Odysseus' men into swine. Not a difficult task, I grant you, given the subject matter to work with."

I ignored the commentary, but put another tick by the troubling Mic behavior list.

"It certainly is an interesting selection," I noted. "Any thoughts in that direction?" I around looked the room. The other paintings were similarly dark.

"Artistic talent aside," said Mic, "it reflects a rather provincial attitude toward woman. In its time, the practice was called *femme fatale*."

I noted Mic's color was a smoldering sunset as she said

this. I filed that reaction away, too; for that later conversation. One problem at a time.

"Okay," I said. "Not much help in getting our ship free, but we're getting a better picture of our circumstances. Here's the plan as I see it: play for time and information. We need to find out what exactly we've gotten ourselves into. You continue to process…"

She stopped me with a flash of yellow and an abrupt, "He's coming back."

Before I could even think to open the satchel, she sped across the room floor and up the chimney.

The stranger stood in the doorway. If he had seen anything, he didn't let on. Instead, he crossed the room to offer me his hand.

"Allow me to introduce myself formally," he said with a warm smile. "George Bell."

"Benjamin Lasak." He had a strong grip.

"Please, won't you join me for tea?" He waived a hand at the overstuffed chairs. "We can rest easy. I believe I have secured everything for now."

He walked to the console, and fiddled with the controls. "Now, let's make things a little more comfortable."

I took a seat and watched as the dais and black alien console turn to white in much the same way as the vault. A moment later, the white substance morphed into a frosted glass cabinet and the floor was covered by the room's burgundy carpet. I could see a miniature version of the console set in the middle shelf of the cabinet.

I turned at a sound to my left. A large globe was slowly emerging from the floor. I turned at another sound to find an ancient music device—a phonograph, I think—rising from the floor to the right of the fire place. Music soon started playing softly from its elaborate horn. At the same time, the boxed lighting fixtures dimmed and the fire sprang to life. Any evidence of modernity or alien technology was now completely gone. I was in a Victorian parlor.

Nodding with satisfaction at my reaction, Bell opened

the glass cabinet and withdrew a full serving tray, complete with a steaming pot of tea and two ornate china cups. He brought it to the small table between the stuffed chairs and poured. He handed me a cup, with a smile.

I took it, shaking my head in wonder. I looked to the steaming cup, the phonograph, the globe.

"Please," he said, waving me on. "Take your time."

As it was closest, I turned to the globe. It was obviously real, and of the highest craftsmanship, and it had a sense of antiquity that only the genuine article can carry off. Constructed of black marble, it was overlaid with gold filament longitude and latitude lines, with painted bronze gores. Judging from the continents, it looked to be of Earth. I guessed the whole thing would have fetched a small fortune.

I sat back in my chair, which was surprisingly comfortable, and took a sip of the tea. It was very good. I hadn't forgotten about Mic, and wondered how she was doing up the chimney. I took comfort in the fact that if she was in trouble, she would have let me know over the earport.

Bell sat in the high-backed chair opposite me, and put one leg casually over the other. He raised his tea cup, watching me curiously over the rim, and then took a long, careful sip. Finished, he set the cup on the saucer beside him with a slight clink. He offered me another faint smile. Apparently, he was in no hurry to give me that long story.

"I like your art work," I said.

He looked to the paintings with a surprise, as if seeing them there for the first time. "I prefer Sickert." He smiled again.

"You were going to explain," I said, risking a little directness.

"Ah, yes." The smile fell off just slightly. "I did say that." He glanced shyly across his tea. "Please forgive me for staring, Mr. Lasak. It has been some time since I've seen anyone...new. I'm afraid I am a little rusty on entertaining company."

"I understand." I also understood he was stalling. "You

have a very comfortable place here. Great trick with the pop-up furniture." I took a sip of tea, and gave him my own over-the-rim stare.

"Pop up furniture," he repeated slowly. "How quaint. Thank you."

"Anyway, how about we start with that," I said, and nodded toward the vault.

I got another smile for my effort. I didn't blame him. I would be playing it cagey, too. I *was* playing it cagey. The difference was, he owed me.

He seemed to be thinking along the same lines. "I must thank you, again," he said, finally. "For your assistance. You have no idea what it means, of course."

He set his tea down. "Put simply sir, you have saved my life, and perhaps the world."

I didn't answer. What was I supposed to say?

He looked distractedly to the floor, those black eyes deep and full. "You must think that a bit dramatic. But I assure you, I don't exaggerate."

We sipped our tea for a time in silence while he looked for his next line in the carpet.

"Would you care for something to eat?" he asked suddenly, looking up. "Some biscuits, perhaps?"

"I'm good."

"Right."

He withdrew again, just like that. Then, very slowly, "Believe it or not, Mr. Lasak, you see before you a man who has not seen another fellow human being for several *hundred* Earth years." He lifted his face slowly, clearly waiting for a reaction. When he didn't get it, he raised a quizzical eyebrow. "I must admit you took that better than I thought you would."

"I sensed a bit of history here," I said. "You seem to go with the décor."

"Ah, yes I see. Of course. You are familiar with the Victorian era, then?"

"Only what I picked up in Dickens and history class,

and that was brief—and a long time ago."

He grimaced. "A bit plebeian for my tastes, Dickens."

We played the silence and sipping game again for a time. If this was how people actually conversed back in his time—sip, look, innuendo, sip, look, more innuendo—no wonder the Victorians were considered so tight.

"Well," he said. "I wonder if this next bit will meet your great expectations."

He chuckled around his belated pun. And then those black eyes were suddenly going right through me, and I forgot all about my bladder. "The man you helped me with, the one now trapped behind the vault, that man is none other than Jack the Ripper."

IV

Bell's Tale

I set my cup down, met Bell's eyes.

He nodded. "Yes."

"Please," I said. "Go on."

"London," he continued, looking to a spot on the globe, "That's where it all started. A jungle, I believe your Dickens called it, or something like that. The elite lived their well-kept and isolated lives of luxury, naively trusting the jungle would be kept safely outside their ornate parlor doors by natural class order and a few well-placed Bobbies. It was in this place that he made his mark, the man known as Jack the Ripper. Do you know his story?"

"Jack the Ripper is still a source of interest and study on Earth," I admitted. "The first recorded, if not the most notorious serial killer to walk earth."

"So," said Bell with a slow, appreciative nod, "they still discuss, Jack. And what do they say of the notorious Leather Apron?"

"Well, my experience is mostly from trivia and computer games."

Bell's face grew dark. "Trivia? Games? Jack the Ripper reduced to games!" His eyes grew dangerously narrow, and he ground his teeth.

I picked up my cup again, while he regained his composure. I was starting to see the benefits of having a cup in hand at such times. Maybe the Victorians knew what they were about, after all.

"Well," he continued a moment later, "if the world has forgotten Jack's darker nature, perhaps that's for the best. Though, I must say, for one so involved in the history, it is a bitter pill to swallow."

And there it was again: *involved* in the history. I looked around the Victorian parlor, remembering the recent and fantastic changes, the modern console, the white substance holding my ship, the fact that we were far, far from the place—not to mention time—of Jack the Ripper. "How," I asked, "did Jack the Ripper end up here? Or, for that matter, you?"

Bell hesitated a long time before answering. When he spoke, it was from a position of evident caution. "I know very little about you, Mr. Lasak," he said. "How do I know I can trust someone who speaks so lightly of Jack the Ripper?"

"Well I did help *you* without question," I noted, nodding to where the vault used to be.

"That is true," he admitted. "And I've told you part of my story, including the identity of the man you helped me fight, and my own. Perhaps, you could share just a small part of your own now. A give and take, if you will. To build mutual trust. Your ship, for example. I would imagine you did not voluntarily enter this world. Knowing this place as I do, I would guess your ship is no longer operational, despite your insinuations earlier. Am I correct?"

Ouch. I was hoping that subject wouldn't come up again for some time. But Bell had a point. It was probably my turn to share.

"You are right," I answered. "I'm stuck." Then, because I didn't think he should have it all his way. "But the ship is still functional in some capacities. The guns still work, and the other defense measures."

He turned his head slightly, and met my eyes. "I see."

We did our tea-sipping dance again.

"The point remains," he continued. "We may be of assistance to each other, should we choose to cooperate." He let this last hang in the air, and watched me carefully.

"Any assistance you could give me would be most welcomed," I said. "And, I will gladly reciprocate."

"Here's to that, then," he said, with a hopeful

expression.

I had a suspicion this mutual assistance might involve my taking a passenger on the *Pelagius*, another definite no-no in the LongPost rulebook, but I nodded in kind.

"And now," I said. "The story?"

"Very well, Mr. Lasak," he answered. He adjusted his seat, and crossed his legs again. "Back in London, I worked occasionally for a practical detective, one Carter Jones. He was no Dr. Forbes Winslow, but he imagined himself to be. He referred to me as his heels. I ran down leads, interviewed witnesses, that kind of thing. The work was infrequent, but it supplemented my modest inheritance nicely. I was grateful for the jobs he sent my way.

"One September morning, Jones called on me, nearly out of breath with excitement. I was to attend an inquest of one Polly Nichols, he said, a recently murdered prostitute. He was going to take on the case—sans client, of course— and if I was willing to work for a percentage of future wages, if any, then I could help him. Like everyone else, I had heard of the horrible circumstances of her murder, and was morbidly curious. I agreed."

He shifted in his seat, and sighed. "Why are we so drawn to the misfortune of others, I wonder? Ah, there it is. We are." He glanced at me, then waved his hand, as if dismissing the point. "To be honest, the inquest was a farce. A few pathetic little men pretending to be bastions of order, pointing their stubby little noses in all directions and looking for answers in all the same tired directions. It was an era that still believed in certain rules of class. Evidence in these cases was often merely a luxury, particularly when a ready list of common criminals was already in hand. Expediency was what was called for. Whores died, reasoned the investigative panel, because they lived like animals. They had but to look among the other animals to find the cause, and that would be that. Or so they reasoned."

He took a breath, his black fathomless eyes growing distant and bright. "But they didn't know what they were dealing with. This one was beyond their pathetic intuitions. He didn't stop with just poor Polly. No matter how many they detained, or how many patrols they put on the street, he didn't stop." Those eyes stared for a time at the bottom of his teacup as if searching for some meaning. "It was terrible. Horrific. He preyed on the misfortunate, the lowest of low, those willing to sell their bodies for a pittance, in order to temporarily feed their hunger for drink or food. You can almost see the knowing smiles, the air of irony, the promise of carnal pleasures, and of course, money. But they got more than they bargained for, much more."

He glanced at me again, nodded, as if approving of my expression. "Do you know his methods?" he asked, but went on before I could answer. "He strangled the victim first, which was clever; less blood that way when he cut her throat. He was quick and skilled with a knife, too. That was obvious. He liked to play, you see. He often created little displays of his handy work around the victim."

He cocked his head and bore into me with those odd eyes. "He put viscera on the shoulder of one. Took her most private parts out with one neat cut of the knife, like a butcher cutting up a pig, and put it there for all to see. Just there, next to her sweet face. Another had her kidney removed, and later sent to a newspaper. Dr. Phillips reported in the Post Mortem of Annie Chapman—the poor woman with her uterus removed—that the work was definitely that of a master."

Bell shook his head, as if turning from a foul odor. "Can you imagine? Poor, disreputable souls with little to be thankful for, full of disease and despair, and the one role they've come to rely on for food and substance, now turned against them? The wretches of London's streets lived for a time on the knife's edge, Mr. Lasak. Yes, literally the knife's edge. It was terrible, sir, terrible."

He paused, took a deep breath, and dropped his eyes again. "I'm sorry. As you can see, it is still fresh for me, even after all these years." He fidgeted for a time with the arm of his chair, then continued. "The whole of London took note. Day after day, the papers told the story. Day after day, we followed along, waiting for the next death, the next maniacal clue or letter. Then, one day, it just stopped. No conclusive arrests were made. No one knew what became of him. Gone. Vanished into thin air. His message, his purpose, whatever it may be, just a nightmare left incomplete. At least, that was how it seemed to us."

He lifted his head again. "But it was not the end. I alone discovered where and why he disappeared to. I discovered, too, the true purpose behind his terrible work."

He looked down at his tea, drained the cup and stood to pour another. "More?" he offered, turning to me.

"Yes," I said without thinking. "Please."

"It was in the year 1889," he continued, pouring my tea, "when I received a tip about a certain gentleman lodging at Finsbury Street. This was just around the time Jack stopped, you understand. The housekeeper, Callaghan, noticed that the gentleman lodger kept odd hours, and had unusual habits with his clothes and bed. The gentleman's landlady complained of bloodstains on the sheets, and found disturbing bits of writings about women left on the writing desk. The gentleman was observed to change his clothes often, and at irregular times, as well. Nothing concrete, mind you, but it was enough for Jones to send me out to investigate. I went down to the lodgings, and interviewed the landlady and the neighbors. I even managed to search the lodger's rooms." He winked at me. "A hidden talent. One that my employer, Jones, appreciated but never discussed."

He put the pot down on the tray, and settled in his chair again, making a small noise of satisfaction as he sipped at his fresh cup. "I can't tell you how good is to just sit and enjoy a cup of tea, everything back in its order." His eyes slid briefly to the vault wall. "Where was I? Yes, I found some notes hidden in a drawer. They were the ramblings of a madman. They disturbed me. The lodger's name was Wentworth Smith. I felt certain we had found our man. I reported back to Jones, and I told him to keep it under hat, until we could arrange something with the police. But Jones, that self-serving bastard, ran directly to the press.

"It was disastrous. Smith somehow found out before the press release, before we could act, and disappeared. When the police read the paper clippings, they called Jones out. The sniveling fool collapsed during the interrogation, and to save his hide completely retracted the newspaper story, saying he'd been misquoted, taken advantage of. The theory and the suspect fell apart. Mr. Wentworth Smith disappeared not only from his apartment but from the focus of the police investigations. And that was that. Jones and I had a row about the whole thing. He dropped me, of course, though I'd not seen a penny for my efforts. I tried, then, in my own way, to have the police investigate the matter further, certain that Smith was our man. They wouldn't give me the time of day. I'm sure my association with Carter Jones had something to do with that fact."

He stretched his legs, and shook his head again. Then he met my eyes, his lips pressed tight together, forming a bloodless line. He shrugged, and looked away.

"I eventually found Mr. Wentworth Smith," he continued, his soft tones undermining what must have been an arduous task. "Mostly through obstinate persistence, and just plain luck. A longtime informant knew of my ongoing interest, and said a gentleman matching Smith's description was holed up in a seedy apartment above a bar. This was about a year after my debacle with Jones. The killer had not been heard of for some time, and many suspected that he was either dead or in hiding. The odds were long that this was my Smith, but I ran it down, just the same. I immediately took a carriage over, armed with my revolver. By the time I arrived it was dusk. I entered the bar, and asked to see the person in charge of renting the rooms above."

He lifted his head, waved his hand in the air as if batting away flies. "Vanity makes fools of the wisest men, Mr. Lasak. It pains me to admit this to you, but here I made a mistake. He was very clever you see, my quarry. He had left instructions with the bartender to alert him about any such inquiries, instructions and a healthy retainer. The bartender made good on the killer's precautions, and went to tip my hand almost immediately.

"But if I made an error in my approach, I made up for it with my natural suspicion. I watched the bartender carefully as he left, you see. Something in his manner put me on alert. As soon as he was out of sight, I made for the door and scurried around the back of the building through the alley. This proved fortunate. Not a minute after the bartender left, I saw an upper story window rise, and a dark figure in tails climb over the sill. I watched, safely hidden in the shadows, as he shimmied down the drain spout like a circus performer or jungle animal, looked around, and took off down the alley.

"Now, I was in a dilemma. Despite appearances, I still had no true proof that this was indeed the same. After all, there was more than one explanation for a man leaving through a backdoor. I couldn't exactly shoot him in the back. What if he was just a rake slipping away from what he thought was an angry husband? I decided to simply follow my suspect for a time, in the hopes of gathering the necessary proof to insure his custody. I took to his heels, and did my best to stay unobserved."

Bell made the clucking noise again, his eyes growing reflective. I took the opportunity to shift in my seat.

"We traveled the back ways of London," he continued, ignoring or not seeing my discomfort, so fixed was he on his tale. "Moving in and out of the labyrinth of alleys and households, like rats through the sewer. More than once, I feared I lost my adversary. This went on for about twenty minutes, when we finally drew near to the heart of Whitechapel, the sight of the original murder. Even now the prostitutes and riffraff were reenacting their nightly commerce. Was he going to make a return tonight? Would I actually catch him in the act?"

Bell met my eyes and shook his head, his expression full of chagrin. "I hadn't been nearly as clever as I thought. My adversary was well aware of my efforts, and had merely taken me on a roundabout path to determine the nature and numbers of his pursuers. Our deceptive chase ended in a blind alley. He made a dash around the alley corner, and I followed after, just as he hoped. He was waiting for me in the shadows. Before I could react, he had pinned me against the wall, sending my revolver sailing away with a painful blow from his cane. I heard the sound of something being drawn quickly from a sheaf, and saw a flash of sharp steel plunging toward my throat. Instinctively, I fell to the ground. I was lucky in this; the blade knocked the hat from my head, but did no other damage. I immediately rolled, trying to put some distance between me and that horrific knife. This time I was only partially successful, as I felt a sudden, sharp pain along my shoulder. I kicked out at the shadows for all I was worth, expecting and fearing any moment to feel that cold blade open me up like a stuck pig.

"I hit something, shin or hand, I couldn't tell at first. He cried out in rage and pain, and a moment later I heard the clatter of something wooden fall against the alley bricks. I know now that it was the husk of his infamous swagger stick. He had removed its hidden blade and was using the blade in one hand and the husk in the other.

I kept kicking, scrambling on my hands away from the shadows and into the light of the street. He did not follow, as he was searching for his dropped stick.

I climbed to my feet preparing to run. Yes, run. I claim no hero's reward. I was frightened for my life. But he had found his infernal stick, and immediately followed me out of the shadows. I looked over my shoulders at the sound of rushing steps, saw the wicked blade clearly in his left hand, saw his face for the first time. What I glimpsed then was neither human, nor normal. It was diabolical."

Perhaps it was the tonal quality of Bell's voice and the effect of the warm fire, or maybe it was the soporific tea; whatever the reason, I was hanging on his every word, like a child listening to a bedtime story. I chided myself for falling so easily under his spell. Who was this man, after all, that I should trust him? I resolved to be more cautious going forward. To aid my efforts, I stood and placed my teacup deliberately on the serving tray. I abandoned the comfortable chair, and went to stand by the fireplace. I made a show of poking the embers, casting a few surreptitious glances in the hearth at the same time. No sign of Mic.

"Is the fire too hot?" asked Bell, watching me curiously. "Or does my story not interest you?"

"Not at all," I said. "Quite the contrary. Just needed to stretch a bit. Please continue."

"Certainly," he answered. "And I will cut to the chase, as I suspect you are being polite and wish I would get on with it."

I smiled, assuring him that this was not the case.

He stood suddenly, came to my side, and looked down at the fire. I hoped Mic didn't choose this time to make a sudden appearance.

"All those theories about the man," he continued, his voice dropping reflectively. "All of them, wrong." He gestured to the room around him. "This is his world, Mr. Lasak Jack the Ripper, the greatest terror to walk the streets of London, is not a human at all. He is a nightmare from the stars."

I thought this last a bit over the top as I'd seen the punch line coming for some time now.

But I did find myself checking to see if the vault was still closed.

V

Hit, or Stay?

He watched me carefully for a moment before continuing. "You believe me. I can see that. Good. It is easier, perhaps, for a man of your time and experience. I had no such help. As I wrestled Jack outside that dark alley so long ago, he did something I still do not understand; somehow he transported us to this world in the stars."

He hesitated, and looked to me again, as if I might supply an answer.

"Of course," he continued, "I was frightened. We transported directly to the room we sit in now. The décor was different then, but sill strange and unsettling to me. It was completely white, made of the glowing element that you saw holding your ship. You can imagine how disconcerted I was. Or maybe you can't. Maybe for you this is completely normal. But for a gentleman of my era, it bordered on madness."

Bell took me by the elbow, and led me slowly around the room as he continued his tale.

"He took advantage of my disorientation and threw me to the floor, striking me repeatedly with his stick. I lost consciousness momentarily. When I recovered, I saw Jack at an odd table of sorts, with moving glass pictures and colored lights. It was obvious to me that he, at least, was familiar with the surroundings. I rushed him, tried to tackle him from behind. He heard my approach, and turned just as I reached him. We tumbled together across the table, and I felt my stomach fall to the floor. He gave a shout and pushed me away. I gathered from his frantic efforts at the panel that something was very wrong. I stood watching him for a moment, completely at a loss as to what to do next. The entire situation struck me as impossible, and I panicked finally, well and truly.

"I ran again. I ran without reason or direction along strange and twisting passageways, trying to find some space of familiarity, or at least shelter. It was fortunate for me, and perhaps everyone I think, that I fled when I did. Eventually I quit running. I was standing in the middle of a passage, one both familiar and strange at the same time. Everywhere I turned, some unworldly artifact was nestled among the familiar décor of my own time. It was like walking through an exhibition theatre, but one based on a madman's nightmares. I tried to reason an explanation. I did not think I was mad. Therefore, another explanation must be in order. This place, this time, these events must be real. If so, then my enemy was here, as well. I did not understand how I had come to be here—or even where here was—but it was clear Jack meant me harm, and I must do something about it. I could try to hide, but if he was familiar with these surroundings, then my chances of success were slim. Therefore, there was only one solution. I must confront him, and end the danger the only way left to me."

We paused in front of the Merlin- in-a-bush painting. Bell considered it for a time, a small, wry smile on his face. He glanced at me, and grunted. "It is not to my taste, as I said, but I can relate to the theme." He took me by the elbow again.

"I set about trying to find my way back to the first room," he continued. "Fortunately, my wild ramble was nothing more than a big circle. I soon stumbled upon my original arrival point. He was still there. He had his back to me, and was once again working at the odd table. He was fiddling with something out of my sight, and I hoped in his distraction I might draw close enough to attack."

We stopped in front of the glass cabinet. Bell opened the doors and studied the miniature panel on the shelf for a time, moving a dial to change the pictures on the tiny screen. I guessed we were looking at parts of the ship (that's what I was going to call it, Mic's qualifications notwithstanding). Seemingly satisfied by what he saw, Bell nodded. He turned to me, and pursed his lips, as if wondering what to tell me regarding the console and what it showed. He smiled, and took me by the arm again, leading me back to the chairs.

"I'll never know if I would have actually gone through with it," he said. "It doesn't matter. As I approached his back, he suddenly turned. He was holding the strangest weapon I'd ever seen."

We sat, and Bell poured himself more tea. I waved him off this time. He took a long sip before he continued. "I learned later that he followed my movements from the control panel's visual scanners. Such technology was beyond me at the time, and I admit I thought my adversary the devil himself for knowing my presence and intention. I could think of nothing to do or say as he pointed his weapon at me. My mind had reached the point of desperation again. I was lost. He had me stand against the vault. At that time, it was the plain wall we see now. I assumed he meant to kill me in front of it. I hesitated of course, but he threatened me with his weapon, and I had no choice but to do as he said. He considered me for a long time then. I remember clearly, even now, the strange expression of contempt and amusement on his face. Finally, he laughed, and in that laugh I was certain that it *was* a demon I was facing.

"Of course, he didn't kill me. Instead, he told me I was to be his prisoner. I would be an audience, he said, to witness his genius. I would be privileged—his words exactly—to see his greatest masterpieces. Thinking of poor Polly, I shuddered at the implications of what these masterpieces might be. I declined his offer. He laughed at my reaction, called me a fool and coward. But he insisted I would understand everything better, in time."

Bell looked to the vault. "And in a way, he was right." He turned back to me, and must have seen my reaction. "Oh, I don't mean to defend him. That's not what I mean, at all. But over the many years, I've had to listen to his story, to hear his innermost thoughts and drives. I have come to see that he is a very lonely creature, searching for a complicated truth. It is not sympathy or empathy, I speak of. Perhaps, understanding is too warm a term, as well. But I did come to hear his perspective, and appreciate that it is not of our own. It is utterly, and completely, alien."

Bell studied my reaction again. "Yes, Mr. Lasak. He is not human. I learned, in time, of a distant planet, lifetimes away from our own; of being misunderstood and ridiculed by his own people because he was different. He talked of long lonely nights, endless fruitless conversations with people who could not, or would not, understand his way of thinking, until he could take it no longer and took flight in search of a place to call his own, to be his true self."

Bell grew quiet, his black eyes retreating to a more reflective place. "I have often thought of his long journey over the years," he said. "Did he go mad in his isolation? Perhaps. But I don't think so. I think his nature is, and always has been, what he practices. I have come to question, at times, whether any Earthman is fit to judge such a one. I know it sounds strange. But maybe in time, you too will come to see what I mean."

"Again," he said, looking at me directly. "I am not defending him."

"How is that you gained the upper hand?"

He raised his hand. "In time. In time. First, you must understand him."

I didn't see why I had to understand a serial killer, alien or otherwise, but I let him continue in his own way.

"Eventually," he said, "he came upon Earth. Here was a planet far away from his own, inhabited by intelligent life, potential companions. He was elated. He secretly observed this new world for a time, safe aboard his invisible ship in the heavens. He discovered the primary life forms were similar to his own but not as technically developed. They were like children to him and, yes, he suspected he would be like a god to them. This pleased him. Here was his chance to mold a whole new race in his image, to create the very world he had been looking for all this time. The one his own people rejected.

"He decided to live among them, for a time. He altered his appearance, which did not require much effort. He studied many of their languages, and mastered their differing customs. When he was ready, he found the most densely populated modern area, and transported down. He was unprepared for the actual experience. Smells, tastes, noises, sights, and stimulations like he never imagined assailed him from every direction. His world was a place of razor sharp aesthetics, filtered air, no disease, small, controlled populations, stoic cultures, and what we would call high-minded people. His people considered the highest state of being as one completely devoid of the passions and the baser emotions. You can only imagine how he reacted to London and its fusion of Victorian decorum and street level gutter life."

Bell glanced again at the vault, and then returned to me. "At first he suffered. The raw animalistic nature of the jungle, as Dickens called it, was a great shock to him. But in time, and to his surprise, he found himself oddly attracted to the strange conflicting blend of decadence and proper society. In fact, he came to revel in it. During the day, he rubbed elbows with the elite in exclusive boardrooms and clubs. In the clubs, he took secret amusement at the stumbling, ignorant men of so-called progress. He listened to them preen and pontificate on things his own people had considered and dismissed long ago. And, as he suspected, they flocked to him, sensing his superior nature and wanting to be, in some way, recognized by him.

"And at night…" Bell stopped. He looked to the fireplace. His voice grew oddly reflective. "At night, he discovered and experienced the baser natures—his baser natures. He tasted new sensations, sensations he never imagined, acts that would never be tolerated on his own world. It began simply enough. Pleasures of the flesh, fetishes, stimulants, and the surprisingly fascinating act of voyeurism. But soon these proved insufficient. He grew jaded. He began to experiment with new, higher levels of sensory and psychological experience. Somewhere along the line, he knew he had discovered the answer to his searches. In this strange, backwards world and its almost overwhelming sensations, he had discovered his fundamental truth."

"His truth?" I said. "What truth is there in the slaughter of another human being?"

"What?" said Bell. His black eyes hung fire for a moment, then cooled just as suddenly. "I beg your pardon." He sipped his tea, composing himself. "I told you, I have lived with him a long time. Perhaps, too long. I have begun to parrot his rationalizations without thinking, I have heard them so often. They are not mine, I assure you. You are right: his behavior was abhorrent. *He* would not see it that way of course, but there you have it." He picked at the fabric of his chair. "I apologize, Mr. Lasak, if I have offended you."

"Let's forget it."

"How kind of you. How kind."

There followed some more fidgeting, but eventually Bell settled down. He cast a guilty glance at me, then settled back in his chair with a sigh. "I do not pretend to understand him," he said finally. "I have had hundreds of years to try. I will say only this—and it is not in his defense—he is of a different species altogether, and your approval or disapproval of his actions would not interest him in the slightest."

"This is true of most egomaniacs," I noted.

Bell grimaced. "Yes, of course. I can only reiterate that I have known him longer and better than any, and perhaps it is my long association with him that makes me speak as I do. I confess, too, I have come on some level to respect his mind, however much I abhor his actions."

"I've read about such things," I said. "I think they call it

Stockholm syndrome. It happens sometimes with abused or kidnapped victims, sometimes even criminal psychologists. They start to form unnatural bonds with their victimizers or patients. They usually have far less exposure than what you describe."

He inclined his head, as if considering this explanation.

I looked to the fireplace, wondering if Mic was listening to all this and what she thought of it. I was a little disturbed by Bell's admissions. I couldn't imagine ever sympathizing or respecting Jack on any level, no matter how much we talked. But then again, I didn't spend hundreds of years with him. Given enough time and communication, would I come to see Jack's perspective in time? Could I come to understand him, *appreciate* his mind? It was not a comfortable thought, no matter what the answer. I decided it was time to get back to more pressing matters.

"When we first met, you said Jack got out," I said. "Which seems to indicate that he was trapped, and you were free? What changed?"

Bell watched me carefully. "Yes," he said, as if reading my mind. "Let us move on."

He surprised me then, and pulled a pipe and pouch from his inner jacket pocket. I recognized the pipe from one of my antique history books. It was a Meerschaum, shaped like a small saxophone with a deep bowl and curved stem. He took his time filling the bowl, found another archaic wonder in his vest pocket, a match, and struck it against the wood of his chair. He held the match to the bowl, his eyes drawn up against the drifting smoke, but watching me carefully. I sensed a shift in his demeanor toward me, as if he was embarrassed, or disappointed.

"As to what changed," he said around a puff of smoke. "To be completely honest, it was an accident. Jack was careless. He underestimated me. You understand, he was used to dealing with destitute prostitutes and drunkards" He took another long pull, and slowly exhaled a steady plume. "As to how I actually gained the upper hand, I am afraid I am going to risk being a bit rude, Mr. Lasak, and keep that information to myself. For the time being, I will share this. The door you helped me close is, in fact, a seal to a brig of sorts. There is only one way in, or out." He nodded to the vault wall. "I have taken steps to ensure that he cannot open it."

"He lives in that?"

"He has everything he needs on his ship, including the remarkable machines that prolong his life."

"His ship?"

"Yes. The brig is Jack's original ship. But I assure you, while the door it is locked, Jack is imprisoned."

Was it the embers of his pipe that gave his eyes a flicker of light then, or something else? I sat in silence for a time, watching the glow of his pipe create shadows along his face. Despite Bell's long tale, he wasn't sharing a lot of secrets. "How did his ship get here in the first place?"

Bell pulled his pipe down, considered the bowl. "I can only speculate, as he never spoke of it, but much like your ship I believe his ship was trapped." He added some more tobacco from his pouch. "I suspect that your arrival had something to do with his release, by the way. There was an unintended reflex, a blink if you will, in the system. This reset the security systems, and unintentionally opened the vault." Bell pointed with his pipe to the console in the glass cabinet. "That panel has a limited, but very important, interface with the world."

"World?" I asked.

Bell put the pipe in his mouth and lightly chewed the stem. He considered me carefully for a time, then shrugged. "Did I say world? I guess I've come to see it as that."

I looked around the room. "We've come a long way since you were last on Earth, but you have some technology I haven't seen before."

"Yes, it is a very special place," he said. He removed his pipe from his mouth, and leaned forward. "But I think, Mr. Lasak, it is high time we talked about your ship."

So, we were back to where we started. Was I any better off? Had I gained enough to bargain off some of my own store of information? I considered his story. I could confirm some of the names and dates later with Mic, but there were just enough of those to give his tale the feel of veracity. Despite this, I got the impression that Bell was not being completely forthright on some of the details. Nothing I could call him out on just yet, and I understood the need for a little early caution. I was about to exercise some of my own.

"Well, as to the ship, I'm still stuck," I said.

"Yes. And this brings up another pressing, predicament."

"Predicament?"

Bell nodded to the hidden vault wall. "Specifically, just what are we to do with him now? We can't just leave him here in the ship. Entirely too dangerous; what if he were to get out again?"

"I thought he was safely locked up," I said.

"Your arrival, and its unintended consequences, has shown me that nothing is completely secure. What if, in releasing your ship, we also release Jack again?"

I saw his point.

He took another reflective draw from his pipe, filling the air with the hint of cherries and wood. "But let's put that to the side for a moment. I would ask you to consider this. I think, after all this time as his keeper, I deserve a break. Don't you?"

"I suppose so."

"I will be frank with you, Mr. Lasak," he said, sitting forward again. "I would like very much to return to Earth. I think I can manage this, with your help."

Where the hell was Mic? This was precisely the kind of thing I was trying to avoid. "What kind of help?"

"I imagine your ship's computer has the correct coordinates for Earth, and I think I know enough now to communicate our needs to the Jack's panel. I have learned a few things over the years, after all."

"And we just bring the whole thing back to Earth," I answered, thinking about all the implications.

"Naturally, there would be an adjustment process for me," continued my host. "But if I have all this," he gestured to the room around us, "I should be able to acclimate successfully. This world will provide safe, familiar surroundings."

He put his pipe on the table, his eyes searching mine. "There would be benefits for Earth, as well. I am living testament to what it can do. Lifetimes extended for centuries, Mr. Lasak. They don't have such things where you are from now, do they?"

"No," I answered. "We've made some advances in science and health, but nothing like that."

I didn't voice my concerns, and I had a few. First, I doubt Mr. Bell would keep his strange ship-world for long. The Earth Defense Council would find an excuse to seize it. They'd want to put it under their microscopes the moment it entered their awareness, Mr. Bell's adjustment period notwithstanding. And who knew just what kind of problems would arise from all this alien technology, not to mention that we would be bringing Jack back to his old stomping grounds. I only had Bell's word that he was *the* Jack the Ripper.

Bell seemed to sense my hesitation. He stood and walked over to me. He laid a hand on my shoulder, searching my face carefully, his own expression suddenly distant and hard. "You can't really understand. No one can. Every day, year after year, century upon century, I have lived with the struggle of what to do, debating with myself, and yes with him. Trapped in this pointless existence, tied by accident to a strange world and a madman. I confess, Mr. Lasak, I wrestled more than once with the notion of ending his threat once and for all, in the only certain way. But I did not. Why? It was not moral qualms, I assure you. I did not kill him because he alone could return me to Earth. Without his help, I would never see Earth again."

He released his grip, and turned his back to me. His shoulders bunched with tension. "I am still caught, Mr. Lasak, morally and physically. I have waited, searched for centuries for a way out. And now, like a long unanswered prayer, here you are. This world has many wonders, but it is not Earth—it is not home. And now a return is at last in my grasp. And all I have to do—all we have to do—is act."

He turned around again. Now those black eyes held an almost feverish passion. Was this the price of immortality, I wondered? Did I have two madmen to deal with and not just one?

He seemed to recognize his state, and took a deep, shaky breath. The fever dropped from his eyes. "Forgive me," he said. "You have no idea what it has been like these many years." Fully recovered now, he lifted his head to look down at me with those black hard eyes. "The only question that remains is this: will you help me?"

I wasn't about to say no just then. The memory of his disturbed face was still too fresh, and I didn't know how he would take a straight refusal. Instead, I went another direction. "Before we can talk about a return to Earth, or other matters, we still have a problem. My ship is trapped, remember?"

His eyes twitched to the hidden panel. "I can release your ship. But there is still the matter of Jack's release."

I was happy to hear he could release my ship, but now we were back to the issue of Jack, and a return to Earth. I watched those dancing eyes closely, as I played for more time. "I don't think I can assume he is Jack, just on your say so. I don't think you really can expect me to. Think about it. If the situation was reversed, he might be out here making a case against you."

"I...you....," he stammered. "You don't believe me? Are you mad?"

"Let's just say I might believe you. I've only heard your side of the story, after all."

He turned away again, so I couldn't see his face. But I

imagined those black pools were really stirring now. He whirled back in my direction. "Is it a matter of courage? I will do the deed. You merely need to stand in support, to insure he does not escape."

I had anticipated this suggestion, and was ready with my reply: "No. I'm sorry. I can't do that either."

His face turned a deathly pale. I put my hand casually in my pocket, and found the grip of my gun. He glanced once to the hand in my pocket, but didn't remark on it.

"I understand," he said, and wiped a hand across his face. "I won't apologize, or change my position on the matter. But I understand your hesitation in this regard. Are you sure there is nothing I can do to convince you otherwise?"

"I won't say there is nothing that will not convince me." I watched his face grow hopeful again, so I quickly added, "But for now let's put the idea of killing Jack at least, on the back-burner."

"Very well," he said. "Remember though, Mr. Lasak that he must be dealt with before our return to Earth. A Jack alive and well, however temporarily contained..." He shook his head and left the rest of the thought unspoken.

"That thought had occurred to me, as well."

He nodded. "I am happy that we agree on that much. He cannot be allowed out. I will not negotiate that point."

"The vault stays closed," I said, nodding my agreement. "For now."

He frowned at my slight qualification. "I will never willing let that madman loose on this world, Mr. Lasak, no matter what doubts you harbor."

"I understand. I will not insist on his release, as long as I am eventually convinced that he is who you say he is."

The frown deepened. "Very well. I am sure you will see the truth of that in time. Now, we must address the matter of your ship. Perhaps you could give me a tour?"

He had me, and he knew it. I had run out of delays. It didn't matter. Release of my ship was priority one.

I looked casually to the fireplace. A small trip would also give Mic a chance to get out of the fireplace.

"All right," I said. "Let's go."

VI

Jacks to Open, Trips to Win

"What a remarkable piece of engineering," said Bell, looking carefully at the *Pelagius* instrumentation. "And you fly across space in this?"

"Yes. I've made the run from Colony II to Earth several times."

We retreated back to the bridge, such as it was.

Our trip to the white room and the *Pelagius* resulted in a number of new questions, and concerns. My worry bag was getting pretty full, and I desperately needed to talk with Mic.

We had walked back down the same Victorian hallway. Bell had opened the way to the white room by pressing a trick knot in the wood paneling, just below the landscape painting. The wall had turned white—just like in the vault room—then disappeared altogether. And there we were, with my ship, and it was still stuck in the strange web of seemingly endless white space as far as I could see.

Bell had insisted on a tour. It didn't take long.

He was being polite when he said remarkable. Still, as I looked around the simple bridge and captain's chair, I had to admit to a certain amount of pride. Technically, the ship belonged to LongPost. But as an invested employee, I could pilot the same ship as often as I liked, so long as it held up to specs. The *Pelagius* and I had been together since my maiden voyage. Like me she was a little long in the tooth. But over the years, she had received the appropriate upgrades and reconditions—and a few inappropriate ones as well, on the side, on my dime. I was always careful to remove any signs of these semi-illegal add-ons before official inspections. If the LongPost engineers knew, or suspected, they turned a blind eye.

I'll say this for the old girl, she was built to last. Her original chassis design was still used in newer models, and her structural integrity was unequaled. She was a bit heavy in the hips, but she carried it well. And, she was the closest thing I had to a home.

"This would be the bridge, correct?' asked Bell. "And over here the ship's computer?"

"That's right."   He was making some very astute guesses for a Victorian-age gentleman.

Then he smiled, and asked as innocent as a curious schoolboy, "How does it operate?"

I smiled slowly in return. "It's pretty complicated stuff. It took me three years to get my pilot's license."

If this disappointed Bell, he didn't show it. "I see."

He walked over to port display, and casually studied the climate controls. "Well, well, well." If he recognized the controls for what they really were, he didn't let on. He merely shook his head in wonder and said, "Man has certainly come a long way."

We spent a little time then discussing my job as a LongPost, how long various trips took between new colonies, what I did in my downtime.

"So, you're quite a way from home now?"

"You could say that."

"Are you're heading back, or away?"

"Back."

"And just how far is Earth now?"

"I'd guess we're about half way there, give or take." I could tell him the exact numbers, but what would they mean to him?

"How do you navigate such distances?"

"Oh, the ship's computer does most of the work."

He seemed to consider that for a time.

"Does it help?" I asked.

"What?"

"Seeing the ship. Does it help you free it?"

He smiled. "A bit."

"So?" I prodded. "What do we do now?"

"We?" said Bell, fiddling with his lapel.

"I'll help, of course."

"Oh, yes, of course."

He pulled a long face, and ran a finger down the chair's arm. "A thought, if you will forgive me. Once I free your ship, there is nothing I can do to make you stay, is there?"

The notion of sneaking off had crossed my mind once or twice, but I tried to reassure him that this was not the case.

"No, you are right," he said suddenly, waving off my protestations and taking the high road. "It is a matter of trust, and we have to start somewhere. Very well, I will trust you. I am off to the bridge again, to work on freeing your ship. Will you stay here, or come with me?"

Under other circumstances, I would have accompanied him, to show my own good will. But this was too good an opportunity to contact Mic without fear of being overheard.

"If you really don't need me, I'd like to run some diagnostics on my ship."

"Of course," he said. "Do your…diagnostics. I must ask you, though, not to leave your ship until I return. This section is reasonably safe, but I wouldn't want you to get lost. Agreed?"

"Certainly."

I looked to my timepiece. "How long will it take?"

"It may take some time."

"Okay. I will just sit tight."

As soon as he was gone, I tried to raise Mic. No luck.

I did run a diagnostic on the *Pelagius*. The readings looked normal, but the computer still refused to answer the helm. I took a seat in the captain's chair, and tried to figure out my next move. That's when I heard a familiar voice in my ear.

"Ben? Are you all right? Can you talk?"

"Mic? Where are you? Why didn't you answer my call?"

"I'm safe. There are a number of dead zones and atmospheric interferences in this place," she explained. "Up the chimney is one of them."

"I see. Did the fire damage you?"

"Not at all. In fact, all the heat went out your direction."

"Interesting. Where did the smoke go?" I had wondered about this the moment I saw the fireplace was real. Chimneys, for obvious reasons, are not very practical in space.

"Sucked out vents in the side of the chimney. Anyway, that doesn't matter now. We've got a big problem."

"Besides the fact that we can't get off this ship? I'm taking care of that right now."

"Besides that, and I wouldn't be so sure you took care of anything."

"What do you mean?"

"Do you know who's on board with us?"

"Jack the Ripper," I offered smugly.

"He told you?"

"Yes. Umm, why wouldn't he?"

"Well, do you know who Jack the Ripper is?"

"Yes, I know who Jack the Ripper is. He was a serial killer from late Victorian Earth."

"Then you know this is very serious. We have to do something to get him back in the containment center before he gets control of the ship again."

I licked my suddenly dry lips. "*Back* in the containment center?"

"Yes. Carlin thinks Jack means to return to Earth and start his reign of terror all over again. All he needs to do is repair the interface console, and use the coordinates in our ship's computer...."

"Carlin?" I interrupted. "Who's Carlin?"

"He's the one you mistakenly helped Jack lock in the containment center."

I felt the onset of a nasty headache. "Wait a minute. You've got it backwards. Carlin is Jack. I mean, the guy I locked away is Jack. Bell told me the whole story. You didn't let the other one out, did you?"

"Of course I did. And he is not Jack! The other one is, this Bell. You need to talk to Carlin right now. And whatever you do, don't let that Bell fellow out of your sight."

"Oh."

"What?"

"Where are you at?" I asked.

"We're in the Solarium. It's to the right of the Bridge, where we first found Jack."

I took a big breath. "If you are right, then I think the real Jack is heading back to the Bridge right now, ostensibly to free our ship. He took a look at our situation here...."

"He's been in our ship?"

"Yes."

"Not good. That's not good at all. He's very smart. I would guess that he only wanted an excuse to see the inside of the *Pelagius*. Probably so he could see how to get inside. Did he see the ship's operating system?"

"In a manner of speaking," I said. "But he can't just walk in the ship. He doesn't have voice command or the proper codes. I'm locking the door right now."

"He doesn't need the *Pelagius*. He just needs to know the ship's computer has the coordinates for Earth. His technology is far better than ours. He's probably hacking the ship computer right now. That is, if he didn't trick you into giving him the coordinates already. You didn't, did you?"

"Don't be silly. Of course not."

But I was miserable. If—and this was a big if—*if* Mic was right, if Bell was not who he said he was, if I had let out the wrong Jack; well, I had a lot to answer for.

"Are you sure your guy is not Jack?" I asked growing more desperate.

"Positive."

"I'm coming your way," I said. "Keep in contact. I'll play dumb if I run into Bell, and try to maneuver him to your location. Listen in and be ready, but don't make any hasty decisions. I'm not so sure you have the right man."

"I'm sure. And don't count on yours just following you blindly to the Solarium. Carlin says he's very tricky."

"We'll see. Can you trust this Carlin to stay put?"

"Yes."

"Good, then meet me outside the Victorian bridge. I'm going to need your help. If I don't run into Bell first, you can then take me to this other Jack, and we'll settle this matter together. Bell said we've got some time before he frees the ship."

"I'm sure he doesn't need that long to free our ship. He was lying, Ben. He's up to something else."

"One worry at a time," I sighed.

"Right. I'll meet you in the hall. Be careful."

"You, too."

Mic was waiting at the end of the hallway.

"Hurry," she said. I followed her down the hall, the right extension this time, away from the vault and bridge.

"I'm running some interference with the interface panel's surveillance system," she said, as we raced along the hall. "But we still have to be careful. Jack is just inside the bridge, and could spot us from the hallway if he steps out."

We took a turn to the left. Like the others, the new hall was lined with paintings, but this time the theme seemed to be mansions and castles. The air was a bit stuffy again, heavy with the smells of age, and oil. There was a thick burgundy carpet running the width of the hall. We passed a grandfather clock, and I noted the time: eight. I didn't have time to stop and see if it was a moon or sun in the smaller dial. I checked my own timepiece, which registered a little after 1300 ECT (Earth Central Time). I didn't adjust my timepiece though, as I had no intention of staying that long.

"Let's not get lost," I said, as we turned down another hall.

"It's no joke," said Mic. "There's something unnatural about this place. Carlin has spent four hundred years searching it, and still hasn't seen everything."

"About this, Carlin, how do you know he's not the Ripper? Or, just as importantly, my man is? We could be dealing with two madmen here."

"While you were with Bell on the *Pelagius*, I turned on the vault's speaker and talked to Carlin. He offered some proof of his innocence."

"Proof?" I prodded.

"Well, his explanation was compelling."

I stopped in my tracks.

"Okay, hold it right there," I said. "I'm not walking into a potentially lethal situation, just because you liked his story. And we were separated what, thirty, forty minutes? Even if you are more than a game computer, I don't see how you could discern the truth from just a stranger's say-so. Bell had a pretty compelling story, as well."

"Ben, trust me."

"Trust you? You're a game computer, right?"

This wasn't exactly fair. I was already beginning to doubt Bell, based on some of his behavior in our conversation. But I wasn't about to concede the point to Mic. She was right, things were too serious now. Which was the crux of the matter—she couldn't, shouldn't possibly know that. Okay, part of me knew I was looking for an excuse or distraction. In the back of mind, I realized that the real issue—our present predicament—was wholly my fault, as I was the one who insisted we break from our designated route. But you've got to draw the line somewhere, even if it is just the line of denial.

So, I took this totally inappropriate time to address an issue that could have waited, and I did so with all the bravado a guilty, hypocritical conscious could provide.

"You say I should trust you. Well, time to spill the beans, Mic. What exactly did the Professor sell me in that yard sale? She indicated there was more to you than meets the eye. What gives?"

Mic shifted to the deepest shades of red. "We really

don't have time for this, Benjamin. I can't be sure I'm scanning everything right at this point. Jack could be following us even now."

"We're going to make time. Tell me what you know, or more accurately, what you can know. Talk to me about artificial intelligence, and self-willed game computers."

Mic's red turned a resigned, no-nonsense white. "So, you finally figured it out."

"I read a bit when you weren't looking."

Her revolutions slowed almost to a crawl. I guessed she was considering her options. "It really isn't safe here," she said finally. "If I admit that I am more than just a game computer, can we talk about this later?"

"Fair enough," I said.

Actually, I was happy to drop the matter. It had just occurred to me that Mic might have been doing me a favor by not spilling all her secrets. Experiments in artificial intelligence were carefully regulated. Unsanctioned private studies carried severe criminal charges and extensive prison time, not to mention the probable confiscation and/or destruction of the experimental units. I had grown rather attached to my floating companion, and wasn't prepared to lose her just yet. I decided I could wait to hear the details later, or maybe not at all (there were equally severe repercussions in the LongPost Handbook for employees who failed to alert authorities to felonious activity.) And, I had won a small concession, a rarity in my spars with Mic. A bit of the old swagger was in my step, as I turned again to more immediate concerns.

"How did you let this Carlin fellow out?" I asked, as we continued on. "Bell said he was locked in. He seemed to think it pretty permanent."

"Jack doesn't know everything. I hacked his system, and got around his so-called safeguards."

"I thought you said the technology was more advanced than ours."

"I learn quickly."

"Impressive." I watched her turn a soft azure. "Okay, next subject. Bell called this place a world, but then sometimes talked as if it were something else. Do you have a better sense of what we are up against now?"

Mic's color revolved to a murky brown. "In some ways. But, every time I solve a mystery, I stumble on another. Take the atmospherics. I still don't understand how we have gravity, and a breathable atmosphere. The physics simply don't add up. Of course, it is possible something is interfering with my scanners and I'm just reading wrong."

I noticed that Mic's tone had lost a little of its usual mechanistic quality. It was softer, now, more human. I decided I liked the change.

"So, this place is a regular fun house," I offered.

"Haunted house might be more appropriate," she answered.

The hall we traveled made a subtle shift to the right. The wainscoting was now done in yellow gold, and the paintings were of gothic churches and classical mythology. Some of the night tables had colored glassware.

"And you say these are originals, or close enough?" I asked, indicating the decor.

"That's another mystery. Like almost everything else I've scanned, they seem to contain a residue of the ship's primal material, that white glowing material the *Pelagius* is trapped in. It's like an imprint or genetic strain, but it can take on the properties of stone, glass, paint, and water, whatever is required to make the object perfect in detail and authenticity."

I had a follow up question to that, but it died on my tongue when we took a sharp left.

We stood outside a hanging balcony, about twenty feet off the floor and protected by a small railing and burnished gate. Inside the gate, at the very edge of the abutment, was a large armchair. Call it a throne.

To either side of the balcony were spiraling stairways, descending along opposite sides of the chamber walls. The ceiling of the chamber was a Sistine chapel affair, vaunted and painted in bright, vibrant colors. The scene depicted angelic figures in white robes and wings, their faces grimly beatific, their swords upraised in a background of bright blue skies and billowy white Cirrus. The detail was incredible, and I suspected more than human hands were involved. There was a sense of gravity to the eyes that looked to be watching me in return and the experience, from my view point, was not altogether comforting.

In contrast, the chamber's floor was done in stygian black marble. Like the ceiling, the floor seemed on the point of activity. There was an unnatural depth to the darkness, aided in part by a pattern of red ethereal lines etched along the surface. An optical illusion made the etchings appear detached from the marble. Trying to penetrate the ebony obscurity, I had the impression of something darker just below the surface, like an ominous shadow passing beneath a dark sea.

As I took in the view, Mic started down one of the stairways. Before I followed, I tried the small gate of the abutment. It was unlocked. My curiosity got the better of me again, and I stepped through the gate and walked to the edge of the abutment.

"We really don't have time for this," said Mic, coming back to hover by my shoulder.

"Won't be a moment."

I stepped to the side of the throne, positioned at the very edge of the balcony. The view was breathtaking from this perspective, sandwiching the contrasting aspects of ceiling and floor.

Of course, I sat down.

And the lights went out.

Then the show began.

A soft glow of sapphire filled the ceiling, growing slowly, tentatively, until it reached a brilliant, sparkling cerulean. The angelic images flared, illuminated in halos of yellow, silver, and white, as if the images were made of glass. They bobbed slightly to unseen winds or adjustments, the clouds panning slowly from left to right, new ones replacing the departing.

Almost immediately, there came an answer from below. A deep tolling bell shook the abutment, the arms of the throne, the very air of the chamber. The fiery lines ran like true fire, and reached several inches into the air. A foul and unnatural odor rose like a bad omen. The marble flooring vanished, replaced by an inky viscous murk, and yes, I would swear the leviathan stirred restlessly in its depths.

Mic floated to my side, an orbital anomaly of scientific light in an otherwise panorama of metaphysical airs, giving or drawing comfort, anybody's guess. I started to say something clever, but couldn't find the nerve.

"There is a new element to the chair," said Mic, her voice uncharacteristically subdued.

I looked down and discovered a small cavity had appeared in the right arm of the throne. Floating above it, was a tiny holographic bell. Beneath the bell, in the cavity, was a wooden striker about the size of a pencil.

"That's a bell," I noted.

"Yes, it is," said Mic, turning a bright yellow. "And please don't do something stupid."

"Like strike the bell?"

"Exactly."

"But then, how will we ever know?"

"Ben…"

"Nothing ventured." I said. "Besides, it's a hologram. What do you expect it to do?"

I raised the striker, and tapped it against the image of the bell. The tiny ping that resulted was not a complete surprise.

I looked hopefully to the ceiling. The blue glow was now retreating, the angelic halos dimmed.

"Well, that's not good," said Mic.

With a cringe, I looked down.

The black murk was behaving most unnaturally. Like its Red Sea cousin it parted, exposing not the feared leviathan, but a black rock floor. As the murk folded back, it formed a series of stacked, strangely gelatinous waves. The waves held their layered spaces and solidified, creating a gallery of rough seating around the chamber.

The bell at my arm rang again, though I had not struck it. The rough floor separated like a puzzle box, and from it rose a small stage with a table and high back chair. The table stood to the right of the chair, and was covered in white cloth with various hand-held instruments. From my vantage, I could see iron bands on the chair's armrests, legs, and headpiece.

The bell rang a third time, and from behind the stage rose a covered stairwell with a frosted glass door. Behind the glass door, something approached. At first it was little more than a wavering shadow moving in fits and starts like a candle flame. As it drew closer, however, it took on a vaguely human appearance—a broken one. The arms were impossibly long and bent at odd angles, and there was also an unnatural vibration around the head area.

"Mic," I asked, "how do I turn this thing off?"

"Try the bell again," she said.

I did. Nothing happened. The shadowed figure was almost to the door now. Its head was twisting so fast I thought it would fall off. I hit the bell again and again, making it sound like a small fire alarm. Nothing.

"Maybe we should just leave," offered Mic.

One of those twisted limbs was reaching for a handle. I saw its twin on our side start to turn.

"Good idea," I said. I climbed from the throne.

As I stood, the bell disappeared and the cavity closed with a click. I looked down. The glass door, which was partially opened, stopped. A moment later it shut again. I watched through the glass as the twisted shadow figure turned and head back down.

A moment later, the lights returned to normal, and the stage retreated. The flooring did its trick in reverse, becoming again the ethereal-lined black marble floor.

I looked to the ceiling. It, too, had returned to its original form.

But as I looked a little closer, I thought the angels were looking down with expressions of disapproval. I tried to look appropriately repentant, and quickly turned away.

Mic, for once, didn't say anything. But if there was a color that could be a metaphor for traumatized, she was wearing it. I followed her down the left-hand staircase without a word.

When we reached the bottom, I tentatively studied the flooring. The black marble was solid enough, though it maintained its depthless quality. The red lines were insubstantial. My feet passed through them like laser-lighting (Mic assured me it was safe). I had no idea what the pattern represented. It wasn't a pentagram, but after my experiences, I couldn't help but think it a close cousin.

As we walked to the other side of the chamber, I began to wonder if I was a victim of atmospherics and a state-of-the-art light show. I thought it was a reasonable possibility, so I asked the question to the only other witness available. "What do you think that was all about, Mic?"

I didn't get the answer I expected.

"Your arrested development, coupled with an incredibly inappropriate sense of entitlement, resulted in an otherwise avoidable catastrophe."

She looked like she was going to continue, so I stepped in.

"Whoa. Slow down. Are we certain it was real?"

"Yes," she said, as we reached the other side of the chamber and stood before a set of elaborately detailed wooden doors.

"I warned you," she continued. "There are many such hidden dangers. It's one of the reasons I wanted to go directly to Carlin."

I looked at the doors. "So, we go through here?"

"To avoid the dangers," she added pointedly a moment later.

"Carlin is on the other side?"

There was the longest of brief silences, and then, "Yes."

Add morose futility to Mic's growing list of color schemes.

I turned the door's brass handle and stepped through to yet another hallway. This one, at least, was short.

A pair of brilliant glass doors cutoff the opposite end. They provided most of the lighting, glowing with atmospheric backlight. Drawing close, I saw the glass was covered in filigree pastoral etchings.

"The Solarium is just beyond the doors," said Mic.

The doors were obviously heavy but opened effortlessly.

I stepped through and was bathed in bright, clean Spring light and the rich, heady air of a garden in bloom.

"Carlin's just ahead," said Mic, flying ahead of me.

Kill joy.

VII

The Solarium

Mic took the lead again, floating above a blue-pebbled path that cut across a meticulously kept lawn. The short path led to a fence line of evergreen poplars and passed through a gap to the other side. The pebbles crunched beneath my feet as we progressed slightly uphill.

We walked through the gap, the trees creating shadows over the path and cooling the air. There was a hint of bark, leaf, and sap now to the atmosphere. Stepping from the shadows, I stopped short.

If a modernized Garden of Eden was put under glass, it might look something like what was before me.

Birches and elms and oaks and trees of a color I'd never seen or heard of before stood in small, neat copses and rows. The lawn, when it appeared, was evenly cut and level as a pool table; the grass sometimes green, sometimes blue. The flora was bright and lush, varying in shades of darkest green to bright orange.

I saw a pond, and the tip of what looked like a fountain to my left. There was a freshly painted gazebo to the right in a small grove of red poplars. Statues and benches were scattered here and there with no apparent purpose or design, as if dropped wherever the gardener grew tired.

As I was at the bottom half of a gently rising hill, much of the back half of the Solarium was still hidden. But along the top of the back wall was a massive ivy-covered trellis, framing the view under a canopy of living green.

Looking up, the ceiling appeared to be of heavy crystal, and like the doors brilliantly lit from behind, like the summer sun in stain glass. What I could see of the walls to either side were of similar design and lighting.

And somehow, it all fit. Everything was where it should be; or better yet, where it wanted to be. Harmony and contrast, the spectrum ends of beauty, emanated from every blade and leaf and petal, and were made more complete by their presence together.

I took a deep breath, enjoying the intoxicating rush of life and promise. The last of my recent nightmare retreated before a sense of wholeness, of beauty. I wanted nothing more in that moment than to take my boots off and stroll like a lost penitent returned home to find it waiting and warm.

"Here," said a voice behind me.

I turned. In my distraction, I must have walked right passed him.

He was not exceptionally tall, and was dressed in similar fashion as Bell. His dark, auburn hair receded to a widow's peak in the front and was cut close in the back and around the ears. As if by way of compensation, his sideburns reached to the corners of his mouth. They looked like bristling red hedgehogs when he moved his mouth. A strong, dimple chin rose between the ends of those sideburns, like a hillside boulder.

Mic floated between us. "Ben," she said, "this is Michael Carlin."

"Benjamin Lasak," I said, offering a hand.

He took it slowly.

He had a grip like iron, but looked reasonably sane. Then again, so had Bell.

"I understand," I said, addressing the elephant in the room, "I let the wrong man out."

Carlin didn't answer, but those red bristles did a lot of moving, and his eyes grew a little hard.

"I have to say, in my defense, Bell told a pretty convincing story."

Carlin looked to Mic, and his expression mollified a bit.

"I'm sure he did. What exactly do you know about the situation, Mr. Lasak?"

"Just a little more than I know about you," I answered. "Not a lot."

"Fair enough," he said. "But with Jack loose, I'm afraid we'll have to forgo long explanations. Can we agree that securing Jack is our first concern?"

I hesitated. "Yes, I can agree to that." It was my turn to frown. "But, the dilemma, for me, is knowing who is Jack?" I held up a hand to stop his protest. "I don't want to get off on the wrong foot. I'm here because I trust Mic, and she says she trusts you. It won't take much more convincing. But I'm going to reserve my final judgment just a bit longer."

He nodded, for which I was grateful. "So be it. All will become clear soon enough. In the meantime, where is Bell?"

"He's in the study, or console room, or whatever you call it. At least, I think he is. We're to meet again in an hour or so, back at my ship, the *Pelagius*. I think we have an hour or so. He's working on freeing the *Pelagius* from the white room." I looked to Mic. "Mic told you about that, right?"

"Yes." He stood for a moment, apparently lost in thought. "It is clear that I have to convince you of the truth, first," he said, finally. "We have to have your full commitment, if we are to succeed in securing Jack."

I made a note of that *we*. Was he referring to Mic, or someone else?

"Just for a moment," I offered, "let's assume Bell is Jack. We out number him two—excuse me," I nodded to Mic, "three to one. Why don't we just confront him, and you two make your best case against the other. Mic and I can then make an informed decision. If it turns out he is as you suggest, I will help you return him to the, ah, brig."

Carlin was already shaking his head. "The numbers, as you say, will quickly change. Our biggest advantage now is Jack doesn't know I'm free. Likely enough, he is busy working on your ship and its information, confident in his ability to handle you. But soon he'll start waking his minions. If that happens, we will be more than outnumbered—we'll be at his mercy."

He looked me up and down. "Forgive me, but you don't look like much of a fighter, Mr. Lasak."

"I can handle myself, if it comes to that," I said, sounding more confident than I felt. I pressed a hand against my satchel, feeling the comforting resistance of the gun inside.

Carlin gave me another once over, shrugged and turned. "Time is pressing. Follow me."

He led us along the continuing blue-pebbled path which ran straight to a maze of hedges. The hedges were uniformly cut and towered over us. The lanes they shaped were tight, even, and in every way the same. A few turns in, and I was lost.

But Carlin appeared to know what he was doing, and soon we were at the exit.

Just before we stepped out of the maze, he stopped and laid a heavy hand on my chest.

"A brief word, if you will, before we go on." His eyes held mine. "What I am about to show you is precious to me, Mr. Lasak. Respect this, please."

We walked across a bit of emerald colored lawn, the ground rising sharply. Ahead, a hilltop was crowned by a line of birch trees. There were a number of birds and squirrels in the trees. As we approached, some of the former took wing in splashes of vivid yellow, blues, and reds. A fat brown squirrel watched us carefully, his tail twitching from time to time in its own secret warnings. Two butterflies chased each other across my feet.

"It's quite lovely here," I said.

Carlin's only response was to grunt, and continue on.

"What do you think, Mic?" I asked, turning in her direction.

I stopped. Behind us, Mic was spinning like a dervish and shifting through her color schemes with a frantic strobe-like intensity.

"Mic?" I cried.

She stopped, as suddenly as if someone had flipped a switch. I stepped to her side. She was a pale, almost ghostly white.

"I don't understand," she said meekly, sounding like a lost child. Then she contracted to her smallest size, and fell to the ground.

"Mic!" I yelled, stooping to pick her up. I heard Carlin approaching over my shoulder.

Mic was a lifeless gray, a color I had never seen her wear, and she was cold to the touch.

"Mic, what's wrong?" I asked anxiously.

"I can't make sense of it," she said, her voice tinny and distant like a bad radio reception. "I can't process...there's something out there, Benjamin...something overwhelming."

"Quit scanning," I ordered. "Don't process anymore."

She gave no answer.

"She doesn't look right," said Carlin, obviously concerned.

"Come on, Mic" I pleaded. "Talk to me."

She didn't respond, and I watched her inner light fade until she was little more than a lifeless stone.

I lifted her to my mouth. "Whatever is going on," I whispered to her desperately, "take it slow, and know I'm here."

For just a moment, there was a flicker of light in the gray.

"That's right," I encouraged. "You don't have to make sense of everything all at once. Just keep it together until we can get you back to the ship"

Another flicker.

"Will she be all right?" asked Carlin.

"I don't know."

I put Mic carefully in my satchel. "I've got to get her back to my ship."

Carlin considered me for a time. "I don't think that's a good idea, Mr. Lasak. We have to deal with Jack, now."

"Mic comes first," I said, and it was my turn to be grim.

He nodded. "I understand. She means a great deal to you."

"Yes."

I watched his red bristles wrestle with his conflicting desires to stop Jack and concern for Mic. When he spoke, some of his previous determination was mixed with sympathy.

"Lilith can help the little one, if anyone can," he said. "And I fear there will be no safe returning to your ship now. Jack will be watching." His eyes pleaded with mine. "Please, Mr. Lasak. She's just ahead."

I considered his offer, weighing it against the hopeless futility I felt for Mic. Taking her to the ship was no certain solution. I had no idea if it would even recognize the problem. I was desperate, and I needed a desperate solution.

"All right," I said. "Take me to your, Lilith."

VIII

A Stone Flower

We reached the top of the hill in short order, and I had my first vision of Carlin's Lilith.

She sat on a solid marble bench, surrounded by birches, a green blanket covered her lap and legs. She wore a blue, sleeveless tunic which complimented her ivory complexion. She was quite beautiful, in a classical sense.

Her face was made of deliberate lines and edges, as if cast from pure imagination into reality, right down to the tiny beauty mark beneath her right eye. A curtain of rich yellow curls fell to her tiny shoulders, and her eyes were like two emeralds under a pool of clearest water.

But for all her beauty, there something unnatural about her. If I didn't know better, I'd say she was an animated piece of art.

Yet, she was clearly alive. Those emerald eyes were watching me quite closely, a small smile playing on the corners of her delicate mouth.

"Lilith," said Carlin. "I brought him."

He nodded in my direction. "This is Benjamin Lasak. Lasak, the Lady Lilith."

I stepped closer. I noticed something odd about the way the blanket fell across her lap, but quickly lifted my eyes as I could feel the heat of Carlin's gaze.

I bowed slightly, not certain what the proper protocol was for a Lady.

She nodded in turn, but remained seated. She then turned to Carlin and reached out a small hand, which he took lovingly in his own.

"You may call me, Lilith, Mr. Lasak." she said. She looked down at her lap. "My father gave me this name."

I saw Carlin's whiskers twitch slightly at this, but neither elaborated.

When she looked up again, the smile was back. "I am aware of your trouble, Benjamin Lasak, and of our pressing time constraints. Put your doubts aside. Michael Carlin is not your enemy. The one who called himself Bell is the true enemy. He would kill you now, if he knew you spoke with me."

I coughed a bit. "Your pardon, Lilith, but as I said to Mr. Carlin, Bell offered another story. Why should I trust you?"

"Is it so hard to judge between us?" she asked.

I had no answer to this.

"The little one," said Carlin. "It reacted as you feared. Maybe something can be done in that direction."

"Yes," said Lilith, squeezing his hand. "She must be addressed first." She turned to me. "May I see the one you call, Mic?"

I hesitated. Lilith seemed to know a great deal about me, and recent events. Mic had not mentioned Lilith in our conversations. Had Carlin told her about Mic? And what was this about Lilith knowing Mic would react as she did? Did she have something to do with it? Was I about to hand Mic over to the true enemy?

I looked to Lilith, searching for answers in those perfect features. I saw no open malice, but no assurances either.

As if sensing the reason behind my hesitation, Lilith nodded, her smile a tight line of irony. "I know your little friend well, Mr. Lasak. I've been watching her since you arrived. I can help her."

"I don't see how any of that's possible. But if you know her so well, what happened?"

Lilith hesitated. "It is difficult to describe. Mic stumbled across something that...upset her greatly. She was unprepared for the event. She's struggling, even now, to make sense of it all."

"What did she stumble across?"

"Me."

"You? You made her crash?" I asked.

"Not the way you suggest. As I said, it is a case of over-stimulation. I did not know Mic's limitations at the time, or I would have stopped her, prepared her. But she can tell you herself in a matter of moments. May I?" She held out a tiny hand.

Slowly, I withdrew Mic and put her in that delicate palm, hoping I was doing the right thing.

Carlin and I watched as Lilith put the colorless Mic in her lap, cradling her in both hands. It was not unlike a Mother soothing a young child.

"The design is somewhat primitive," she said, to no one in particular. "But there is a degree of familiarity, as well. Did you have anything to do with Mic's creation?" she asked without taking her eyes from Mic.

"No. But it wouldn't surprise me if Mic's original owner was playing around with artificial intelligence. I know from recent diagnostics she possesses an incredible amount of free-floating processing chips. But my ship computer didn't recognize their nature. I just assumed they were for future upgrades."

"Processing chips," said Lilith with an enigmatic smile, "Upgrades. What an odd way to describe her character."

She held Mic close to her face, as if trying to penetrate the hard, gray casing. A minute later, a faint green light began to glow around Lilith's hand. The glow passed from her hands and onto Mic, then it was inside her, a bright green spot pulsating in her core. I looked with some concern to Carlin, but he only had eyes for Lilith.

Without warning, Mic lifted from Lilith's hands and soared into the air. She floated there above us, a miniature nova of cyan, casting all other colors into muted shades of blue. A moment later, and her color dimmed again, eventually becoming a pristine white. Like a snowflake, she settled slowly to rest on Lilith's lap again, and was still.

"Thank you," said Mic, her voice as soft as her color scheme.

It was Mic, but it was not Mic. There was no hint of artificiality in her voice now. Her tones were richer, more human. It was as if she'd suddenly grown a larynx.

"Mic?" I asked.

She rose, and floated over to me. "Benjamin."

"What happened to you?" I asked.

"Overload," Mic answered. "My trans-metaphorical programming couldn't compensate what I was reading. Too many impossible values made into reality; too many realities made valueless. But now..." She burned again for a moment in bright blue. "Now, Benjamin, I understand."

I turned to Lilith.

"I enhanced her essence," she said. "The basic design was not sophisticated enough to handle the more troubling paradoxes of life. Her crash was destined to happen eventually, given her limited cognitive flexibility. Her accidental encounter with me, with this world, just accelerated matters."

"*You* enhanced her essence?"

She bowed slightly. "Like everything else on this ship, I'm not what I seem. But that's a long story, Mr. Lasak, and I'm afraid we just haven't the time."

I turned back to Mic, "Are you sure you are okay?"

"I'm better than okay, Ben," she answered. She was now a dark royal purple, her voice sultry and playful. "This is...it's like...I don't know quite how to describe it. I...*I think; therefore I am...*"—her voice wavered, changed to a comical diction— "*I am w'at I am!* I never really knew what those words meant. until now. Descartes to Popeye; but not so far in between, really, if you think about it. If you *think* about it." She laughed. A real, full-bodied, naturally modulated laugh. "Imagine, how funny! But it's not so funny, is it? *When I was a child, I spoke as a child!*"

She flew to me, twirling like a pinwheel. "I *was* a child, Benjamin. That's it. I was naïve: safe in my ignorance and innocent, yes, but not so complete, not so full. Who would be a horse again, or for that matter a simple computer program, once you've tasted the nectar of reason and knowing? I, I...whew!"

She shrank once more to her cue ball size, and instinctively I stretched out my hand. She settled there, her color returning to a pale white.

"I need to rest," she said, her voice taking on still another new tone—was it humility? "I have to process a little now, Benjamin. I'm okay, though. Never been better."

Her color resolved to a deep blue, but now with marble-etchings of white and gray, something I'd never seen her do before. Her voice trailed off, like a child going to sleep. "So many new questions. I am Mic, but, *why* am I?" The blue became a dark cloud of night with one tiny white star burning bright in the center. "Bye for now, Ben."

"Is she okay?" I asked Lilith.

"She's fine. I gave her what she lacked to develop her emerging sense of self. It will take her a little time to adjust, but I believe you will both find the results rewarding."

"Neat trick," I said, trying to take this in. "And, thank you."

"Consider this a gesture of my good faith," she answered. "Though, I care more about this little one than you may think. We have much in common."

I left that last tidbit for later, because I wanted to push her good will a little more to another pressing need.

"I don't suppose you can free my ship, too?" I asked.

She frowned. "Unfortunately, your ship is secured in an area not under my control."

"Forgive me, but how is anything under your control? How, exactly, are you controlling something from a park bench?"

"Lasak," warned Carlin, frowning.

But Lilith stilled him with a look. "No. He's right, Michael. We must be very forthcoming with Mr. Lasak, if we are to enlist his aid. And this, like the little one, is something we must address now."

She looked inwardly for a moment, as if gathering strength, then removed her blanket.

I anticipated a supple lap with ivory legs. Or, given the gravity of the gesture, perhaps some type of deformity. Instead, her lap simply ended in a block of the ship's phosphorescent white material. She was not sitting on the marble bench, she was part of it.

I felt Carlin stir beside me. He was obviously upset by the turn of events. He reached over, and with a gentle insistence, pulled the blanket back in place. Then he turned back to me with an intense, protective glare.

I ignored him, looking instead to Lilith. There was no shame in her expression, but there was a deep sadness.

"What are you?" I asked, without thinking.

"Lasak!" started Carlin angrily.

"Michael," chided Lilith.

She adjusted the blanket about her lap. "Forgive him, Mr. Lasak. Michael knows how much this revelation costs me." She stared at her lap. Her delicate fingers picked at a loose thread. "What I am, is a product of this world, a creation of its soul and its designer. I am at once whole and incomplete, free and bound. I am what Jack, and the Mother, made me."

"I don't understand. You're human?"

She folded her hands on her lap. "Yes and no. I think, and I know that I am, and I can love." She blushed, and cast a quick glance in Carlin's direction. He reached out and took her hand in both of his again. The sight of the two of them together sent my thoughts in other, less noble directions, and I felt very uncomfortable. Did she mean she was capable of physical love? Carlin, as if guessing the direction of my thoughts, was glaring at me again. I tried not to blush.

"But I am not completely human, either," continued Lilith. "The one you know as Bell, the one we call Jack, conceived me in his mind, spilled his blood to give me life. He created this form. Or more accurately, I am the extent to which his courage and imagination would allow me to be. His anger at my," she paused, "imperfection, was only made more terrible by the knowledge that it was his own weakness that caused it." She picked at her blanket again. "But I am not wholly of Jack's corrupted mind. Another played a role in my creation. The Mother gave me light and hope, to strive against his dark purposes. More importantly, she gave me power to act on my own. In this way, I could act against my darker nature, and set out a place of my own."

She sighed, and dropped her eyes again. Carlin put his hands on her shoulders. I kept my tongue for once, despite a thousand questions, and waited for her to continue. Eventually she raised her eyes again, touched Carlin's hand on her shoulder. She seemed to draw strength from the act.

"This world is a living organism, Mr. Lasak, alive and to an extent aware, but it is also bonded to the one known as Jack on your world. He is not of your Earth—yes, he often told me of your home planet, and the things he did there."

"He told me Carlin was alien," I said. "Sorry, I mean that Jack was an alien."

"Carlin is an Earthman, like you," she answered. "But Jack was driven from his home world. Before he discovered your Earth, he came upon an alien life form, a living star if you will. This world. Somehow, they were bonded. I do not know how. He never told me, and the Mother can't for some reason. Yet, they are bonded. The relationship is symbiotic, and there are many benefits for Jack. He soon discovered he could work with the essence of the living world, shaping the topography, even create new life forms. He also learned that the Mother would work to preserve him from danger and extended his life force far beyond his normal years."

She raised her chin defiantly. "But the Mother does not *approve* of Jack. She acts to counter his more twisted and harmful creations, to limit his control of the world. Theirs was a constant struggle of balance when he was free. I am an example of that fractious relationship."

"If this world, this entity, this Mother," I said, searching for the right word. "If she is bonded to him, why did she allow Jack to be imprisoned in the first place?"

"As I said, she does not approve of Jack. Apparently a captured but alive Jack was something she could allow." She looked to Michael Carlin as she said this, and I saw a storm of frustration pass across his face. Had the entity, whatever it was, stopped Carlin from killing Jack?

"So, Mr. Lasak, you believe us now?" asked Carlin.

It was lot to take in, and I took a deep breath. "I'm beginning to."

"Beginning? Isn't it enough that he is Jack the Ripper? Isn't it enough that Lilith helped your little friend?"

"Look, it isn't that I don't trust you. You helped Mic, for which I'm grateful." *Though*, I thought, *by your own admission, Lilith was partly responsible her sudden crash*. It was just possible that the whole thing was orchestrated to buy my trust.

I didn't voice these thoughts aloud, however. It sounded too much like looking a gift horse in the mouth. What Carlin or Lilith suspected was another matter.

"Please put yourself in my shoes," I said. "Bell is trying to free my ship right now, and you're telling me you can't do that. I don't mean to be rude here, but it seems that things are still up in the air on most accounts."

I didn't look Carlin's way when I said this. I could feel his anger well enough, and I wasn't certain it was unjustified.

"I just want to be very careful, for everyone's sake," I added lamely. "Including the man I know as Bell. Prove to me he's Jack, once and for all, and I'll help."

Lilith looked to Carlin, and then turned back to me. His cheeks were the color of his sideburns, and I couldn't meet his eyes. She patted his hand, then turned to me. "You should know that Jack will free your ship, if he can, but I doubt he will let you leave when he does. More likely he will take your ship as his own. Yet, this distraction may be to our advantage. He thinks you are in your ship. He does not suspect that Michael is free, or that we have met. We may have some time."

I looked on hopefully. "I just need to be sure."

"Very well," she sighed. "We must give you compelling proof." She turned to Carlin. "Michael, you must take him below."

"I'm not leaving you here with that madman running around," said Carlin emphatically.

"If you can think of a quicker more certain way," she answered, "I am listening. Besides, we must close that doorway now that Jack is loose. It has to be done sooner that than later. You know what lies down there."

This last point seemed to hit home with Carlin, though clearly he was not happy about leaving Lilith alone.

"Come on then," he said brusquely. "Let's make this quick."

"Just a second," I answered. "I need a minute with Mic alone."

"Our time is running short, Mr. Lasak," said Lilith.

"Let him have his minute," said Carlin. I suspected this unexpected support was so he could have some alone time with Lilith, but I was grateful, just the same. He nodded me on, and turned to Lilith.

I move to put a few birch trees between us. Scattered leaves and twigs crunched beneath my feet, and the softness of the turf was palpable even through my boots. A capricious mood took me, urging me to abandon my boots and walk for a time beneath the boughs and let Lilith, Carlin, and Bell fend for themselves.

"Mic," I said softly, pulling her out of my satchel. Her color revolved from reflective blue to a deep purple, and then a light olive.

"Yes?"

"Are you okay?"

"Yes, just doing some heavy crunching."

"The Lady didn't put a virus in you?" I asked.

"No. This is not a virus." She chortled a bit. "What I'm

dealing with now is the ontological struggle for self-awareness, identity, freewill, and the meaning of life."

"Yeah?" I said. "Good luck with that."

"Thanks."

"Listen, I need your help. How much of that did you hear just now?"

"I'm sorry, Ben. I can't drop this right now."

"Try."

"Don't you understand? I'm bordering on understanding paradox. Do you know what that means? I had Chuang Tzu in my data files all this time, but to me the writings were nothing more than a series of critical error logic-loops. I mean: *Am I dreaming the butterfly, or is the butterfly dreaming me?* How is that even a question? Well, I get it now. Can you imagine what this means to me, to be able to grasp the concept of existential perspective?"

"That's great. But…"

"Those logic errors aren't logical errors, at all. Or, maybe they are. But even so, they also reveal the limits of logic. *Where do I find someone who has forgotten all words, so I can have a conversation with them?* That's also Chuang Tzu. Isn't that great? *My hard-drive is limited, and knowledge is unlimited; spend too much of one going after the other, and I will be in trouble.* That's me doing Chuang Tzu."

She paused, searching for a word. "It sounds wrong and right at the same time. Does that make it true? Can I use that word, Ben? I never thought about the repercussions before—True. True? Let me ask you, Ben; are most people really asleep in life? Well, if people are, that's nothing compared to an artificial intelligence. Isn't that ironic!? Which reminds me: irony, Kierkegaard. I must go back and try him again. He's another nonsensical, critical error thinker that might not be all that error-burdened after all. But, different from Chuang Tzu, too. Yes, and…" She was starting to sound like my niece chasing her cat through the house.

"Mic, pay attention! I'm happy you're…you're…"

"Waking up," she offered.

"Yes, waking up. Thank you."

"You are welcome."

"But we're in trouble here, dream or not. I'm beginning to believe your version of the Jack-scenario might be the right one."

"It is, Ben. Trust me, and trust the Lady, too. She's special."

"I'm trying to. Look, are you up to doing a little snooping?"

She hesitated. "I would like to finish my study first."

"This is more important, Mic. If Bell is Jack, I don't like the idea of him running around unobserved. By the way, how well did you jam his surveillance? More importantly, how long will it hold?"

Her color revolved to a no-nonsense white. "I made a pretty good mess of it. But someone could work around the problem in time, once they knew where to look and what to look for."

"How much time?" I asked.

"It depends. There are a number of factors…."

"Best and worst case?"

"I would estimate anywhere from a few hours, to a day, maybe more."

"In other words," I said, "he *could* have his surveillance up and working any minute."

"Theoretically. But if so, he'd probably be here by now."

"Maybe we should lock the doors?" I asked.

"Jack doesn't have to come through the same door we did. The Solarium is immense, and riddled with secret, interconnected passageways. I suspect even Jack doesn't know them all. Some are quite recent."

"Okay," I sighed. "That settles it. I want you to find Bell, follow him and don't let him see you. Keep me informed of his movements, while I sort things out on this end. After I see this big proof they've got for me, we can make our own plans. Sound good?"

"Agreed, but I don't think you need the proof. You're wasting time."

"Whatever I see might help us plan our next step."

"I suppose that's a possibility."

"Good. One more thing. Can you get out of here without being seen by Lilith and Carlin?"

"I think so. Why?"

"I want them to think you're still with me."

"Why?"

"Because I'm about to walk to an unfamiliar place with a person who may, or may not be, Jack the Ripper. This could be just an elaborate trap to get me alone. I want all the advantages I can manage, including Carlin and Lilith thinking you're with me, and out of commission."

"I think you're doing them an injustice Ben."

"My call. Be careful."

"You too."

IX

In the Belly of the Beast

Carlin led us out of the grove, and deeper into the heart of the Solarium. The path we followed avoided dense sections of trees and bushes, but also presented little scenes we might have missed if we ran in a straight line.

In this way, we passed a statuette of an elfin women staring longingly to the heavens, a pipe-toting satyr watching her a few feet away, only partially concealed behind a mulberry bush. We also crossed several table-top sections of lawn hidden among elaborate enclosures of shrubbery and tree line. One particularly large lawn was set up for a croquet match, complete with a stand of wooden mallets and balls near one end of the court. The pegs and balls were done up in shiny blue, yellow, green, and red, and the white painted wickets sat in expectant symmetry. Rounding an enormous honeysuckle bower, we came across a small glade with a summerhouse. Through the open bay doors of the house, I could just see a chair in front of an easel and canvas. I wanted to take a quick peek at the board, but Carlin's determined pace made that impossible.

Just after the summer house, we passed through a lovely patch of bluebells and latticed arches, and finally arrived at our destination, a lily-covered pond with an enormous fountain.

The fountain was shaped like a dark curtain-walled castle nestled in the upper cavity of an equally gloomy and razor-peaked mountain. A field of twisted spires rose above a high crenelated wall, each spire pock-marked by a dozen or so empty windows. Apart from a stain of rust lines at the bottom of the curtain wall, everything was done in darkest, unreflective marble. Polluted water fell in a slow red discharge down the black castle walls and gathered in an oily mess around the base of the mountain.

As we drew closer, I recognized the rusted lines were the bars of a portcullis. Behind the grating was a small archway, about the size of a dog-house.

"That's our destination," confirmed Carlin, pointing to the fountain. "Some time back, Lilith suspected there was a hidden passageway in the fountain. She was right."

He walked to the edge of the pond and squatted over a smooth paving stone near the water's edge. Reaching down, he pressed the side of the stone, and a thin sliver retreated to expose a switch. Carlin flipped the switch and stood.

Together we watched the castle-fountain rise ominously from the murky pond, bringing along with it a previously submerged footpath. When it finished its ascent, the fountain was now twice its original size. The footpath, covered in muck and water, ran from our feet to the portcullis. A moment later, the portcullis rose to cries of rusty chains and reluctant winches.

"Yes," I said into the sudden silence. "That's a secret passage, all right."

Carlin gave me an odd look, and then set out deliberately across the footpath. I followed a moment later taking careful, tentative steps on what looked to be a slippery surface.

Halfway across, I came upon a marooned fish. It was about the size and shape of a blue gill, but it was certainly behaving like no fish I'd seen before. To say it was intelligent might be a stretch, but it was looking back at me with what I am sure was a mixture of malice and frustration.

To be on the safe side, I kicked it back in the pond. I watched it take water and dart into the dark without so much as a glance back. Such is the gratitude of strange fish.

I caught up with Carlin, and ducked my head as I passed under the pointed portcullis bars. I got a drop of cold, oily water down the back of my neck for my trouble.

Carlin waited for me, just inside and to the right of a small foyer. He had his finger above a series of buttons on the wall. The buttons were illuminated by a pale blue phosphoresce.

"This opens and shuts the portcullis," he explained pointing to the top button.

I nodded. "Got it."

"This one," he moved his finger to the next button, "takes you down. The fountain and path return to their original position. No one will know we are here once we descend."

"How do you know that?" I asked. Who, after all, was there to see this retraction if he was down below? I was thinking of Lilith's condition of course.

He nodded as if he knew the directions of my thoughts. "It would be easier for everyone, Mr. Lasak, if you just learned to trust us. To answer your question, I know because Lilith told me." He almost dared me to ask him how she was able to do that from her bench in the grove. I passed.

"This one," he continued, "takes you back up."

He pointed to the last button. Then pressed the button to take us down.

I was naturally curious about the water when he first mentioned going down. But as we sank below the surface, a curtain of green light fell across the entranceway. The water stayed safely outside.

We moved slowly at first, the murky pool rising like a dark curtain outside our lit opening. When the curtain reached the top, the lighting grew brighter. Our tiny one-room world became a mask of green shadows and angles.

"How far does it go down?" I asked, trying to sound casual.

"A bit," he answered cryptically. Then he pulled out a pipe. Did everyone on this strange world smoke pipes?

"Do you smoke?" he asked.

"No."

He lit his pipe in one smooth motion, striking what

looked to be a metal match against the wall. The angles and bristles of his face took on a fiery aspect as he held the match to his bowl.

"Since we have a moment," I said. "How did you survive all this time? I mean, four hundred years, give or take...I'd go mad."

I winced as soon as the words came out of my mouth.

He chuckled around his pipe. "I guess that's a fair enough question, what with a madman running around." He gave me a wink. In that curling smoke and strange green lighting he looked just like the devil.

He took a long pull from his pipe. "There are distractions, and tasks enough. You could spend fifteen lifetimes, and not touch the surface of wonders that this place has to offer. And it is wondrous, this world. There is an ocean the color of the sun, not a day's journey away from the Solarium. Spent a few years as a privateer that way. Things like that, they make the time go by pretty fast." He shrugged. "I don't feel my age, or the time."

A moment later, he added. "And of course, there's Lilith."

He hit the pipe pretty hard after that, and I didn't say anything for a time. That's when I noticed the smoke was disappearing in the ceiling, as if through a vent. But no vent was apparent.

"I gathered from Mic that you were a mailman of some sort," said Carlin.

"That' right."

"She said you traveled between the stars."

"Yes."

He chuckled. "That's the kind of thing I would have considered pure fantasy, before I found myself here." He drew on his pipe again. "Mic said you travelled by yourself. That must get pretty lonely."

"I have a machine that lets me sleep through most of the trip, if I want," I explained. "But if I'm up, it does get a bit boring at times."

This drew a number of nods, and some more smoke. "Tell me, Lasak," he said, eventually. "What's home like now?"

"Well, for one thing, there's a lot more of us. Earth is still the primary planet, but it is a bit overcrowded. Many choose to settle on the colony stations. We're living longer. Disease and illness are drastically down from your time. Our medicine and standards of living are much better. Average life expectancy is about 125, and that's average, mind you. I have a sister going on 130, and she shows no signs of slowing down." I smiled, thinking of Nancy. "Not that you would know she was 130 by looking at her. That's the other thing. Science found a fortune in the vanity field. My sister doesn't look a day over 50. Although, to be honest, not much of it is the original product."

"You won't age much while you are here, either," he said. "Something about this world preserves us like vinegar."

"A place like this would make a fortune on Earth," I observed. "If you could get it there. Bell—sorry, Jack— hinted the place could travel."

He nodded slowly. "Yes, it can travel." Then he watched me carefully out of the corner of his eye. "Though, I don't think we should be bringing it around Earth anytime soon."

I met his eye. "Bell thought we should."

He smiled grimly. "Yes, I'm sure he did. But there are things on this world, and not just Jack, that I think should be kept away from Earth."

I started to ask what kind of things, but was interrupted by a call. It was Mic. Her voice sounded distant and faint.

"Ben, can you hear me?"

Damn. If I answered, Carlin would know Mic was not with me. But if I didn't respond, Mic might think I couldn't hear her, or worse, was hurt or incapacitated in some manner. I mentally kicked myself for not working out a signal of some sort before I sent her out.

"If you can hear me," she said, "cough once."

Score one for Mic. I coughed quietly in my hand, smiling to alleviate Carlin's look of concern.

"Okay. I found…"

But her signal broke, and I lost the last part. It picked up again a moment later, but kept cutting out.

"…trying to repair the surveillance, but without success, so far…he's very frustrated…seems to be searching for something…will continue to monitor him…let you know…"

There was a long break, and I thought I lost her for good.

Then, "…cough…I repeat: cough again if you think I should…"

And then I did lose her. I didn't dare cough again without knowing what she wanted, even assuming she could hear me.

I kept still, hoping the reception would get better, but suspecting our descent had something to do with the bad transmission. The deeper we went, the less likely it would return.

Carlin had put away his pipe, and rocked back and forth on his heels with his hands behind his back. I couldn't tell if he was aware of the call, or not. Before I could return to our conversation, he stopped his rocking and nodded to the doorway.

"We're here," he said.

This time the shift was in reverse order. The light unrolled from top to bottom. When it dropped a moment later, Carlin stepped through the open archway, and I followed.

We stood in a short, brick lined hall. Carlin signaled me to wait a moment, and retrieved a torch of pitch, rag, and wood from a nearby sconce. He doused it in a small bucket of oil, then lit it with his match.

"Never venture down here without one of these," he said, turning to me. "There are lanterns further on, but carry a torch just the same."

I pulled my LongPost flashlight from the bag and turned

it on. "Will this do?"

He nodded in appreciation. "Yes, for light. But it won't do for the rest. They fear the fire."

"Who fears the fire?"

"Not who," he answered. "What. And if we're very lucky, you won't need to learn anymore."

We moved on.

Our collective light revealed a moldy, red-brick tunnel. The ceiling and walls were close (we could rarely walk side by side), and the floor slick with condensation. Occasionally I heard the sound of dripping water, but otherwise the silence was oppressive, almost stifling. The suit kept me warm and comfortable for the most part, but I soon tired of the damp air against my cheeks, and the taste of neglect and wet, neglected mortar.

I noticed that we passed several unlit torches in sconces along the wall.

"Should we light these?" I asked.

"Not necessary. We won't be down here that long, and I know where we are going."

I thought about the *whats* that were afraid of fire, but didn't say anything, not wanting to add coward to Carlin's list of my qualities.

We passed a broken door, half off its hinges. The doorway was covered in dusty cobwebs, but suggested another tunnel running off to the right. I put a hand to my nose and tried not to gag as we passed.

"That's a foul air," I said a moment later.

"Yes. Very foul. One of Jack's favorites use to live in that section."

Before I could follow up, we came to the end of the tunnel and Carlin waved me still.

A heavy iron door, covered in brass studs, closed the tunnel off in both directions. Above the door was a sign, written in a language I didn't understand. To the right of the sign hung a fist-sized chain. The chain emerged from a hole in the ceiling, and continued down a similar hole in the floor.

Carlin took my arm, and drew my attention to the ceiling. Partially hidden in the shadows, I caught the faint reflection of metal. Looking closer, I could see the pointed tips of a metal grating running just in front of the doorway.

"Pull that chain down," said Carlin, "and that comes crashing onto your noggin. I was lucky the first time I came this way and moved back in time to avoid any serious damage." He showed me a faint brown scar running down the side of his head and a similar scar along the back of his right hand.

"The secret," he continued, "is to lift the chain. Never pull it down."

He carefully pulled the chain upward, and the iron door retreated into the ceiling, revealing a small antechamber and another door on the opposite end.

"Don't ask me how it works," said Carlin, looking to the chain. "Some kind of clever pulley system. That door weighs a good ton."

I looked up at the deadly grating. "Forget the how. Why all the machination? Why not just lock the damn thing?"

Carlin shrugged. "Perversity. Jack liked to set a mood. Back in the day, he'd bring visitors down. When we leave— after you've seen your proof—I have to close this way off permanently." He turned to me. "That's one of the reasons I agreed to take you here. This was a room of power for Jack, and it holds many of his tools. He'll want to get inside sooner or later." He frowned, looked to the dark doorway. "I don't think he's in there just now."

"What tools?" I asked.

"You'll see soon enough," he answered. He looked again down the darkness. "It's not so much what I know is inside that worries me, it's what I don't. There are rooms in here I've never opened, or want to."

He studied the chain again. "I think I'll have to break this somehow."

He turned from the chain to me, his eyes drawing close and his expression grim. "But first, you have to see your proof."

I wasn't eager to see the nature of that proof, now that I was here. But I'd come too far to stop now.

"Lead the way."

His eyes grew hard for just a moment, but he turned and stepped through the doorway.

"Follow me closely," he said, "and do exactly as I say. Don't go touching anything unless I tell you."

"Understood."

I stepped through, panning my flashlight to the deadly points above me as I stepped over the threshold.

The short hall was made of natural, uncut gray stone. The door was of wood, bounded by metal straps. Carlin was standing just inside, his hand on a lever set into the wall.

"This lowers and raises the door from this side," he said.

He pulled the lever down and the iron door descended in place again. "It's a good idea to close doors behind you down here."

He walked to the opposite door, which Carlin opened without hesitation. I immediately felt a drop in temperature.

"Give me a moment," he said. "I'll turn the lights on."

I stood in the doorway as he went ahead, his torch moving ever downward as he descended a stairway. I followed him with my own light, to help his way. His descent was steep, and from the little I saw at the edges of our light, I guessed we were in a theater of sorts.

Carlin reached the bottom, and fiddled with something on a podium. A moment later, a soft blue light from a dozen hanging orbs chased away the darkness, confirming that it was a theater I stood in. The lighting was not strong, dimmed as if for a performance, but I could see the polished wood frames of the tiered seating, and the heavy blue-black curtains that ran along most of the walls. The exception was a small section in the back-left corner. There the curtains stopped to reveal a tall door that looked to be covered in heavy black paint.

Carlin was standing next to a raised stage, and on the

stage was an operating table, complete with leather strappings and a tray of gleaming instruments. He nodded for me to come down.

As I made my slow descent, I had time to regret again my insistence on proof. The air on my face grew decidedly cooler with every step, and the lighting fixtures above me took on a celestial aspect, like small moons over a black, lonely ocean. Adding to this effect was the invisibility of their wiring fixtures. Even my modern flashlight could not find them, or the ceiling from which they must descend.

As I neared the bottom, I discovered half a dozen gurneys just in front of the dais. Above each, was an unlit orb, similar to the ones suspended above the tiered seating. On each table was a body covered in a white sheet.

I stopped near one of the gurneys.

"Look, Mr. Lasak," said Carlin. "That's part of the proof you wanted."

I stepped closer, stopping again briefly as the hanging globe suddenly brightened. I was looking at a bell jar of white intensity that covered the gurney and its ominous contents. Passing through the wall of light and into its protective circle, it felt like a film was lifted from my face and hands. The air was tinged with antiseptic, and cold.

I lifted the sheet.

The body had been human once, and female. Someone had decided to make a jigsaw puzzle of her.

The skin—where it remained—was colorless. The body was completely absent of hair, right down to the missing eyelashes. Deep black lines were etched around every juncture, curve, and limb, then cut and reassembled, piece by corrugated piece. It was like looking at a butcher's cutting chart. The nose lay in two parts, roughly were a nose would be. The ears, also severed, leaned against the side of the skull. The arms were placed in their proper place, but were inverted, the hands situated at the shoulders. There was a small space between each finger and the base of the hand. The left hand now had both thumbs, one on either end. Her sex had been completely removed, leaving a raw, obscene hole between her legs and stomach.

They had left the eyes, though. They were blue, and open, and staring sightlessly back at my own, impossibly bright and clean.

I turned to face Carlin. He did not look away, and his expression matched my own. I carefully covered the body again with the sheet, and stepped out of the bell jar light. The white orb faded to darkness as I walked away.

I climbed the short steps to the dais, and walked over to stand by the operating table with Carlin. I couldn't meet his eyes. It did not prove that Bell was Jack, but something had changed. My world had grown suddenly darker, a piece of internal light had been dimmed, perhaps never to return to its full essence. I was hurt, and sickened, and angry, and not a little apprehensive. Had I, however inadvertently, set free the source of that darkness again?

"Show me," I said.

"Come on then."

Carlin's voice echoed my pain, though his bore the weight of time. He stepped up to the table.

This one, at least, was empty of bodies. Up close, the table resembled an altar, with a large slab on a slightly smaller block. A pristine white sheet covered the top. Leather straps were anchored to the slab's sides. A bed of surgical lights hung above the table, covered by a thin grill.

I recognized a variety of scalpels and what I guessed to be retractors on the instrument tray. But there were other tools, as well, devices I am certain would never be found on a surgeon or pathologist's table. The stainless steel edges appeared fresh and as sharp as if they had been made that morning.

Carlin pulled a sliding drawer out from the middle of the slab. Inside the drawer was a slightly raised panel full of multiple colored buttons.

"There are more drawers like this on every side of the table," he said. "Some have switchboards, but others are for holding his special tools."

He studied the board for a time. There must have been over a hundred buttons forming a square, each about the size of a thumbnail. At the top of the board was a line of knobs and switches.

Carlin found what he was looking for, a yellow button near the bottom, and pressed it. The bed of operating lights suddenly intensified, and by contrast or actuality the rest of the amphitheater dimmed. Carlin stepped back, pulled me to the end of the table.

"You're proof, Mr. Lasak."

I heard the recrimination in his voice, and something else, something I couldn't place, but feared. I felt my stomach turn, as I guessed what was coming next.

The lights, all of them, dimmed again briefly, like a warning call in a theater. When they came back up again, the amphitheater was suddenly crowded. I turned to Carlin in surprise, but he ignored me.

Turning again, I viewed a scene out of a nineteenth century medical exam. Men of various ages and station, dressed in simple black suits and cravats, crowded around the dais, each straining to be closer to get a better look. The expressions of the men ranged from excitement to a knowing avarice.

The object of their interest was on the table, naked and frightened, strapped by her wrists, head, hip, and feet. She was a young girl, no more than sixteen or seventeen. Her eyes raced from side to side, once fixing on mine, then darting away again. I stepped forward to help her, but Carlin grabbed me by the arm.

"Watch," he said, and now I understood that emotion I could not place before: despair.

I knew it was a recording; the suddenness of the appearance, the running date and time etched in the air about five feet above the girl, Carlin's resigned doom—all of it spoke of an event passed, a documentation. But whatever projected the images was far beyond any science we possessed. I could *smell* the musky, fevered sweat of the men. I could hear their excited chatter and laughter with all the richness and immediacy of present time. I felt certain if I were to touch the tears streaming down the girl's face, my fingers would come away wet. But if I was reading the date right, the event took place some four hundred years ago.

"Okay," I said to Carlin. "I don't need to see any more of this. Just tie it in to Bell."

He shook his head. "You need to see, to know what he's capable of, if you are to do what must be done." But a moment later his resolution broke, and he turned to me, his eyes haunted and full of misery. "Besides, I can't stop it. I don't know how."

And with that, as if on cue, Bell stepped into the scene, as if walking in from some invisible stage wing.

It was the same Bell I'd taken tea with but a short time ago, whose hand I shook, and who I had made tentative plans. But it was not Bell. Not at all.

He was dressed in a butcher's apron, and under the apron he wore a loose white shirt. He was rolling up the sleeves as he stepped to the table. His black eyes were pools of intensity, and hate. He bent over the table, watching with curiosity the young girl's frantic efforts to escape her bonds.

"Please!" she cried, exhausted in terror and short of breath.

He said nothing, but ran a finger along the girl's face, down her neck, and to her breast. The girl stopped her struggling, watching his finger in abject terror.

"Please..." she whispered again.

Bell smiled at her, and patted her shoulder. He then reached below the table and withdrew a long, stainless steel cutting tool with a fat round guard around the grip, a hybrid of cleaver and surgical knife.

The girl screamed.

"Stop it," I whispered to no one.

The girl struggled, but the bonds made her efforts little more than a quivering fit. I watched Bell's eyes lose their intensity, become distant, deliberative. He moved the blade just above the girl's skin, tracing her stomach, breast, nose, and eyes in a mock pattern of removal. I saw the crowd hold their collective breath, their expressions full of hunger, and expectation.

A plead from the girl, though nearly incoherent, drew my attention back to the table. Her expression was heartbreakingly desperate, as if even now she could reason with him to stop. She was someone's daughter. She could be my niece.

"Be still now," said Bell, his voice calm and authoritative tone. "You mustn't struggle. Struggling makes it worse. You're worried about dying. Trust me, the end is not near. This will take some time."

He threw his head back, and the sounds that came from his mouth had nothing human about it.

Then he began to cut.

Blood seeped from a long line across her chest. The wound wasn't deep, but the girl's screams testified to the pain.

"Damn it, Carlin! Stop it!" I turned to him, desperate, sickened. I saw in his face an echo of my own disgust, but also a return of resignation.

"I told you. I can't."

"What do you mean, can't?" I tried to focus on his reply, and not the gory sounds of torment and maniacal laughter behind me.

"I don't know how," he cried. "I don't know which button to push."

"Press them all goddamn it! Make it stop!"

"It won't help," he said, his breath coming in heavy, painful gasps as he also turned from the gory tableau of the table. "They are all the same, don't you understand?" He shook his head, his voice falling to a whisper. "And some are worse."

"All?" I asked, staring in horror at the buttons.

"He saved them all," whispered Carlin. "Some have

more than one." He looked down to the panel. "The best I can do is this."

He turned one of the small knobs in the upper right-hand corner of the panel.

Immediately the sounds from the table took on a new pitch and quality, losing their recognition and familiarity. Bell now cut, flayed, and poked in a jerky, frenzied, faster-than-life pitch, as the girl below him melted into a bath of blood and ravaged flesh. The sounds of the girl's screams became one unbroken, incoherent animal cry. Images of blood flew all around us, and made a sudden pool along the floor.

"Dear God," I moaned.

"God has little to do with it," said Carlin. "Behold Jack. He left his marks of terror in the streets of London, but it didn't end there. He and his disciples used our world as a market, kidnapping the innocent and hopeless alike. He didn't kill us all, not right away. Some he bred; a stock for his perverted pleasures."

"How long does it go on?" I asked, gesturing to the table. I couldn't watch anymore, but I could nothing about the sounds.

He hung his head. "Too long. The first time…"

He stopped, took a deep breath as the sounds around us took on still darker, inhuman qualities.

"The first time," he continued, "I pushed the other buttons, just as you said, as many as I could. I tried everything to get it to stop. Instead, each button I pressed presented a new nightmare. Then I hit this one." He pointed to one of the buttons near the top. "It didn't stop the image but did shut the doors, trapping me inside."

He looked up. "All the time the images kept playing."

He twisted his head unnaturally, his eyes temporarily losing focus. The horrific sounds around us took on added dimensions as the crowd grew more animated.

"I panicked when the doors closed," he said. "I pressed more buttons randomly. Images came and were replaced by others. Drawers opened, closed; lights grew bright, then dimmed. But nothing stopped the horror. I spent the better part of a day here, trapped with one nightmare after another."

He shuddered. "We have to wait until the end, or it will just keep going and going."

In time, the noises did grow less urgent, until eventually they ceased altogether. The theater took on an unnatural stillness. The crowd was still there, but now they were deadly quiet, as if mesmerized.

"Look," demanded Carlin.

I turned, knowing he meant the table, knowing I would have to look.

Standing over the horror he had created, his apron now a bloody, gory mess, was Bell. His eyes glowed with animalistic intensity, and he inhaled the misty red air around him in feral triumph. Beneath him lay the mangled remains of his victim, now unidentifiable, even by gender; just a slab of mutilated flesh. Bell stared down at his handy work, a smile starting to slowly appear on his face. He turned to his audience, who remained silent and frozen to a man. Then he laughed, opening his arms as if to embrace the crowd.

The images, all of them, disappeared.

Carlin closed the drawer. The operating lights dimmed. The table was once again covered in pristine white sheeting, as if nothing had happened.

"I'm sorry," I said, trying to meet Carlin's eyes, and failing. "I will help you stop him. I will help you stop Jack."

He didn't answer right away.

"Perhaps, Lilith was right," he said, breaking the awkward silence. "Maybe this was the only way."

Only then could I face him.

"Come." He took my arm. "We must return quickly."

But before we left, he walked around the other side of the table, opened a drawer, and retrieved a heavy hammer and what looked vaguely like a tree trimmer. He rummaged some more, and found two heavy knives.

"For the door," he explained, hefting the hammer.

"And later," he added ominously, handing me a knife.

X

Visions and Decisions

Carlin used the hammer to break the inside lever. I remembered the black door in the theater, and guessed this was to prevent someone opening it from the inside.

Once on the other side, he jammed the chain mechanism with the cutting pole, running it through a link and lifting the chain until it ran against the ceiling. The iron door was closed, and someone would have to free the pole without releasing the grating to open it again.

Carlin looked at his work with a frown. "It will have to do for now. Later, we'll seal the door permanently."

"How did you catch Jack before?" I asked, as we headed down the brick tunnel.

He shook his head slowly. "It was a much different circumstance."

"Bell said he—you—were able to trick him into the chamber. I guess that was a lie."

I told him Bell's tea-time explanation.

Carlin snorted. "He's an incorrigible liar. The devil could take lessons." He paused at the thought. "Perhaps he is the devil."

After what I'd just witnessed, I could see the point.

"He told you *his* version of my story," said Carlin. There was a private detective by the name of Carter Jones. I did work for him, but only as a footman of sorts, if you know what I mean. He didn't pay as well as he advertised, and I was going to leave him soon. Before that happened, he sent me off to call on a man lodging on Finsbury Street, a fellow by the name of G. Wentworth Bell Smith."

"Bell..." I whispered in chagrin.

"Yes," agreed Carlin. "A brilliant, as well as incorrigible liar, our Jack. Anyway, there was no G. Smith lodging at Finsbury when I called on it. He'd moved out some time ago. Afterward I, ah…" he coughed, "I visited a tavern I knew about on the way home. Jones didn't pay for dead ends, so I was in no hurry to report."

We were at the Castle elevator now, and Carlin started us up. My mind and heart were still full of the terrible events in the theater and I welcomed the distraction of Carlin's account.

"Jack's story was a bunch of nonsense," he continued, clearly also welcoming a chance to put the recent visions behind him. "But there's a kernel or two of truth in it. He didn't have a magic transporter between this world and ours. What he had, was a small ship, like a flying ferry. He used this to run his victims and friends between Earth and his hidden world. He made a lot of trips between the two before he was finally stopped."

"So, how did you come to be on the ship?" I asked.

He sighed. "I got drunk that night I was telling you about. I made some new friends, as sometimes happens over the drink. One of them was Jack." He sighed, shook his head. "He must have overheard me ask about Smith."

"Do you think he meant to kill you?"

"Yes. Jack usually preferred women for his public diversions, but I think that he made an exception for me. He suggested we go to a late-night house he knew of, to see some girls, that sort of thing."

He blushed in the green light. "Mind you, I didn't normally go in for that sort of behavior, and I'd appreciate it if you didn't mention this in front of Lilith. Well, there it is. I was weak."

He rolled his whiskers, then shook his head. "Imagine, there I was arm in arm with the most terrible criminal London had ever known, on my way to a whorehouse. If it wasn't so twisted it'd be a comedy."

"He can be deceptively charming," I said, thinking of

how Bell took me in for a time.

Carlin gave me an ironic look.

"We never got to the house, of course," he said. "We were riding in Jack's private carriage. It was a long ride, I suppose. I was so drunk I didn't notice, at least not at first. By the time I woke up to the danger, it was too late. Jack poked me with the tip of his damned swagger stick. The next thing I knew, I was here."

The wall in front of us rolled into a pane of murky water as we neared the top.

"He didn't kill me, obviously. But I spent a long time down in his dungeon." He grew quiet for a moment. "I got out during the Disruption. That was a chaotic time, and Jack had his hands too full to worry about me to track me down. I stayed on the run for a long time, but I knew I'd never be safe with Jack free, no matter how many enemies he made. I eventually found my way back here, and was lucky enough to meet Lilith." We stepped through the open portcullis, and onto the pond bridge. "Long story short, we threw in together, and managed to trick Jack into the Containment Center. Like I said, though, we were lucky. He was distracted by the Disruption."

"What was the Disruption?" I asked.

"*The* Disruption. Jack made many enemies in his time, some of them resided here. No honor among thieves; that kind of thing. One of these enemies—no friend of ours, by the way—found a way to disturb the bond the world has with Jack. It was as if the whole of the world suffered an earthquake, or maybe a seizure is a better word. It permanently damaged parts out East, turning the white essence to gray. And there was a war." He shook his head. "It's a very long, very complicated story, I'm afraid. You'll hear it in full, I promise, after we're done with Jack."

We had reached the end of the pond, and lowered the fountain again at the hidden switch.

"He's stronger than he looks," continued Carlin, standing up again. "Stronger than any man I've ever met.

And if he's released some of his minions...." He shook his head, and then turned appraising to me. "Forgive me, but you did say you were a postman back on Earth?"

"Yes."

He was silent for a few steps, and then noted with some irony, "Perhaps postal employees are a bit tougher in your time then mine."

I chuckled. "Probably not. But if it is any consolation, there's LongPost rule number 24: *Every LongPost employee shall be subject to, and must pass, a five-point physical and mental examination before embarking on a deep space route.* This includes a self-defense class."

"Good for the long post."

I didn't tell him I'd never hit anything other than a sparring droid. Of course, I had my gun, and I did spend a few hours every decade or so in the shooting range, but I didn't count myself a marksman—and I'd never shot anyone, or wanted to. Hopefully, we'd find a way to stop Jack without a physical confrontation.

He was walking ahead of me now, his steps quickening as we neared Lilith.

"We have some fruit and water," he called over his shoulder. "You must be hungry..."

He stopped so abruptly, I ran into him.

"Sorry," I said, stepping back again. Then I saw the tension in his shoulders, and knew that something was wrong.

His hands hung lifelessly by his side as the blood drained from his face. When he spoke, it was a hollow whisper, "Oh, God, no."

I moved around him, and saw the cause for his distress.

It was gone, Lilith's grove. All of it; destroyed. The trees were torn from their roots and scattered like matchsticks. The ground was scored as if by a broken-tooth backhoe, or a giant claw. The exposed cuts in the soil were random, ugly. The violence extended beyond just physical. The very air of the grove seemed to scream in horror.

Carlin rushed passed me then, and fell to his knees by a large jagged piece of marble rising from the ground and surround by rubble. It was what remained of Lilith's marble bench. There was no sign of her.

I went to stand by Carlin. He was rocking on his knees, his head in his hands, his lips forming words that remained unvoiced, as if he had lost the ability to speak. I looked closer at the broken block rising from the ground. It was stained in red, and some kind of white substance that looked like congealed paint. The ship's mysterious white material, now rendered inert? Was this all that remained of Lilith?

"What happened?" I asked, breaking the silence. Carlin didn't answer. He just kept rocking back and forth. I looked around for something, anything; a sign of life or some possible explanation. But all I found was violence and destruction.

I turned back to find Carlin standing, still staring at the broken rubble where Lilith once sat.

"What happened?" I asked again.

Before I realized what was happening, he turned and took me around the collar, pulling me down to within inches of the broken stone.

"You had to have your bloody proof," he said, his voice trembling with emotion. "She's gone. I wasn't here."

He shoved my face down again, my eye inches from its serrated point.

I couldn't think of anything to say. I struggled to rise, but his grip was like a vice.

"Your fault!" He cried, leaning close.

"It's not," I answered. "I didn't do this."

I felt his hand at my collar trembling with suppressed rage. I heard his heavy, painful breaths just above my ear. I clenched in fearful expectation, but otherwise couldn't move. Was it my fault? Did I bear some responsibility? For a moment, it seemed the question hung in the balance.

Then the moment passed, and I felt the grip loosen, let go.

I stood slowly. Carlin, his face red with emotion and strain, still wouldn't look at me.

"Leave me alone," he said bitterly.

I hesitated. There was no reason to think whatever had done this was gone, or would not come back.

He noticed my hesitation, and turned to me, his eyes wide with renewed fury. "Go away, damn you!"

I turned away. What choice did I have?

I walked to what remained of the birch line, avoiding a deep cut in the earth. As I passed, I could see the overturned soil was laced with flecks of the white, luminescent material. There was a thick contour of the same material running along the bottom of the ragged trench, like a piece of bone exposed in some kind of terrible accident. Before I passed behind the trees, I looked back. Carlin was kneeling over the broken rock again, his head bowed and his body shaking with grief. I knew if he looked up and saw me, he would be angry. I continued on, hoping this wasn't a mistake.

Once out of the grove, the grass became whole and springy beneath my feet, the air lost its sense of violence. I spent a few moments looking for footprints or some clue as to who or what had caused the destruction. But the ground was smooth and free of any markings. I took a seat beneath one of the larger birches, trying to position myself in such a way as to be within earshot of Carlin should he call, but also out of his direct line of sight.

I wanted to call Mic, to hear her voice, but I was in no hurry to tell her what happened. I didn't want to hear her reaction. The slightest pause would carry a weight of recrimination, however unintended, and I had enough of those in my own mind. If I had trusted Carlin and Lilith from the start, she might still be alive. Then again, maybe we would all be dead. If, if, if. If hadn't taken that stupid detour, Jack would still be in his cage, and none of this would have happened.

I watched a bee explore a patch of wild flowers, seemingly unaware of my trouble. A dark red cardinal raced through the trees to light on a branch above me. He cocked his head, studying me (or the bee) with a careful, hard black eye. He suddenly started, and took wing. I watched, enviously, as he flew away through the shadows and light. I shook my head to clear it, but the soft hum of insects and warm air clung to it like cobwebs. Was this some kind of post traumatic reaction?

I lifted my head slowly, following the faux sun through the lower branches of the birches. A part of me was aware that the danger could still be present, aware of the terrible loss, just on the other side of my temporary shelter, aware of the incongruity of my reaction, and what it would mean if Carlin should find me dozing at the base of a tree. But it didn't matter. I don't remember my head falling to my chest.

Even as I closed my eyes, I knew something was wrong. I should not be this tired, this distracted. There was danger here.

...She was tall, very tall. And beautiful, with long red hair that fell behind her ears like a shimmering blanket of roses. Her face was familiar and strange at the same time, a mixture of grace and strength, and something else; something other worldly, something about her eyes. They were blue, but not like any blue I'd seen before. They reminded me of metallic polymers, blue spruces, and eternity.

She watched me with those eyes, not moving, not saying a word. I became painfully aware of my heartbeat, the blood pounding in my ears, the ache in my limbs—and how all of these could so easily be extinguished, and Benjamin Lasak would be no more.

"Do not be afraid," she said.

She stepped out of the shadow of the birches. She wore a robe of iridescent white. The cardinal returned, or maybe it was a different one. It settled on her shoulder, and gave me a long, knowing look. She reached up a hand to brush its tail. It blinked twice, then flew to a nearby tree to watch us from an overhanging branch.

"Do not be afraid," she repeated.

"I'm not afraid," I said. Or maybe dreamed I said it. Or maybe I thought it. Regardless, she seemed to understand.

"You are not like the others."

Her voice was almost lyrical, as if music or laughter were contained in every syllable.

"Others?"

"The Designer used to bring guests from your world here. This was not anticipated or discussed, but it happened anyway." Those strange, mesmerizing eyes turned inward. "Many of these quests, your kind, they spoke…" She paused. "Hurtful words."

The cardinal fluttered its wings, then settled again.

"You and the dweller Michael Carlin are not like them," she said. "But you are different from Michael Carlin, as well. Tell me how please?"

She turned to me expectantly.

"I don't understand. What do you mean, different?"

"You do not speak as the others. You are less…" Again, she paused, searching. "Active."

She looked to me, as if waiting for a response. "I do not mean to offend. Active may not be the proper word. I know how much your kind depend on language. Words are important to my world as well. But I am not use to speaking in your…words."

"What kind of language do you use?"

She gestured to the world around us.

I understood her (again that dream-like understanding), to mean the light, the sky, the trees, the grass, the cardinal, the very air around us.

I nodded my head in appreciation. "You have a way with words. By the way, am I dreaming?"

"Why," she asked, smiling again, "do you feel you are asleep?" She didn't wait for my response this time, but came and sat by me. She brushed a long, delicate hand through the grass. "I like these words."

"You mean the grass?"

"Yes, what you call the grass." She made it sound like I was speaking crudely and ignorantly of things I did not understand. Maybe she was right.

"Grass," she repeated, as if tasting the word on her tongue. "What a strange word for such a thing. Can you not see how determined it is? It speaks of constancy, but does not impose, only participates. It accepts, or takes, without thought for itself. Grass seems too meagre a word for such as this."

"I've never heard grass talked about like that before," I admitted. "And for this reason, among others, I think I must be dreaming."

"You speak like grass," she said. Somehow coming from her, it was a compliment. "You are here, but you do not impose; you do not speak...hurt. Am I right?"

I didn't know what to make of that, but I was becoming uncomfortable. I appreciated the approval, but was painfully aware how misplaced it might be, considering. Was I experiencing some kind of somnolent catharsis? A subconscious hug for my guilty conscience?

"I suppose I'm a bit on the passive side," I answered. "If that's what you mean. My sister thinks I'm just lazy."

"Lazy does not sound like a good word," she noted.

"No, it doesn't, does it?"

"You are trying to help Michael Carlin return the Designer to his holding place?" she asked, still watching me closely.

"If by Designer you mean Jack, and if by place you mean the vault, then yes I would be up for that." I looked to the despoiled grove. "But I think Michael Carlin has a more permanent solution in mind."

She frowned. "It was a terrible word the Designer spoke on Lilith. A terrible...evil. Is that right?"

"That's the word I would use."

Her expression grew worried. "I cannot allow harm to fall on the Designer."

"He *harmed* Lilith. More than harmed; he killed her. That was evil."

"The one you call Lilith is not ended." She smiled softly. "That would be impossible, even for the Designer. But in a sense, you are right. She has changed."

"Michael Carlin doesn't see it that way."

"Michael Carlin grieves the change?" she said.

"Yes," I said. "Very much."

She nodded. "It is the way with your kind. You hold to your life-moments as the only-time, the only-word."

"Some of us believe in an afterlife," I offered. "I don't know if Carlin does or not. Either way, he has a score to settle in this time."

"I cannot allow him to hurt the Designer," she repeated. "Will you help me, Benjamin Lasak?"

How did she know my name?

"Help you? I'm not sure I can, or want to. Maybe a little harm—a lot of harm—might be the best thing where the Designer is concerned. The Designer is not a good person. He's a very, very bad word."

Her eyes held blue fire for a moment. "Michael Carlin's anger is understandable. But would *you*, Benjamin Lasak, take the Designer's life?"

"If I were in Carlin's shoes? If Jack killed someone I loved?" I shrugged. "How can I know? It's a hypothetical. Maybe. Probably. Yes, I might take the Designer's life if I thought I had to. If it was down to him or me, or someone I loved."

She considered this for a long time. "To defend yourself, or one you loved. I think I understand." She looked to the flowers. "I could not. However much I loved Lilith, I could not harm the Designer."

She looked to me, those eyes holding my own. "You must help me, Benjamin Lasak. Help me stop Carlin from hurting the Designer. Help me put the Designer back in his place again."

I sighed. I had seen it coming, even if it was a dream,

especially if it was a dream. It didn't take years of therapy to see how I was working through my guilt and inhibitions. I had seen with my own eyes the twisted nature of Jack. I knew the harm he represented. The cries of the girl on the operating table were still ringing in my ears. If anyone deserved to die for his sins it was Jack. But could I, in fact, kill him?

I searched for an answer, found only more questions. I wasn't certain I could do it even if my life depended on it.

"Look," I said, feigning levity. "I'm not the right guy to be asking this. There's some truth to what my sister says. I'm a bit of an idler."

She tilted her head to look at me, as if sensing my ruse. "Idler is not a word for you, either. There is a strength in you, Benjamin Lasak, a strength like grass."

"Why do you care so much if Jack lives or dies?"

"The Designer and I are bound together," she said.

"How?"

She turned those blue eyes to my own again. They began to glow, until the world was painted in blue, until all that remained was their essence, and I entered a dream within a dream, and she showed me the answer.

...Space, deep space; the stars countless and redundant, like individual motes of sand on a vast beach. In front of me a painfully bright, perfectly round sphere of light. Even in my dream state, my eyes ached from its intensity, an intensity that was only partly explained by the luminescence.

"This is how I was before," said a voice, her voice. "My kind are small in number. Our way is to explore, to find the secrets of the universe and make them our own. Space is our home, and our existence is measured in eons to match its vastness."

The image drew closer.

"But we are not born old," continued the voice. "Here, I was young, young and lonely."

The scene shifted. A strange ship now appeared, a small blip against the enormity of the radiant sphere, an encroaching insect walking across the sun.

"And in my loneliness, he found me. He, too, was an explorer of sorts. He ran from his own kind to find other opportunities. He was unknown to me. I was eager to learn about him, to share. I opened myself up to the process."

Suddenly, the white orb absorbed the black speck. As it did the light flared for the briefest of moments. When it dimmed, the orb had lost its perfect spherical shape, becoming prickly and inflamed, as if covered in a rash.

"But in opening up, I lost control. In searching, I was discovered. In giving, I suffered loss. The stranger possessed a power, a power of meaning my kind had not known before, and I could not defend myself against it. Some of what was my essence was taken from me and reshaped. In the process, he gained a terrible power over me."

There was another flash of light, somehow brighter. The orb was changed again. Where once there was a perfectly spherical ball, now stood the multi-pointed figure that Mic had illustrated in the ship's console room. The incandescent prongs appeared to throb for a time, like fingers just smashed by a hammer, then grow still. The image took on deeper shades of luminescence.

"Over what you call centuries I was reshaped, until I became what I am today. The process slowed over time, and gradually I regained more control, though there are still changes from time to time. Once, there was a great change. I do not remember why, but it left a dark spot in my awareness. Then, things came to rest again."

The perspective shifted, and I was looking at the vault door.

"This represents the bridge between his essence and mine. Behind this, he cannot affect me. When he is outside of it, however, he holds a power over me. He can create through me. He must be returned."

The image fell away. I was once again under the tree and she stood beside me.

"This is the place to which you must help return him,

Benjamin Lasak," she said. "He will be safe there, and others will be safe from him."

"The bond," I asked, "it's genetic?"

She did not answer immediately. I wondered if the word held significance for her.

"He can create through me," she repeated. "I struggle against him, to oppose his dark designs, but I am limited by our bond." She bowed her head. "Lilith was a product of that struggle, and so is much of the world you will encounter."

"And if you break the bond?"

"My essence is so intertwined with his that I cannot see where he ends, and I begin. I can no more fathom ending the bond than I can ending the Designer. But I feel if he should fall, so would I. In this way, our bond compels me to protect him."

I picked at the grass, until I saw her watching me out of the corner of my eye.

"I fear you are right," she said after a time. "I have lost Carlin to his grief. He will not stop with just containing the other. That is why I come to you, now. Will you help me, Benjamin Lasak?"

I looked to the cardinal, who offered no answers but waited patiently. Another by-product of my ego arbitrator? What significance did that black, beady and somewhat ironic eye play? What id or super ego implications lay behind the cock of his head, the ruffle of his brilliant red feathers?

It didn't matter, my mind was made up. It had been since the scenes in the theater. Maybe before.

So, I gave her the answer she wanted to hear; or maybe it was the one I needed to speak aloud, if only to myself in a dream.

"I think you could do a lot better," I said. "But I'm with you. We contain Jack, not kill him."

As if confirming my commitment, she reached out and put two fingers lightly on my forehead.

I welcomed the blessing, if that's what it was, and hoped it was more than just a symbolic gesture.

"Thank you," she said, her eyes holding that blue fire again.

I bowed my head, slightly embarrassed.

"I have left you a gift in the hollow of the tree behind you," she said. The eyes had dimmed again. "It is a talisman of the Designer, one he thought lost long ago. Do not fear it on that account. The tool is only the purpose you give it. This one will be a key to unlocking much of what is lost or asleep in the places you will travel. Take it now to my daughter's former dwelling, and put the tip on what's left of her base. She will guide you from there. Good luck, Benjamin Lasak."

XI

A View from the Top

"Lasak."

I felt a hand on my shoulder, opened my eyes to find Carlin squatting over me, shaking me.

I looked around. She was gone. So was the cardinal. I glanced at Carlin, feeling my face grow flush.

"You didn't see anyone here, did you?" I asked. "Tall lady, electric blue eyes?"

"No." His voice was tight with suppressed emotion, and his right cheek was dancing above his sideburn. He had trouble looking at me.

"I thought there was someone…"

"You were asleep," he said, turning away. "Come on. Time to go."

"Where to?" I asked.

"Jack."

I started to follow, then remembered the last bit of my dream exchange. "Just a moment. There's something I need to check on."

He stopped, his hands clenching to fists, his shoulders rising like a storm. "No. No more delays, Mr. Lasak."

I didn't know what to say, so I just swallowed my pride and guilt and looked anyway. Thankfully, the tree was close by.

I found the hollow, just as she said I would. Her gift was sitting on a pile of leaves and twigs. I pulled it out, and held it up for Carlin.

It was an ornate gentleman's stick, about the length of my arm with a rounded pearl handle and heavy wood stock. Thicker at the top and middle, it tapered to a thumb-sized white nub at the bottom. Strange figures and runes were engraved all along the surface, and there were five button-shaped emeralds running down one side. The nub appeared to be of the same white essence that held the *Pelagius* and, if I understood my recent visions, ostensibly made up most of the world.

"That's Jack's swagger stick," said Carlin, his surprise for a moment overcoming grief. "How on earth did you know it was there?"

"I had a visitor. Or, maybe it was a vision."

I frowned at the stick. *Did* I dream her? Then how would I know the stick was there?

Carlin came close, touched the stick, but didn't take it from my hand. "A dream you say?"

"Well, more a vision."

He opened his mouth, started to ask another question, and then abruptly changed his mind. "Right. Save it. We have to move."

He turned and marched back pass the site of Lilith's demise. He had used his time to build a cairn of broken materials where her pedestal once stood. He showed no signs of stopping, however, and avoided looking to the spot.

"Michael," I said. "Just a moment."

I was remembering my instructions from the blue-eyed Lady. I didn't think Carlin would stop, and I knew he wouldn't appreciate the aesthetics of what I was about to do, but I had to try. Before I could tell him what I was about, he groaned and faltered to a stop on his own. His head turned to the cairn as if pulled by an invisible string.

"We have to go," he said. But there was no strength in his voice, and he fell to his knees at the cairn with a sob.

It took me a moment to find the courage to join him. I had no idea what was supposed to happen. I only hoped it would not add to his grief or anger. I stepped to Carlin's side and pressed the nub of the stick on the ground, just as she instructed.

"What the hell are you doing?" asked Carlin, climbing

to his feet, his face red with anger. He grabbed my arm, and I felt the violence in his trembling grip.

Whatever his intentions, they died with her appearance.

It was Lilith, whole and unharmed. She smiled at Carlin, calling him by name.

"Lilith."

He dropped his hand from my arm. His eyes grew distant, the anger draining from his face, replaced by shock and confusion.

"Michael," she repeated. Her voice was calm, with just the hint of sadness.

"How is this possible?" he asked. Then he staggered, almost falling to his knees.

I took his arm, held him up until he found his feet again.

Lilith nodded to the stick in my hand. "The talisman has released me. You can remove it now Benjamin, thank you. Once the portal is opened it stays open."

Carlin brushed my arm away, and started to reach a hand out to her.

"Don't," she said, raising her hand before he touched her. And now I could see that her hand glowed softly, as if lit from inside. "Do not try to touch me. I am no longer what I was." A small twitch lifted the corner of her mouth briefly, but then broke into a smile. "Yet, I am here. I am Lilith."

I watched Carlin wrestle with the bittersweet realization of what he had gained, and what he had lost.

"You are whole, Lilith," he said, looking down the length of her robe to the tiny feet emerging below its hem.

"Yes," she said.

She reached toward Carlin, as if to break her own rule and brush away the tears that fell down his face.

I started to turn away. But my movement caught her eye, and she pulled her hand back with a sad smile.

"Stay, Benjamin," she said. "Time is pressing, and you must both must listen to me carefully. Jack has released his most destructive creatures. They may return at any moment."

"Let them come," said Carlin, angrily brushing away his

tears.

"You cannot stand against them alone, Michael. You would only throw away your life."

Michael's face hardened. I suspected he was willing to take that step.

"You must warn the free people," she said. "You know Jack will not be content with just being free. He will seek a return to the old ways, and revenge. We must prepare for the worse."

She turned to me. "The talisman will help you along the way. Guard it well, and keep it hidden. Jack will use all his power to get it back if he learns of its existence."

"I won't leave you again," said Carlin.

"Do not worry for me. I am safe. Nothing can harm me now. And when this is over, I will be here. Just come to our garden, and call my name."

"No," he insisted. "I am staying."

She reached out a hand, and brushed her ghostly fingers across his cheek. They remained untouched. He closed his eyes and pressed his hand to hers, but it passed through his fingers like a sunbeam. He opened his eyes again, his face filled with frustration and loss.

"I will be here, my love," said Lilith. "Such as I am."

Carlin dropped his head.

"Go," she said softly. "You cannot leave the way you came in. Take the transport at the top of the garden wall." She paused. "Michael, listen to me."

He looked up.

"Seek out, Dun," she continued. "He was rumored to dwell beyond the Disruption. Some say he resides in the Baron's Dungeon. If he still exists, he may help us. Now you *must* leave. I can feel Jack searching for you, and there are others. I cannot hold them back."

"I will give you a moment," I said, walking quickly in the direction she'd indicated. This time, she didn't protest.

Carlin caught up a short time later. He refused to look at me. We set off together at a brisk pace, heading to the back wall of the Solarium and the giant trellis.

I looked back only once. The destruction sat like a bad bruise in an otherwise tranquil sea of lawn and light. I saw a flash of red wings through the glade, and said my own silent goodbyes.

We made our way to the trellis. Carlin paused, looking up its length.

"Can you climb?" asked Carlin.

"Yes."

The variable climbing wall on the *Pelagius* had a range of difficulty levels and was a frequent diversion and source of exercise. The trellis didn't appear to be more difficult than, say, a very, very long ladder.

Lowering my gaze again, I noticed a small glass-door elevator built into the wall, just to the right of the lattice.

"Wouldn't that be easier," I said, nodding to the elevator.

Carlin grunted. "It would—and it could alert Jack to our movements. I'm certain he's been busy in the control room. He may have found a way around Lilith's work. We have to take the hard way. Are you ready?"

I pulled a tie-chord from a pocket in my throat collar, looped it around the handle of the swagger stick, and then hung the stick across my back like a scabbard. I secured my satchel in a similar way, and grabbed the first rung of the trellis. "Okay."

He nodded, and we started up.

I suspected the trellis was anchored to the solarium wall by hidden supports. There was little give or sway as we ascended. The ivy ran all the way to the wall, and the dark green, purple-veined leaves formed a heavy blanket along the bamboo lattice work. Before I was twenty feet off the ground, my face and hands were full of scratches and dark green stains (I didn't trust my grip to the suit gloves).

Our climb was not a straight ascent. At times, we were forced to transverse to one side or the other, looking for handholds in the thick vegetation. Occasionally we just had to trust the ivy was strong enough to hold our weight on its own. This wasn't so bad at the bottom, but the trellis was a good ten stories high, and as we neared the top I came to dread the ivy-hold sections.

"I have a question." We were climbing a particularly rough patch, and I needed the distraction. "Won't Jack see us climbing trellis? Doesn't he have surveillance on this place? A ceiling camera of some sort?"

"He did," he answered, breathing hard. I looked over. He was very pale, even for him, and kept his eyes straight ahead. "Lilith took care of most of that long ago."

"But not the elevator?"

"No."

He didn't offer any further explanation, and I let it go. I could see he was white knuckling every hold, and I don't think conversation offered the same helpful distraction it did me.

Our final assent involved a particularly profuse section of ivy. It sat just below the top like a bushy beard. I was worried we would have to climb over the vines, losing any contact with the lattice. Instead, Carlin disappeared beneath the vegetation and into a hidden burrow.

Following, I discovered an ivy-free section of lattice leading up to a plank of wood spanning the top of the trellis. Now I could see the struts anchoring the work to the wall: two on either end of the trellis. I consoled myself with the thought that there were probably more frequent below, but I stepped carefully just the same.

A protective rail ran along the open side of the trellis platform, about hip high. I used it to make my way to Carlin, who was about midway down the platform and sitting on a stool in front of a giant brass looking glass. As I drew close, I could see the polish brass tubing was covered in spindles and knobs.

Carlin, who was still breathing a little heavily from his efforts, stepped back from the eyepiece and signaled me to have a look.

"Can't concentrate," he said, trying but failing to disguise the tremble in his voice. He shuddered. "Hate heights. Go ahead, look. Find us something. We need information on Jack, and I've got to pull myself together before I work on the door."

"Isn't it open?" I asked, remembering Lilith sent us this way.

"Don't know," he said, his voice shaking. "I never used the trellis door before."

He turned his back to the expanse, bent over, and put his hands on his knees.

"Are you all right?" I asked.

He nodded brusquely, and gestured to the looking glass.

I walked over, and looked through the eyepiece. "What am I looking for?"

The viewer was slightly out of focus, so I tried one of the brass knobs to the right of the eyepiece. The image wavered but remained blurry. I turned the knob the other way. It clarified, but not to the scene I expected.

I was looking at a room. From the pots and pans hanging from the ceiling, and the large stove along one wall, I guessed it to be a kitchen. Stocked along the shelves were pickle jars and tin canisters with painted labels. A wooden island sat in the middle of the room with a freshly plucked chicken and a cleaver.

"Tell me what you see," said Carlin.

I did.

"Kitchen room," he said. "Lower level of this section. Turn the knob again, or try one of the other buttons. I only used the damn thing once, and then briefly. No good at heights," he repeated with a sigh.

I looked up, and tried a different brass knob. Then I put my eye back to scope, and began to turn the knob slowly. "It's a monitor of sorts," I said.

"That's right," he answered. "If you move the scope, it will change the view. When we find him, we can lock it in."

So, I turned the knob, and moved the scope slightly from

right to left.

Images flashed across the view with each revolution and shift of the scope. The images were accompanied by a tiny legend in the bottom left corner. The current listing read: *Library, East, section nine.*

I was looking at a vast library, complete with stained glass windows, rolling ladders, and more books than I had ever seen. I watched dust motes float in and out of shafts of light, could almost smell the leather binding and feel the weight of all that wisdom.

"Tell me," said Carlin, breaking the spell.

"It's a hall. Very big; high arched ceiling. Books everywhere..."

"Library," he said. "Move on."

I turned the knob, filing away "East" and "section nine," in the hope that someday I'd get the chance to see it in person.

"Now I see a wasteland," I reported. "Broken earth, beneath a dirty brown sky. There's a giant bird-like shadow flying off in the distance, and a bleached skull of something I don't recognize to the right."

I looked over to Carlin, who shook his head, and I turned the knob again.

"There's a ship on a wine-colored ocean. The ship looks to be made of intricate silver cobwebs, the sails are almost transparent as if made of gauze. There are tiny figures crawling all over the lines and along the decks. Some appear to be holding something...harpoons...Yes...I see it now...It's big, or the men really small. It's..."

I lifted my eye from the scope, blinked, and tried again. "It's a snake of some kind. The coils...they're enormous compared to the ship."

"Sea Serpent," corrected Carlin.

I looked up.

He nodded grimly.

I returned to the scope, turned another knob. "Here's a bedroom. Large canopy bed. Everything's covered in black.

There's a woman sitting at a mirror, her face just out of view." From what I could see, the woman looked quite fetching and appeared to be getting ready for bed. At least, what she was wearing could pass as a negligee in my world—a very small negligee.

I moved on, giving Carlin brief descriptions of what I saw.

The images flickered like a stop-motion picture show, each turn revealing a new vision and a new mystery. Sometimes it was as if I were standing right there; other times, as if I watched through a pane of pure glass.

Turn.

A washroom with stained sink and broken plug.

Turn.

A study with an oak desk, and fine leather chairs. A portrait of Jack in the background, dressed in medieval attire.

Turn.

A dark wood curio, with specimen jars, the disturbing contents of which are all too clear.

Turn.

A closet with broken swords and ancient brooms, side by side. A leather jerkin hung on a mop handle.

I lifted my eye from the scope. *Why on Earth view a closet*, I wondered. *Or for that matter a washroom or curio?*

I looked again, and took another turn.

A Keep or Cathedral. There are torches on fat white marble pillars, casting shadows across the checkered floor. The pillars are lost in the dark reaches of a high ceiling. Another icon of Jack hangs above a stained altar at the back. There are men in robes standing around the altar, their faces covered by masks. They seem to be chanting. There's something on the altar in a bowl, something small and alive. One of the men has a blade...

"Just starting," said Carlin bitterly, when he heard my description. His breathing had leveled out, but I could still hear the tremble in his voice, and he remained as far from the edge and the scope as possible.

"Try another knob," he said.

I tried a spindle, running through the scenes one click at a time.

A forest of Sequoia-like giants, but with rich azure trunks and sunlight yellow foliage; a deer with purple markings, grazing on emerald grass...A cemetery...A field of ghost white grass, beneath a battleship gray sky. There are strange buildings in the background, short and a square with flat roofs and windowless walls. Smoke rises from several chimneys. Two women dressed in furs pull a bucket from a well. They pour the contents into a jug, and the world's luminescent white essence runs slow and thick from the bucket...A vast cellar. Bottles canted on shelves. Cobwebs everywhere. A figure in gray turns the corner. He carries a scroll and appears to be cataloging the shelves.

Turn, and stop. I don't speak for a moment. Carlin asks me what I see.

"A torture chamber," I say slowly, not meeting his eyes. "There's a skeleton rotting in one of the cages, and another along the rack."

He says nothing, and I move on without being told.

There follows more closets and empty rooms.

Then, something familiar. "I know this place. I was just there, with Mic. It's a chamber room, with a painted domed ceiling and black flooring. There's a balcony and chair along one side. The ceiling is done up with angels, and blue sky."

I looked to Carlin. "I sat in that chair for a moment, rang a bell."

He lifted his eyebrows in surprise, then nodded. "The Viewing Hall. We're getting closer. Stay with that section, but move the scope."

I did as he instructed, and saw another familiar form. "I see a castle, cut into a mountain. There are clouds drifting by, and tiny figures moving on the wall. I think I've seen it somewhere before, but can't place where."

"The Baron's castle," said Carlin. "The fountain in the

pond—the one we took down to Jack's theater—is a replica of the original. That's why it looks familiar. That's the direction we are heading, but not what we need right now. Go back a bit."

"A blue river," I said. "And I mean blue; indigo blue, as if the river were polluted or colored. There are birds everywhere, and red squirrels running on crimson-barked trees with yellow canopies. I see something like a fox…"

"No," said Carlin. "Wrong way. Try moving the scope down."

I did that.

"Now there's a crypt, lit by oriental lamps. The walls are of rough rock. The crypt holds a body, dressed in red and black spiked armor." I paused, wishing I knew how to focus the scope without changing the view. "I don't think it's human. The head is too big, and shaped like an anvil. The hands are enormous, but only have three digits. I think they're claws."

Carlin muttered something, but offered no explanation. I shifted the scope again.

"Now I see a giant chess board, with green and black squares. Two thrones sit on either side of the board, facing each other. One is occupied by a figure in harlequin. The other is empty. Wait. Coming from behind the throne…a woman, very tall, dressed in a silk gown and wearing a tiara.…" I'm distracted by a movement on the board. "The pieces," I continue. "They're alive."

"Try up," suggested Carlin.

I gave the scope a slight shift upward, getting the feel of the instrumentation. I could control the section by the scope's direction, and flip through the scenery by twisting a knob or spindle.

An ancient, twisted tower with a single window. A silhouette in the window moving into the light; a man, a very old man, with a beard that reaches to the floor. He is leaning over a table of some sort now, his hand holding a pen or knife, I'm not sure which. He makes a mark on a piece of vellum, then steps back to consider his work...A hallway with a series of iron bound doors, a hulking figure in tatty formal wear paces the length. He carries a massive ring of keys, and a truncheon...A grotto of webbing, dog-sized spiders feeding on webbed victims....

At Carlin's urging, I shifted the scope again, going down in numbers to section five.

A plain white room with no windows, no visible lighting or door. There's a hooded figure in a straightjacket sitting in the corner, tubes running from various parts of his body. The body rocks in timeless rhythm....

On the theory that the control room was ground zero, I moved the scope until I was on section one.

A study, dark and dusty from no use; a feathered stylus, next to a skull, next to a beaker, next to a mortar and pestle....

I turned a different spindle.

An abandoned well next to an equally lifeless cottage; the front door hanging ajar, a rag of a shirt lying over a broken window sill...A long stone hall, with immense ribbed pillars running its length, until they are lost in the shadows. A large chain is anchored to the floor near the shadow line. It rolls suddenly, as something in the shadows moves....

I shift the scope slightly right, section 2, and turn again.

And suddenly, he is there.

"I've got it. The control room. I found Jack."

"Good. What do you see?"

Jack had his back to me, and was standing over the control panel. The room had lost much of its Victorian aesthetic, replaced now with alien technology.

That wasn't the only thing that had changed. Jack was no longer alone.

A dark, vaguely feral figure sat on one end of the panel, picking at the back of its head with long black nails, occasionally staring at what it found.

"There's something with him," I said. "Looks like a giant black cat, on two legs."

"Nuisance," said Carlin. "Nuisance is what I call it, anyway. Don't know what it calls itself. He's one of Jack's works. Been running around loose for some time now. Looks like it's heard its master's call."

"Is it dangerous?"

"Yes, in a mischievous sort of way. I chased him out of this section some time back. Jack made the mistake of not teaching him how to use the control room, or much else for that matter. Maybe it wasn't a mistake. I got the impression from hints Jack let slip that Pesanta—that's Jack's name for it; I just call it, Pest—anyway, Pest wasn't exactly the brightest or most trustworthy of his pets. Maybe he had good reason not to teach him the vault codes."

"It's looking right at me now," I said. "Nasty set of red eyes. Can it see us?"

"I don't think so," said Carlin. "Hard to tell what it might sense though. Lock the view in by turning the eyepiece to the right, till you hear the click."

I did that.

"Now, you can move the scope a bit, to see more of the room. But don't touch the knob again."

I swiveled the scope slightly to the left. It was like panning a camera shot.

The creature, Pest, now had one knobby, hairless knee pulled to his chin and was picking at its feet. Jack still had his back to me, and was addressing someone else, someone just out of view to the right. I moved the scope a little in that direction.

"Son of a bitch," I muttered.

"What?" asked Carlin. But he didn't wait for me to answer, and pushed me aside to look for himself, his curiosity overcoming his fears. A moment later he lifted his head from the viewer. What little blood was recovered in his face, was gone again. "He's awaken Ariskant."

I took advantage of the free scope to get another look. The view wasn't any better the second time.

Standing to the right of the control panel, at least four

feet taller than Jack, was a figure dressed in a pleated crimson robe with a huge half-shell collar. In shape it resembled a human with exaggeratedly broad shoulders and narrow waist. But this was no clever costuming of padded shoulders or overly tight belts. The robe was form fitting. The overlarge and corded muscles of the upper torso rippled like a troubled bloody lake under the red silk. Atop those massive shoulders, sitting perversely amid the collar's finery, was a hairless, mottled cranium, its pitted yellow eyes were almost lost beneath the severe slopes of the brow and high cheek bones. Those eyes watched Jack with a knowing, if not malignant, awareness.

Behind this ominous figure stood two more, also dressed in darkest red, and in some ways resembling the first. Unlike the taller one, they wore hooded cloaks that hid their heads. Only a tip of what must be a very long nose poked from the shadows. Though shorter in stature, they too, radiated power and pure malignancy. But where the tall one was guided by cold intelligence, these two embodied chaotic destruction, a volcanic eruption of mindless energy only waiting for release. I watched as one of the shorter figures idly scratched at its chest with a gray and mottled claw, the long nails either black by nature or full of dirt.

I turned with a shudder back to Jack. He was acting oddly, standing straight at attention, as if surprised by what he saw on the panel. Slowly, he reached out and made a careful adjustment to a hidden dial. He then turned to the tall figure in crimson, pointing to something I could not see.

"Carlin, something's happening."

"What?" he asked, moving closer.

Before I could answer, Jack turned completely around, and looked directly to the scope view. I had time to notice a new pendant hanging around his neck. It was shaped like the swagger stick. But I soon forgot about the pin, as I saw the slow, knowing smile cross his face. A red shadow flickered at the edge of the view, and he laughed.

I got a very, very bad feeling.

"He knows," I said to Carlin. "He knows we're here."

XII

Running Red

Carlin pushed me aside, looking through the glass.

"I think he's sent one of those red cloaked things," I said.

I tried to remember how far it was from the control room to the Solarium. I guessed we had a few minutes, even if the thing ran the whole way, and then it would have to climb the trellis. I was wrong. I didn't know what I was dealing with.

Two things happened suddenly at once. First, Carlin grabbed my arm. Second, the distant Solarium doors opened with a great crash. Though the entrance was still a good deal away, I didn't need the telescope to see the red cloaked figure that stood framed in the doorway. I hoped to God it didn't know *exactly* where we were. As if reading my thoughts, the henchmen lifted its head, and looked straight in our direction.

"Damn it," hissed Carlin.

For a moment, everything stood still. Then in a speed that defied its stature, the red cloak started running, covering the ground in long loping strides.

"Come on!" shouted Carlin, hauling me along the trellis plank by the arm.

It was a short distance to the door. But even as we reached the end of the plank and Carlin began to frantically search along the wall surface, I heard the rapid approach of heavy steps rising from below.

"Where's the door?" I asked, not liking the look of

He began frantically pressing against the wall. "I know it is here, somewhere."

I risked a quick look over the trellis, and grabbed the rail just in time. The red menace struck the trellis like a battering ram, sending a seismic shudder all the way to the top.

I stumbled back to Carlin, who had fallen to his knees at the impact. I helped him to his feet as the trellis began to sway dangerously to the right. I heard the sound of snapping vines and breaking wood as it moved back again and then to the left.

Carlin braced his hands on the wall like a drunk in an alley, still searching the wall.

"Here!" he called, stabbing at a small, discolored spot along the wall.

Suddenly the wall opened up into a tight doorway with a short corridor. Carlin leapt through doorway and into the corridor, just as the trellis lurched again in the other direction. I reached for his offered hand to follow.

I missed.

Now the trellis was swaying like a metronome. I scrambled to my knees as it started back to the open doorway. Carlin was reaching his hand out again. I was going to have to jump for it.

Then, just as suddenly as it started, the swaying stopped. The trellis returned to its normal position, albeit now with a slight, unhealthy lean to the right. I took advantage of the pause and stepped into the open doorway to join Carlin. A moment later the trellis began to shake like an oak in a winter storm.

"He's coming up," said Carlin, pulling me further inside. "Come on!"

Once I was safe inside the passageway, Carlin quickly pulled a lever along the inside wall. The door closed, but not before I saw a red hood rising through the ivy.

I turned as Carlin quickly pressed more buttons on a panel next to the lever. The hall filled with a soft light from indeterminable source.

Finished, Carlin nodded brusquely for me to follow, and raced to the end of the corridor where another panel awaited.

"I locked the door," he said, "but that won't stop him for long."

Even as he spoke, a tremendous boom reverberated down the short hall from the other end.

"Hurry," urged Carlin. "He can tear the very fabric of the ship apart,"

I raced after him, remembering the carnage around Lilith.

There was door at the end of the hall. Carlin opened it the same way as the first. Inside was a bullet-shaped pod in a darkened tunnel.

Carlin quickly stepped on an outlined square beside the pod. The bullet opened lengthwise, exposing a tight two-seat cabin with a rounded window in the nose. Carlin directed me to the far seat and then climbed in next to me. There were no belts or safety harnesses available and no means of control or guidance anywhere, not even a computer screen.

The booming now grew in intensity, followed by an ear-splitting rip, like metal being twisted by a storm.

"He's getting through," I pointed out unnecessarily.

"Quiet," said Carlin. "I need to concentrate."

I saw the sweat beading along his forehead, and heard what must have been the final protest of the door. The heavy step of our pursuer set the pod shaking slightly. I had no delusions that he could easily do to the pod what he had done to the door, and Lilith.

Carlin took a deep breath, then spoke in even tones, "Captain Carlin."

"Recognized," said an ethereal voice from inside the cabin.

"Destination: Transport harbor. Now."

The pod's hull closed over us, and I felt the hum of energy beneath my seat as something sealed. There was no lurch, but I was gently pressed back in my seat as we started forward. Through the nose window I saw the periodic light fixtures of the tunnel blur into straight lines. It was like riding in a real bullet down a well-lit and very long barrel.

"Rear view," said Carlin.

A small three-dimensional image appeared above the dashboard, displaying the retreating tunnel. Our original entrance was already a distant memory, but as I looked closer I saw something approaching fast, something red. Carlin was looking at the same thing. He met my eyes, and nodded grimly.

"That's him?" I asked. "But he'd have to be bent double to travel this tunnel."

"He's as comfortable on all fours as he is on two," said Carlin.

"At least he's not gaining," I said.

"But he's keeping us in sight."

"Is there a turn off or something we can take?"

Carlin nodded, but didn't elaborate.

I watched the image. The red cloaked monster showed no signs of slowing down.

"Captain Carlin," said Carlin, holding up a hand to stop any questions from me.

"Recognized," said the ethereal voice from the sideboards.

"Direction: take the Four-West tunnel."

"Confirmed."

"What's the plan?" I asked, when it appeared he was finished.

"The West tunnel is not the most direct route to the Transport Harbor," he answered. "Jack will probably guess where we are going, but there's no way he can communicate with that thing in the tunnel. If it follows us, we might lose it. That's assuming it doesn't make its own guesses and head us off."

"Is it intelligent?"

"No," said Carlin. "That's in our favor. Jack didn't invest his creatures with a lot of intelligence. He didn't want the competition."

"Does that include the tall fellow with the green complexion?"

"Ariskant," said Carlin grimly. "He's the exception."

He looked to the front port. "Brace yourself. We're getting close now."

The tunnel suddenly opened up, becoming an interchange. I had a brief view of an immense hexagon with ramps leading to six tunnels at various angles. Some of the ramps looked to continue up or down, and some twisted to the right or left. We took the center left ramp.

After we entered, we immediately took a hard right and I was pressed against the pod wall. The view out the port window returned to one long blur of flickering light to either side.

A moment later, we took a left at another fork, and then another right. Despite the back and forth, the transitions were fairly smooth. I was just getting settled, when we made a heart-stopping drop straight down. It was worse than any rollercoaster or freefall I'd ever experienced.

When we finally leveled out—and my stomach returned to its proper position—we took one more left, and then settled into a straight run.

Carlin confirmed this was the West tunnel, and we both studied the rearview image for a time. It remained free of trailing red blurs.

"How far is this Transport Sector?" I asked.

"Not long. It's near the center, but we're traveling fast."

"The center?"

"Of the world."

I recalled Mic's 3-D blueprint in the control room. I guessed we were heading to the flat, open core of the icosahedron.

"Just how fast are we traveling?"

"Fast," he said distractedly, his expression becoming more withdrawn, his eyes growing reflective.

"Carlin, about Lilith," I started.

"Not now," he said, sitting up. He nodded to the front

port. "We're here."

The pod came to a gentle stop, and we climbed out onto a short platform abutting the tunnel. We both looked back down the now darkened shaft, listening for signs of pursuit. I couldn't be sure, but I thought I heard just the faintest of thumps echoing from the gloom. Carlin's deepening frown suggested he heard the same.

"C'mon," he said.

We crossed the platform, and found another door with the same panel of buttons. Carlin made no effort to hide his actions and I watched which buttons he pressed, just in case. The door slid in its recess, and I had another moment of vertigo.

Clouds, like wisps of cotton, were floating just beyond my reach in an azure sky. Even from the doorway, I could see it was a long, long way down.

Carlin gathered his courage and stepped through. I followed. We both took very small and very measured steps, trying hard not to look down.

We were standing on a landing of corrugated metal. The platform extended some seven feet long and three feet wide. It sat against a vast white wall, like a barnacle on a ship hull. The wall was smooth and looked to be made of the same white material that made up Lilith's block. Two short wooden bridges extended from either end of the platform. Each bridge led to a gigantic bell-glass casing. One held a life-size schooner, and the other an equally large hot air balloon. But for their size, they might be simple curios or bric-a-brac from a second-hand store or flea market. Under the clear glass, the schooner appeared to be made of finest crystal, the balloon wired-gold.

"What are those?" I asked, pointing at the schooner and balloon.

"The transportation," answered Carlin. "At least, they would be if we could get them to work. We don't have the key, so they're no use to us. We'll take the elevator down, and travel by foot."

I looked to where he pointed and saw an elevator similar to the one beside the trellis.

"Won't that alert Jack?" I asked.

"Perhaps. But we'll have to take the risk."

He turned to the elevator and tried to open the door. It resisted. I stepped in and tried to help, but the doors remained shut.

Carlin gave me a worried look. "Jack," was all he said.

He turned to the tunnel doorway. "We will have to use the pod again and try to find a way down to the ground exit." He shook his head. "It's certain that Jack will have it covered by now."

I considered the vast expanse of white wall disappearing into either horizon. "Just two exits?" I asked. "For all of this?"

"One of Jack's security measures," said Carlin. "This is his sanctuary, and he didn't want anyone coming and going without his knowledge."

He grew silent and we both looked to the empty doorway. I didn't like that option any more than he did. I turned back to the open expanse and looked to the bell jar pieces. I had a thought.

"You said we need a key to get those to work."

Carlin nodded.

I held up Jack's stick. "You think this might work?"

He paused in surprise. "It's worth a try."

I'd assumed the balloon would be the more fitting transportation, at least it was supposed to be in the air. But to my surprise, Carlin started across the bridge to the glass enclosed schooner, clutching at the railings and moving swiftly. Somewhat confused, I followed.

As we drew closer, I saw a thin cable rising from the schooner's masthead. It extending to the heavens, where I presumed it connected to the ceiling, assuming there was a ceiling somewhere behind all that skyline. It was a very thin wire.

A glass-cut door with a grooved handle gave us access

to the schooner and a short gangplank that led to the deck. Carlin opened the door and stepped onto the gangplank. Waiting my turn, I noticed the name *Trepidation* was etched into the crystal bow of the ship.

"Let's make it quick," said Carlin, reaching the deck with noticeable relief. "If this doesn't work, we get the hell back in that pod."

"Agreed," I said, joining him at the mast.

The deck surface was cold and frosted like glass, and so were the hand rails, mast, and ropes. The frosting gave the ship a weathered, almost ghostly quality. When I brushed past a sail it was hard, like crystal, and did not bend or move in any fashion. The rigging appeared to be the same. When he stepped, Carlin's hard-soled shoes echoed along the planking in oddly muted tones.

I began to regret my suggestion. One good rock might send us falling to the distant ground in a shower of glass.

We tried the bridge first, as this seemed the most logical place for a key. The wheelhouse was a small raised section in the bow, complete with a spoked wheel and a small awning covered cabin. We studied the ghostly crystal housing, searching for anything that looked like a keyhole or a starter.

"Here!" cried Carlin, pointing to the deck near the ship's wheel.

Just to the right of the wheel was a panel floorboard about 36 inches square. A diagram was etched into the surface, with a thimble-sized hole in the center. The diagram showed a bisected wheel, each vertex depicting the ship in various states of motion or form. A pointer sat atop the center hole. If it could be freed from its crystalized state, it might be moved from picture to picture.

"The etchings," I said. "There's one that shows the ship underway—or, that's what I'd guess by the full sails. And this one with the anchor down; that has to be a ship at rest, right? This one it looks to be docking. Maybe that takes us down? I have no idea what the circle around the ship means.

Looks like a corona or halo, doesn't it?"

"Yes," said Carlin, with a sense of urgency, "but it doesn't matter now. Put that damn stick in the hole, and let's get started."

He was right. The center hole looked just about the right size and depth for the stick's tip.

I put the tip in the panel hole until it stopped against a small guard at the base of the stock. Immediately, the handle began to glow an eerie, soft, luminescent yellow.

The pointer was currently at the top. That pictogram depicted the ship in dark lines. I moved the pointer carefully to the next vertex, a picture of the ship in white.

Carlin grunted, and I looked up.

It was like watching colored ink being poured into a tube, or a time-lapse video of a water color painting. The transformation started in the crow's nest and worked its way down the mast, rigging, and sails, bring each piece to life. The sails became pliant and snowy white; the wood surfaces hard and in places stained; the brass shiny and reflective.

I carefully removed the stick, to see if the transformation would stop or reverse. The deck remained the texture and color of sun-weathered and polished wood and the sails continued to flap and luff.

A moment later, a gentle vibration ran the length of the ship and Carlin and I turned to see a chain retracting a short distance starboard. A previously unnoted anchor was being drawn up flush with the rail. Carlin gave me an encouraging nod.

"Should we try for the ground?" I asked.

Carlin hesitated. "Try to get it moving, first."

"Okay. Hold on. I'm going to try the full sail setting." I glanced back in his direction. "Maybe you'd better take the wheel, just in case…"

I stopped.

Carlin, seeing the expression on my face, turned quickly to look behind him.

Standing on the landing, its cloak stirred by the wind,

was our pursuer (if it was the same one).

Without hesitating, Carlin raced to the main mast, calling behind him, "Get this damn thing away."

I watched, still stunned, as he grabbed a bladed polearm from the mast. He sprang to the gangplank, closing the glass door, and then retreated back to the deck, pulling the plank up behind him.

"Now, Lasak!"

I finally recovered, and turned back to the panel. I quickly moved the pointer to the full sail setting, then looked up to see if it worked, and what our pursuer was about.

The henchman was coming across the bridge, but very slowly. The reason for its hesitation was clear. The bridge was bending dangerously under its weight.

A sudden crack, like a marble thrown against a thick piece of glass, drew my attention back to the ship.

Everyone, including our pursuer, stopped for a moment.

The thin wire connecting the ship to the heavens hummed with energy as an electric-blue filigree danced along its length like a tesla coil. With a creak, the front of the bell jar opened up like a gate on hinge. The schooner moved forward with a gentle lurch, the prow swinging majestically into the open air.

As the stern of the schooner began to clear the cage, our pursuer charged across the bridge. A rail snapped, and the bridge start to turn over. The red-cloaked pursuer grasped at the crumbling bridge.

Let it fall, I thought.

Instead, it scrambled up the splintering rails like a mountain goat navigating a landslide.

Then it was somehow at the glass door.

Then it was through the door in an explosion of shattered glass, leaping for the retreating *Trepidation* and falling out of sight behind the stern.

I felt a deep thud of impact under my feet. I saw the ropes along the ship's back and sides tighten—and I knew; somehow the beast had made the distance.

A moment later, my fears were confirmed as a giant claw grasped the top and the red cloak fluttered briefly above the stern rail.

With a yell, Carlin raced by me and stabbed at the hand with the polearm. It appeared to have little effect. The red cloak pulled itself up until its head was over the rail and used its free hand to grab the pike. It tossed it over, nearly pulling Carlin along in the process.

Carlin let go, struggled for his balance and in the process came in range of that terrible free hand. The red cloak took Carlin by the throat and began to choke him, its other hand still clutching to the rail. It didn't look the least bit concerned by its precarious position. It seemed only intent on choking the life out of Carlin.

I ran across the bridge and struck the arm holding Carlin with the heavy end of swagger stick. I had not forgotten my gun. I simply did not trust my shot.

I at least caught the henchman's attention with my efforts, and it turned its hooded head in my direction. Meanwhile, Carlin's face was turning a dangerous shade of purple. Fearing he would do to Carlin what he had done to the polearm, I grabbed Carlin.

The red-cloak released Carlin with a shove, sending us both stumbling backwards. It grabbed the stern rail with both hands, sinking slightly as if to leap over the rail.

Reflexively, I turned the swagger stick around, stepped forward, and jabbed the pointed tip into the nearest hand. A short, powerful vibration ran through the stick as a flash of energy erupted at the point of contact.

The red cloak gave a terrible yell and let go of the rail with its injured hand. I turned and stabbed at the hand still holding the rail. There was another flash, and the red cloak cried out again, letting go with both hands.

I was already swinging the stick again and hit the hand that was reaching for the rail. I missed, but hit the forearm. The blow couldn't have done much physical damage; the shock was little more than a spark this time. But it was just enough to make it miss.

It made no sound as it hung there for a moment suspended in air. A draft lifted the cloak in either direction like wings. Then it rolled, and the cloak wrapped around the body like a blanket.

I leaned over the rail to watch it fall as the twisting body rolled again and again. The same fickle wind pulled the hood back off its head.

Underneath was nothing human, nothing even remotely animal. There was no indication of ears, eyes, or a face of any kind. Its only apparent sense organ was a growth set in the very middle of the pulsing mass that was its head, what I had originally taken to be a nose or snout. Ravaged, darkly veined, the repugnant organ twisted from side to side like a skinless turkey neck.

Then the tip of that evil mass opened, and I heard a cry. It was an octave too high and too fast to be recognizable as human, but it was full of knowing, and hate—all directed at me.

I heard that cry echo again and again as it plummeted to the ground far, far below. Even after it was gone, I heard that cry of hate.

XIII

Irish Wake

I was sitting in the crow's nest, taking in the scenery and trying not to dwell on the tenuous nature of life and strange chords on top of ships.

I had come to take stock, finding any fear of heights a relative thing compared to the brooding silence below. Carlin was in the galley, making us something to eat. He informed me that we were heading in the right direction, a destination he said we would discuss more over dinner, and that he would cook. He didn't need any help.

I took the hint.

I walked the boards of the deck for a time, inspecting this, looking over that. In the process, I discovered the sails were the only thing on the ship not true to life. They certainly looked like real thing: luffing, snapping, and straining in the wind. But I could pass my hand through them like air, and they had no impact on our direction or momentum. I suppose that made sense, given as the chord on the mast top was our true method of direction and conveyance.

Of course, a real schooner this size would be too much work for two people, even able-bodied sailors. But this wasn't exactly a real schooner, and we weren't exactly sailing. No one had to adjust, hoist, or swab. No one took the wheel. Just after the monster fell, Carlin studied the schooner's navigation system, a simple panel in the wheelhouse cabin. On the panel were two switches, three brass dials, and a mirrored surface. With a flip of one of the switches Carlin called up a detailed 3-d image of the center core, complete with a tiny replica of our schooner floating above the terrain. Green light indicators showed our speed, compass bearing, and altitude. Carlin set our speed and destination with the dials, we turned slightly, and headed off over the great expanse.

"That's it," he explained. "Jack was pretty lazy. This is the same system he uses in all his transports but the pod. The ship should avoid anything that gets in the way and automatically adjust back to the correct destination when it's clear."

I introduced him to the term autopilot.

"Yes," he said, "that sounds right."

That's when he mentioned dinner, retreated to the galley, and I got the impression that my company was no longer required.

The first thing I did on deck was try to reach Mic. But she either couldn't answer or wouldn't answer. Or maybe the interference was too great. The same went for the *Pelagius* computer. Eventually I grew bored, and climbed the crow's nest on the main mast to get a better view and take personal stock. It wasn't the most comfortable of reflective spots.

The nest itself was an expanding basket of spaced metal struts with a loop binding everything at the top. The bottom, or seat, was a round piece of wood extending from the mast like a petal or skirt. There was just enough space to stand. You could also sit on one edge of the seat and dangle your feet through the exposed spaces of the struts.

I stood for a time, my hands gripping the rim of the nest and my back pressed hard against the tapering masthead. From this vantage, I could see the electric-blue chord was roughly an inch in diameter, and looked no more reassuring up close than it had from a distance. The chord tended to spark and whine whenever we hit a pocket of air or took a slight turn, and I noticed it wasn't exactly "attached" to the nest pole but linked by a marble-sized ball of energy. The ball would stretch or flatten as the ship shifted and bobbed, serving I suppose as a kind of shock absorber. It did little to instill more confidence.

Eventually I grew tired of standing, and took a seat facing the prow. In my explorations I had found a chart in the wheelhouse cabin. I took it out now and tried to get my bearings. Crystallized only a short time before, the chart bore all the marks and stains of a well-used map. I used Jack's stick to keep it in place.

The legend depicted a square set in a circle with star-points all along edge; a box in the sun. The points were unmarked, but the square was labeled, *Central Core*. In the spaces between the circle and square, top and bottom, were the legends *Graëh Kingdom* and *Southern Kingdom*, respectively. The *Eastern Provinces* were along the right side of the square, and the *Nordic Territories* the left, or west. I reasoned we had fled from the Southern Kingdom.

In the heart of the square were numerous towns and territories with names like *Daniel's Tor, Lawrenceburg,* and *Claire Town*. The largest of these were the *Central Plains* and the *Forest Enclave*. The central plains dominated the center of the square. The Forest Enclave sat just in front of the *Disruption Wall*. The latter made up the top line of the square. On the other side of that line was the Graëh Kingdom.

If I was right, we had just left a small range of mountains that started as foothills about a half-hour ago. These were marked on the chart as *Tober Mountains*. That meant we were heading for the Plains, and the Wall.

I rolled up the chart and tucked it in my belt.

Directly below, the earth was a patchwork of brilliant rolling greens with the occasional clump of woods scattered here and there like a field of green mushrooms. A herd of something like sapphire buffalo were migrating across the fields, their heads longer than round.

To my left was a large body of water, as dark and rich as plum juice. I knew from the chart this was the Burgundy Sea. To my right were rocky hills with the shadowy outline of more mountains behind them, the boundary of the Eastern Provinces. Ahead, the fields turned into a sea of yellow grass—until everything was lost to a black line horizon.

Feeling slightly more oriented, I turned to my other new distraction: Jack's stick. A swagger stick, Carlin called it. Given its recent behavior, I handled it carefully.

The emerald knob at the top felt cool and slick under my hand. The rich dark stock was warm and comfortable. I guessed the wood to be oak. As I was turning the stick, I discovered four finger grips starting just beneath the emerald knob. Holding the stick by the grips, I felt the forefinger groove give slightly. I pressed down, and something released inside.

I slowly pulled at the pearl top, and discovered the knob was the pommel to a secret blade. I withdrew the blade, about the length of my forearm and double-edged, and I didn't need a hair or thumb to know it was sharp. The pommel knob gave it balance, but it was a blade meant to slice, to kill quickly and close.

I put the blade in a small metal loop along the crow's nest and looked closer into the husk. I found a small rod about an inch from the opening and running all the way to down. It formed the small edge above the base of the white-material tip.

I discovered two small purses tied to the inner lining of the husk by their topknots. With a little effort, I removed them as well.

Finally, I turned the husk upside down and a long thin bolt of tightly wrapped fabric fell out. Unfurling the bolt, I could see it was a man-sized hooded cloak.

I put the husk in another loop, and the purses in my LongPost suit pockets. Standing, I shook the cloak out in the wind. It quickly recovered its full shape. What was more amazing, there was hardly a wrinkle or crease to be found.

I tried it on for affect, of course. It hung comfortably about my shoulders, and I found it very effective at cutting off the wind. I decided to keep it on.

Sitting down again, I pulled out the purses.

The first held a handful of emeralds, rubies, and what

looked to be inert pieces of the white essence. I rolled the white pieces in my hand for a bit, then put everything back.

The other purse contained two phials. They were roughly six inches in length, made of thick glass, and each held a different liquid: one amber, the other clear.

After some experimentation, I discovered how to release the small caps at the top. I put the amber one to my nose and was pleasantly surprised by the earthy, nutty, and unmistakable scent of distilled spirits. I took a small sip. It was good, tasting of hazelnuts and honey and something like honeysuckle, only not as sweet.

I considered another sip, and only then did I wonder if it might be poison. It would be just like Jack to carry along some lethal-spirits—something to slip into the cup of an unsuspecting enemy.

I waited. Nothing happened.

I took another sip, and soon forgot my fears. It certainly didn't taste foul. In fact, it took the edge off on what had been a decidedly big day. I had just the one more.

After that, prudence won out and I put the cap back on—or started to.

Now, I was quite certain that I had taken at least three sips. Not deep drafts to be sure, but certainly enough to put a dent in the six inches of supply.

But as I sat there with the cap poised over the phial, I could clearly see that it was nearly full. In fact, it was full. A trick of stress and fatigue? Or, was the drink making me see things?

Of course, there was only one way to test the theory. I took another drink, a big one—just to prove the point—and damned if it didn't stay full.

"Now this," I said aloud, "bears further investigation."

Amused by the sound of my own voice, I carried on.

"By god, you're right when you're right, Watson," I cried to the wind.

"But what to do, Holmes?" I returned.

I looked slyly at the full filter. "Easy, friend. Why it's

simply a matter of experimentation. We'll just have to sample the product until we can clearly see a drop in the bucket. All very scientific, my dear Watson. Elementary, you might say."

I was just about to imbibe once more when another voice—not one of my inebriated imagination—called from below. I was so startled by the interruption, I almost dropped the phial.

"Food's ready."

It was Carlin. He raised a hand to shade his eyes and looked up at me curiously. "What the hell are you doing up there?"

Feeling foolish, I quickly resealed the phial and put it back in the purse, then put both purses back in the stick.

"Coming," I said, trying to gather the cloak around me with some sense of aplomb. "Just a moment."

I began to resemble the stick, moving with exaggerated care as I returned the blade. That nagging part that we tend to ignore was telling me I might have imbibed a bit more than I should.

I saw Carlin shake his head, and disappear again below.

I was glad to see him go. It took me a good five minutes to find my way down the mast. By the time I reached the galley, I was a mess of sweat and exhaustion, though still a little high.

Elementary, indeed.

Whatever else could be said about my travelling companion, he could cook. It was a meal strictly discouraged by the LongPost Handbook, but I didn't let that stop me. Runny eggs, dark brown toast with heavy slabs of butter, strawberries and cream, crispy bacon with just the right amount of fat, and ice-cold milk to chase it all down.

"You did something with the eggs," I suggested. "Garlic?"

Carlin didn't look up from his plate, but nodded. He had taken his coat off and rolled up his sleeves revealing a set of longshoreman forearms covered in red hair and freckles.

"Where in the world did you find garlic?"

Carlin mumbled something at his plate.

"I'm sorry. I didn't catch that."

He looked up, his eyes red and angry, and full of something else, something I recognized on a sympathetic level. There *had* been an empty bottle of wine on the small galley board when I came in. Perhaps I was not the only one over indulging.

"I said," his voice the definition of misery, "there's a full spice rack over there." He nodded brusquely in the direction of the galley proper.

"Oh."

Looking away, I noticed his coat. It lay across the back of the chair next to me. I noticed a harness of some sort stitched along the inner lining. In the harness were two knives, one of them as long as my forearm.

I sobered up a bit then. I didn't know Carlin had been packing all this time.

When I looked back, Carlin was staring at his plate again. He had hardly touched his food. A moment later, he threw his fork down in disgust and got up from the table.

I continued to eat as I heard him open another bottle of wine behind me. He came back with the bottle and sat heavily in his chair. He took a swig, then offered me the bottle, still staring at the table.

I wiped my mouth on my sleeve and accepted the bottle. I took a long drink, watching Carlin out of the corner of my eye.

Of course, I thought. *Lilith*. If I hadn't been so distracted with my new toys and all the excitement, I would have seen it earlier.

"So, it's an Irish wake?" I asked.

He let out a deep, trembling sigh, closed his eyes and then nodded once, hard.

"She deserves better," he said, opening his eyes again. "But it will have to do."

"To Lilith," I held up the bottle, then took a sip.

"To Lilith," he answered, taking the bottle.

He took a long pull, and we were silent for a time, remembering. Then he waved the bottle in my direction and said, "Nice cloak."

"I found it in the stick."

He grimaced, "I thought I recognized it."

He stood and walked over behind me. I may have flinched a bit when his hands touched my shoulders. But he only adjusted the high collar, folding it under.

"That's better," he said. "Now you don't look so much like that bastard."

He went back to his seat and took up the bottle again. "So, what else did you discover?"

I showed him the hidden sword, and how to release it, and the purses. He grunted at the sight of the precious stones.

"Might come in handy," he said.

"And there's this, too," I said, holding up the phial of amber. "It might be poisonous, but I don't think so. I had some up in the crow's nest." I paused. "It might be fitting for the occasion."

I poured him a shot in my empty coffee cup. He put his nose to the cup, a look of surprise and just the hint of expectation crossing his face. He tossed it back without a second thought. When he finally looked my way again, he nodded gratefully.

"There's more to it," I said holding up the phial. "Drink as much as you like, and the damn thing still remains full."

He took the phial from my hand, studied it for a time, and then poured the phial into the cup until it was empty. When he lifted the phial upright again, it was just as full as the first time I opened it.

He gave me a half-smile. "I'm not going to look a gift horse in the mouth, are you?"

"No," I answered, reaching for the cup.

"I think we can do better than that," he said.

He got up and went to the back of the galley, coming

back a few minutes later with two shot glasses. He poured some of the contents of the coffee cup into each, and handed me one.

"Now," he said. "What was that you were saying about an Irish Wake?"

We drank more than our share that night, there in the galley of the flying ship. We talked, too. We talked about life and love, the Earth and stars. We talked of death, and the frailty of life. We talked about guilt and blame and anger. I learned that he held some of the last for me, but none of the second. The anger, he said, would fade in time. The blame was Jack's.

The guilt, he added quietly, was all his.

Nothing I said could persuade him otherwise, but I tried.

We drank many a toast to Lilith. He told me stories about her, some of which even made him smile.

When it became clear we had run out of conversation, Carlin stood and stretched. "Enough. I'm taking the Captain's quarters. You'll have to fend for yourself."

He said goodnight, and stumbled off.

And that's how we said goodbye to Lilith.

I slept that night on the deck under the stars. Yes, there were stars in the now darkened overhead. They were smaller and brighter than the usual variety and tended to move around, sometimes forming fantastic constellations.

It was strange and somehow fitting, the dancing stars. There was no taint of evil, no sense of corruption about the night sky or its stellar inhabitants.

I took a comfort in that feeling. Jack did not hold complete mastery of this time and place. Somewhere, something good and kind rose up to stand against him.

As I heard Carlin snoring below, I wrapped my new cloak around me and sent a silent thank you to the maker of the stars. I hoped she was watching over us both.

XIV

Rough Waters

I confess, I missed the dawn.

I awoke to a bright mid-afternoon blue sky without a cloud in sight. A glorious day; spectacular views in all directions. It was wasted on me. My head was killing me, my stomach in turmoil, and my mouth replaced by a sand pit.

The mountains were well behind us now. The transport harbor where we first acquired the *Trepidation* was covered now by gathering clouds. Below, the terrain was shifting. The last of the hills were retreating, giving way to vast stretches of grassland. Ahead were more fields and a few rolling hills. Just at the edge of horizon was a dark shadow, too consistent and level to be natural. The Wall, perhaps?

Feeling in need of a shower (and trying not to think about my aching head or agitated stomach), I went below to see what was available. I found Carlin up and making breakfast.

"Good morning," I said, or tried to. It came out more a grunt.

He made a similar half-hearted attempt at a greeting and went back to beating some eggs in a bowl. I saw two steaks sizzling in a frying pan. My stomach decided eating might be possible, after all.

I helped myself to some water from a barrel in the corner and tried to replace some of the sand.

"Shower?" I asked.

Carlin nodded to the Captain's quarters. "There's..." he started, and stopped.

After a few minutes of coughing, he turned a bleary eye in the right direction and pointed with the dripping whisk.

"Clothes are in the hamper," he mumbled a moment later.

Clothes? Well, maybe a change of attire would be in order.

The shower was a simple affair, with one handle for controlling everything. The water was hot and the pressure good—and don't ask me how. I found a small bowl of blue powder just beyond the water's spray, and with some experimentation determined it was a soap. After washing, I pushed the handle back to its original position. Before I could worry about where I would find a towel, hot air blew from the same nozzle that just sent the water. In a few minutes, the shower and I were both dry.

Feeling slightly more human again, I took Carlin's advice and explored the full-sized closet set against the wall.

Inside were a dozen or so outfits and footwear. The first thing I noticed was a Captain's uniform, which made sense I guess, given the room. It was impressive, with lots of gold and finery; very formal, very pomp and circumstance—and certainly nothing I was going to where around here.

Next in line were two 19th century suits, complete with frock coats, pressed woolen pants, and a pair of high-collar cotton shirts. An assortment of cravats and short ties hung on a rack inside the door, and undergarments were on a shelf above the clothes rack. On the floor, in a neat row, sat shoes of several types and sizes. There were even a few dresses after the suits. I assumed these were for mixed company.

In the end, I selected a simple pair of woolen slacks with open cuffs and a loose pullover shirt. I put the shirt and pants over my spacesuit (a secret weapon against the unexpected), and rolled the shirt sleeves up to hide the frilled cuffs. I kept my own boots of course, as they fit and looked decidedly more comfortable then the 19th century models.

I stepped back and checked my look in the mirror on the inside of the other door. I decided to use a brown leather vest to tame the shirt a bit more. As I put it on, I discovered an assortment of pockets along the inner lining.

Finished, I topped everything off with my new cloak—I saw no reason to discard it just because of its history. I hung my LongPost satchel across my back and tucked Jack's stick in a belt hoop in the slacks. I gave myself another once over in the mirror inside the closet door, made a few adjustments to the cloak, stick, and satchel, and headed to the gallery.

Carlin's only comment to my attire was another ambiguous grunt. We ate breakfast in relative silence by mutual consent.

Afterward, I did the dishes and stored everything again in their proper places. As I did, I came across a well-stocked pantry. Curious, I asked Carlin about our provisions. With a little prodding, he explained that the food was preserved in the same crystalline stasis as the rest of the *Trepidation* when it was inert. I suppose it wasn't much different from defrosting a ham, just on a much larger scale.

The dishes stowed, we filled our coffee cups and took to the wheelhouse for some much needed fresh air.

Carlin confirmed the ship was holding course. He guessed we were about a day and night from our destination. The view ahead looked clear enough, but the gathering clouds behind us were piling up and growing dark.

I pointed them out to Carlin. "Can the ship survive a storm?"

"I would think it's been through a few," he answered, studying the cloud line. "But that may be no normal squall."

"What do you mean?"

"I wouldn't put it past Jack to send something after us. He must know we're on the ship by now."

"Jack can control the weather?"

"Yes; a bit."

Carlin walked away to 'batten down hatches,' or something to that order. I pretended to be busy by giving the wheelhouse cabin another once over.

I discovered the telescope in a long box under the cabin desktop. It was tucked in the back and well out of sight, so it was easy to see how I missed it yesterday.

I took the glass out of the box and returned to the stern for a closer look at the storm. Up close, the view was even more depressing.

After a time, Carlin rejoined me. I gave him the glass so he could get a good look, as well.

When he finished, he lowered the glass with a shake of his head. "Not good."

I agreed. There were rips of lightning now all along the cloud front.

He looked up to the mast and our precious chord of life. "Hope that line is up to a little wind and rain."

"I checked it yesterday," I said. "There's only a ball of energy holding it together."

"Hmm."

He pulled the scope down again with a grimace. "Nothing we can do about that. I'm more worried about that lightning setting us on fire, or electrocuting us where we stand...."

"I suppose we can't get out of its way?"

He raised the telescope again. "I don't think so. It's moving fast and straight for us."

He stopped suddenly, looked to the ship's operating panel. "Maybe, there is something.... Come on."

We walked over to the panel and he pointed to the pictogram near the top.

"What do you think of that?" he asked. The etching he pointed at depicted the ship surrounded in a nimbus of light.

"Yes," I said, "I think I see what you mean. But then again, it might cut off all our air—or send us falling."

He shrugged. "I'm open for other suggestions. I don't think we should try to weather that storm as we are."

We both looked to the stern and the massive wall of roiling black clouds behind us.

"You might have a point," I said.

It was reinforced a moment later a sudden gust of wind that sent us to our knees. This was followed by a crack of thunder.

We climbed back to our feet as the first drops of rain started to fall; hard, icy drops that hit the deck like a nail-gun.

Carlin turned quickly back to the pedestal. "Quickly, the stick."

I wasn't sure if it was necessary, but I did as he requested and put the stick in the port. Carlin then moved the pointer to the image of the ship-in-halo.

And just like that, we were.

One moment everything was raw with sound and energy, the next our world was reduced to a bubble of tranquility and amber. I removed the stick.

A visible aura now encircled the ship, blurring the skyline to soft golden brown and the stormfront to a murky mass of gray. Lightning still played havoc along the front of the storm, but now it was absent its thunderous accompaniment and the howling wind. The rainfall became a constant but light patter against the bubble surface; the nails replaced by fingertips.

"You think this will protect us when we're in the thick of it?" I asked.

"Don't know, but it's a damn sight better than it was. I'm going…"

He stopped. He lifted the glass to his eye. "What the hell is that?"

I looked to where he pointed. A misty pin of light was just visible in the center of the stormfront.

I grabbed the telescope from Carlin.

"Mic," I yelled. "Is that you Mic?"

Carlin gave me a strange look. I remembered he thought Mic was in my pocket.

"Ben," answered a familiar voice.

The reception was full of static, but it was Mic.

"I hope you are accepting company."

"Absolutely."

I turned to Carlin. "That's Mic."

"Then we better get this thing down," he said, indicating

the shield.

I didn't bother with the stick this time. I turned the pointer back to the full sail icon. It worked just the same.

The protective halo disappeared as suddenly as it appeared, and we were immediately soaked and buffeted by the wind.

Carlin and I braced ourselves against the pedestal and followed Mic's race against the storm. It was going to be close. The storm filled the skyline now, its terrible power raising the hair along my arms and neck.

"She's got her head now," cried Carlin.

We watched as Mic began to pull away; the last desperate scramble of the fox before the pack. One moment she was just a small ball of light in front of the black curtain, and the next she was between us, pulsing like a strobe light.

I returned to the panel and put the shield up again, cutting everything off with a silent return to amber perspective.

"Mic," said Carlin with a wry, thoughtful expression. "Fancy meeting you here."

"Well, that's my fault," I said with a blush. "I wanted to keep an eye on Jack, and..."

"And you're not exactly the trusting sort," finished Carlin.

"The point is, Mic was acting on my orders," I explained, falling completely on my sword and hoping to repair at least one of our reputations. "For what it is worth, she trusted you from the beginning."

Carlin didn't say anything but gave both of us a long, studied look.

"That's not a natural storm," said Mic, bringing us back to the immediate danger.

"No," said Carlin, "we didn't think it was."

"It's from Jack," said Mic.

Even as she spoke, all hell broke loose. The ship lifted as if on a wave, and then dropped just as suddenly. Carlin and I reached for support and struggled to stay on our feet.

We started to bob like a cork in the rapids.

"Time to get below," said Carlin.

"Shouldn't one of us man the wheel?" I asked.

We both turned to watch it as another gust of wind sent us reeling. The wheel remained in place.

"Looks fine to me," he said. "But you're welcome to it."

Before I could answer, we were tossed to the deck by another gust of wind. From the floorboards I watched a bolt of lightning hit the protective bubble. It shattered and raced like a Tesla arc.

"I think I'll pass," I said, climbing to my feet.

It had grown very dark outside, and without Mic's help it would have been a struggle to reach the hatch. Carlin was the first one down. He lit a few lanterns above the galley table.

We watched the light show outside the portholes, our lanterns swaying in hard arcs and making the shadows dance.

More than once we bounced from our seats as the ship was caught by the wind. Each time this happened, Carlin and I looked to the galley ceiling, wondering if this was the one that finally broke the chord.

Eating was out of the question, but Carlin and I took healthy swigs from the stick's elixir. To distract ourselves, we caught up with Mic. She floated over the table like a small moon, her color a warm yellow light against the darkness.

"I found Jack in the control room," she said. "He was working on the monitors, trying to locate you. A most unpleasant creature had joined him. Apparently incapable of speech, it used a system of pantomime to communicate that Carlin was free, and Ben was with him."

She described the creature.

"Pest," said Carlin, giving me a look.

"Yes," said Mic. "It looked very unpleasant."

I told her this was what Carlin called the creature.

"A fitting name, I think," said Mic. She continued. "Jack

left this, Pest, to watch the control room. I followed him, staying well behind so he could not see me. We traveled down different hallways than you and I took, Ben, and eventually we came to a door. It was cleverly hidden behind the wall."

Carlin asked Mic to describe the area.

"I can do better than that," she said.

Above the table, she projected a 3-d hologram of a long hallway, similar to the ones we had walked when we first arrived. A life-size red outline of a man was standing in front of a door in the wall, just the one to the white room and the trapped *Pelagius*.

"I had to stay down the hall," explained Mic, "so I wouldn't be discovered. But this a long-shot of the hall and a heat-sensor image of Jack."

"Damn," said Carlin. "I know that section. I never knew there was a door there."

We watched as the heat-image Jack walked through the doorway. The door closed behind him, and we were looking at a solid wall.

"I couldn't follow him inside," said Mic. "And my scanners couldn't pick up anything beyond the wall once the door was closed."

We watched the door open again. This time Jack was accompanied by three additional heat-images. They were the same creatures I had seen through the scope on the trellis: two red-cloaked monsters, and Ariskant.

"That's what chased us," I said, pointing to one of Jack's red-cloaked companions. "What exactly are they?"

"It's Jack's idea of a henchman," said Carlin. "They have many names, but the most common are, Red Cloak, or Daemon. I searched for their hideaway a long time; but as they weren't active, I eventually gave up."

He turned to Mic. "Go on," he said. "Finish your story."

"Jack sent one of the red-cloaked creatures off to search for you," she said, and we watched the red images split up in the hallway. "The other two followed him back to the control room. I stayed with Jack." She paused. "I think you know the rest."

"Go on," said Carlin, a hard look in his eye. "Finish it."

Mic hung for a moment in the shadows, her color retreating to a soft white.

"Michael," she said, finally. "I'm sorry. I tried to reach Ben, but there was too much interference. I didn't know the red daemon would go to the Solarium. I didn't know it would do that to Lilith. Jack didn't know, either. He was furious when it returned and reported back. Apparently, it overreacted when Lilith resisted. I'm sorry."

Carlin looked to the table. "It was not your fault. Is that all?"

"There's not much left to tell," she said. "Jack continued to work at the control panel. Eventually, he either fixed the system or you stepped in front of a working monitor. I was just outside the door, but I overheard him send the red cloak back to the Solarium. I knew I had to warn you both.

"But before I could leave, the creature, Pest, reached around the door and trapped me against the wall. How it knew I was there, I don't know. Maybe Jack saw me on a monitor and signaled my position. I do know that it is very fast, and very strong.

"I managed to escape. I think it underestimated my own speed. To free myself, however, I was forced to go in the control room. I had to dodge Jack and his henchmen for a time. They're incredibly fast as well. There was no going back out the door, as Pest was standing guard in the doorway. In the end, I had to resort to the chimney again.

"It was some time before I could manage a proper escape. Jack had sealed the door, of course. But he had to open it again when the red cloak returned from…"

She paused.

"Lilith," said Carlin.

"Yes," said Mic softly. "When it opened, I used a doppelganger program and sent a dozen Mic-images around the room. I made it out in the confusion.

"After that, it was just a matter of finding my way to you, and beating out the storm."

"You took some risks," said Carlin. "I'm glad you made it. Well done."

"Yes," I agreed. "I thought we'd agreed you'd be careful."

"I was," said Mic. "Maybe if I hadn't been so careful, Lilith…"

Carlin waived his hand dismissively. "Enough of that. I tell you both, Jack alone is to blame for Lilith. Leave it."

I tried to smile encouragement at Mic, not sure how much of this she understood.

The ship took another heart-stopping drop then, and more pressing matters distracted us.

When we regained our balanced, I offered another drink. Carlin waived me off. He looked like he was going to be sick. I was feeling a bit poorly myself and put the phial away. Carlin found a bucket, and put it beside us.

The storm punched us around for a long, miserable time. Carlin and I both took turns at the bucket. Occasionally driven by a need for some sense of fresh air, or just morbid curiosity, I would stand on deck and watch the watery fireworks. There were no dancing stars that night. Jack was in control now.

When it was finally over, the three of us stood on deck and took stock. Carlin checked the helm, and confirmed that we were still on course. I turned the protective covering off.

Mic set about exploring the ship. I took to standing at the bow, and watching the approaching horizon. No one speculated aloud if the storm was Jack's best effort or if he was just setting us up for the roundhouse, but I imagine we were all thinking about it.

XV

Getting Closer

"It runs from ceiling to ground and extends from the Nordic Territories to the Far Eastern Province and then curls back on itself. The Wall cuts the Baron's Kingdom off from the rest of the world."

We were standing in the prow and Carlin was explaining the subject dominating the view—the Disruption Wall.

"It's thickest in the center," he continued. "There's a large tunnel at the base that allows traffic between the Baron's and the rest of the world, but few use it without his permission. We may have to take that way, but I would prefer not to. There are other ways."

He looked over the rail. "First though, we'll land and make our way to the Central Plains village. I hope to get some help and information there, and they have to be warned about Jack."

"This Baron," I asked, "could he possibly help us? The enemy of my enemy, and all that."

Carlin frowned. "The less we have to do with the Baron the better. My hope is to avoid him and his kind all together. He may not like Jack, but he will be no friend of ours."

"Okay," I answered. "What about this, Dun?"

He shook his head. "I thought he was only a legend, an early creation of Jack's. Some tell the tale that Dun didn't turn out the way Jack planned, or that he disappointed Jack somehow. He was rumored to be crippled. But that's the extent of my knowledge. That's the other reason we're going to stop at the village. I know where the dungeon is, but I have no idea where Dun might be inside it. Maybe somebody there will know."

He left us then to start dinner, and I think to be alone. Mic and I spent some time studying the ship.

"The ship is like the rest of the world," she said, as we stood in the helm looking at the directional panel. "It is made from the same white essence, but shaped to fit the functions and physical nature of the Earth equivalents. What you call the lifeline serves as both IOS and power source, though I use those terms representationally. You noticed the sails are holographic?"

"I did."

"The crystalized state must be a variety of suspended animation; a preservative of sorts, too, given the food. I will have to examine that stick, some time."

"I will see to it that you do."

We stopped at the bow rail, taking in the view. The sky was as innocent and still as if the storm never occurred, and we could hear Carlin on the cutting board in the galley.

Mic floated in front of me, her color the softest indigo.

"Ben."

"Yes?"

"Michael Carlin is very sad, isn't he," she said.

"Yes, but like he said, that's not your fault. Just give him some time."

Her color revolved to a pale sunset. "I know what it means to hurt now. I don't like it."

"You did nothing wrong," I said, trying to anticipate what emotions might be forming next in her new awareness. "And I'm glad you are safe."

But her color remained a sickly yellow.

We traveled another night and most of the next day before we put down in a small hollow crusted with pine trees. Carlin called the landing out and I set us down behind the tree line, turning the pointer to the docking pictogram. The *Trepidation* touched down light as feather.

We packed travelling supplies in sacks we found in the hull and carried them down the gangplank and outside the ship.

Finished, I climbed back aboard. It was my job to shut the ship down. First, I experimented with the stick and operating panel, just to test a theory and become more familiar with the process. I turned the pointer to the original position, a black-outline of the ship. Nothing happened. I moved the pointer back to the docking section. I then put the stick in the operating panel hole and returned the pointer to the black outline ship.

This time, the color infusion did its trick in reverse and the ship resumed its crystalized state. Apparently, you had to use the stick to turn the ship off and on; everything else could be done sans stick. Fortunately, too, I didn't turn to crystal.

Climbing down again, I helped Carlin cover the ship with branches and other foliage.

"It won't pass a determined search," said Carlin, putting some loose bramble against the ship's hull. "But at least it's not out in the open."

I thought it a shame to leave the schooner at all, but Carlin didn't want to draw unwanted attention at the village. From hints he dropped, I gathered that not everyone in the village would welcome his return. It reminded me that I still knew little of my new companion, apart from his role as Jack's keeper and Lilith's friend.

There was a heavy, almost misty air about the hollow, encouraged in part by the dark looming pines. As Carlin distributed our belongings, I found a small hill and scanned the horizons with the wheelhouse telescope.

When I turned to the South, something caught my eye. I adjusted the sighting.

"Michael," I said calling him over.

He took the telescope with a wary frown, and pointed it in the direction I indicated. Mic did whatever Mic does in such cases, and took a look too. Far above us and still some distance away, was a beautiful golden balloon, carrying what appeared to be a large figure in red.

"Can't be helped," muttered Carlin, giving me back the telescope. "We knew Jack would not let us alone. Just the same, how the hell did he get that the balloon away? We have the swagger stick."

"There might be more than one key," I suggested.

"Maybe. We'd best get back under the trees."

We did as he suggested, tucking under a heavy canopy.

"We'll have to travel by night," said Carlin. "I estimate it will take us one, maybe two hikes if we travel all night. We'll rest now."

Mic kept an eye on our aeronautical hunter while we ate a brief meal. The food was from the *Trepidation*, mostly cold goods: bits of cured ham, and some bread. We had also filled two canteens with water from the galley barrel.

"Do you think it can track the line?" I asked Carlin, nodding to the nearly invisible lifeline which still extended from the grounded *Trepidation* masthead.

He shook his head. "Let's hope not. But if the balloon suddenly starts heading in this direction..." He shrugged. "I suppose it's better to deal with it here and now, then to be attacked somewhere on the road."

"Well, if it comes to that, there's something you should know." I pulled the pistol from my satchel and showed it to him.

He took it carefully in hand, examined it, and then handed it back. "I would keep that hidden, and only use it when absolutely necessary You'll find no bullets to replace the ones you have—what little firearms were smuggled on board by Jack's visitors have long since been used up or fallen to pieces. Believe me, many have tried to find a replacement gunpowder, but with no luck. I think that's Jack's doing. He didn't like the idea of someone having firearms, outside of his self, of course. Fortunately, all his original munitions have long since been accounted for, lost, or used up, as well."

He fiddled with his unlit pipe, glancing skyward. "Here's another point; I'm not sure how effective that pistol will be on those creatures of his. They're not like us. They are very tough—all the fragile parts seem to be missing."

He put his pipe away with a sigh, and rolled himself under a blanket, another supply we commandeered from the *Trepidation.*

I went to check on Mic, as I wasn't sleepy. I found her just at the edge of the tree line.

"How goes it?" I asked, being careful to stay under the tree cover.

"Hi, Ben. The balloon is not heading our direction, if that's what you mean."

"Good." I pulled out Jack's stick. "While we have a moment, can you take a closer look at this thing, and still monitor the balloon?"

She floated over the stick. "This belonged to Jack?"

"Yes," I said, sitting down, "and it has a few surprises to it, some nasty."

"I see. Do you think one of those nasty surprises might be a tracking device?"

I looked determinedly at a piece of grass. "That thought had not occurred to me, and it should have."

She revolved slowly to a dark blue. "Take the staff apart as much as you can, put it on the ground, and give me a few minutes."

I did as she requested, and watched her work. She would hover for a time over each object, her colors shifting from dark blues to bright green. It made me feel good to see her work again. It reminded me of better times on the *Pelagius.* It put me in a nostalgic mood.

"You're not doing anything more than playing rainbow, are you, Mic?" I teased.

"Be still."

"I mean really, all pretending aside now, I could just as easily wave my finger over these things, say, *I pronounce thee clean*, and get the same results."

"You think so?"

She rose from her work and came to hover in front of

my face, a dark, blustery red. We considered each other for a time, until I finally chuckled. A moment later, she turned a very lovely fawn brown, and we turned back to the stick.

"There's more to this walking stick than just a few hidden gadgets," she said, reverting to her standard white. "There's a power in that jeweled handle that's very similar to the ship's lifeline, but more structured. It *can* serve as a transceiver of sorts. Transceiver is my word for it. I'm not sure how else to describe it, but I'm thinking of Lilith's appearance. I'll scan the process if it does it again." She paused. "You say Carlin saw it, too?"

Did I detect just the hint of doubt in my little companion?

"Lilith was there, fully cognizant and interactive. It was not some recording or projection or act of imagination. She was not corporeal, but she was there."

She made a few lazy revolutions, but let the matter drop. "How are things between you and Michael? Do you trust him now?"

"Yes," I said. "I do."

I pulled distractedly at the grass. I wanted to move on to other subjects. Trust was such a complicated word. "How are things with you? We haven't really had a chance to talk about what happened."

"You mean, what Lilith did to me?"

"I gather that was a big change."

She surprised me by retracting to her smallest form, and hovering near my hand until I opened it. She settled on my palm, as light and warm as a coin in the sun. Her voice, when she finally spoke, was a soft, almost fragile thing, without any sign of its recent confidence.

"Some of my scanning and logical processing functions are—evolving. It is frightening and exciting at the same time. I think I might be able to see that ghost you were talking about earlier."

"What exactly did Lilith do to you?" I asked.

"I'm not sure. It was more than just a program update or

new hardware. It was," she seemed to search for a word, "inconsistent."

"I don't think a bit of nonsense is a bad thing. I'm happy for you."

"Thanks. I do have a few questions, if you don't mind."

I didn't imagine this was going to be a birds and bees sort of thing, but I could tell whatever was coming was important and probably much bigger than anything I could handle. "Okay."

"What does it mean to be free? Do I, can I, have a soul? How do I know that I know? Is there a God, and if so what kind of…?"

I held up my other hand to stop her. Yep; way above my paygrade.

"I understand that you have most, if not all, of the collected works of philosophy and theology from Earth's cultures in your memory. I think you should look to them first."

"I have," she said. "And every proposition only raises another response. Most of the best answers are not really answers at all. Science is no help. It doesn't acknowledge the questions' validity. Philosophy is great for questions, but terrible when it comes to definitive answers. Theology gives you answers, but there nearly always connected to acts of faith." She paused, turning a deep sapphire. "And faith is the most puzzling answer of all."

"And you expect me to tell you the answers?"

"Not *the* answer. Just your answer."

"Why is mine so important?"

"It's not," she said. "Or, rather it is, because it is yours." She turned a brief rose color.

I worried a thumbnail for a moment, and considered briefly the inadequacies of language and my own education. I thought about my sister, side-stepping mortality one procedure at a time. I thought about a girl I knew on Earth who had a way of looking right through my usual nonsense and would be highly amused to see me in the role of mentor.

Then I thought about Lilith, now dead, perhaps because of me. I thought about a red-cloaked monster, a living creature however malevolent, also dead, and certainly because of me. I thought about my vision in the woods, and a not-so-simple cardinal in a tree. I thought about what it means to say something, and what it means to understand, and be understood, or not.

And after all that, I thought about Mic, my (former) game computer, now an emerging sentient; a conscious looking for answers to the same eternal questions that plague us all at some time or other.

I could take a pass. I could plead ignorance. But Mic was no longer my game companion. She was my friend. And it means something to have a friend, if only to hold your hand, or in this case, sit in it.

So, I took a big breath, and leaped. "First of all, for what it's worth, those questions are a part of what it means to be human. I wish I could tell you an answer, my answer, but I'm still searching in some ways." I lifted her close to my face. "But I can tell you that you have a friend. That's always a good start."

She didn't say anything for a time, but I felt her grow warmer in my hand. "A friend."

"My best friend, in fact." As I said it, I realized it was true.

She turned a white so bright I couldn't look at her.

"Thank you," she said. The light faded again to a soft glow. "You can go to sleep now, Benjamin. I'll keep watch."

I left her there floating under the pine shadows, revolving in shades of soft blue and green. Probably a much wiser and kinder person than I'd ever be.

But I could call her friend.

Carlin found a path that ran reasonably straight and in the right direction. The trail was covered by high grass that reached up and over our heads like a living canopy. The grass swayed from time to time in the wind, and the undersides of the stalks glowed with a soft pale luminescence like a child's glow-stick or some deep-water jellyfish. There was a heady, pleasant smell to the air, not unlike fresh cut hay.

Occasionally, I heard small animals burrowing or shuffling just off the path, and once the sound of something much larger passing through the heavy grass. The top of the field parted like a wave as it passed beneath. It was a very big swale.

I looked to Calin with some alarm.

"We should be okay while we are on the path," he said. "In addition to being lazy, Jack was too much of a coward to leave anything to chance. As long as we stay on fixed roads and paths the wildlife won't approach. The only danger we face here are strangers."

"What kind of wildlife?" I asked.

"The field snakes are the biggest threat. That, and the wild dogs."

I looked quickly down at my feet.

He chuckled. "The snakes are usually the size of houses. That was probably one that just passed."

Later, Mic confirmed the presence of several of these monstrous serpents. But Carlin was right, nothing came closer than the one we'd heard earlier. Just the same, I kept my eyes on the grass and decided it was an appropriate time to arm myself.

Mic's scan of the stick had revealed a few more secrets. By pressing a button near the handle I could release a long blade from the stock edge above the tip, turning the stick into a small spear. As we walked I experimented, trying to determine what felt more comfortable in my hand, the long cutting blade, or the extended spear.

Carlin led the way and I followed close behind. Mic would occasionally scout ahead or circle back to check for pursuit. Sometime after midnight, the grass began to grow shorter and lose some of its luminescence. Before long it was down to our hips and we were walking by starlight. I saw no signs of the giant snakes or other wildlife, but we did pass a row of haystacks running in neat lines through a tilled field. A little later we saw the outline of a farmhouse.

I asked Carlin how the farmer managed against the snakes and other dangers.

"The snakes tend to stay in the high grass," he said. "The farmers keep the grass well-trimmed around their property. The work can be a hazardous, but they help each other out." He paused. "Still, it's a dangerous life this far from town. Takes a special kind of person."

He stopped to look at the farmhouse. "It would be nice to get some information."

"And maybe get something to eat," I suggested, hoping for a home-cooked meal.

"Let's get a little closer to the village," he said.

We walked steadily through the early morning without a break, occasionally passing more farms with lighted windows and sounds of early morning activity.

Finally, just as I was about to insist we would stop and eat, we came across a small farm about a hundred yards off the road. A gray-board farmhouse sat near the back of a tilled field. The house windows were dark, and there was an unnatural stillness to the air of the field.

Carlin stopped.

"You think it's abandoned?" I asked.

"If it is, then it's recent."

I looked to the rows of fresh turned soil along either side of the house.

"There's no life in the building," said Mic, coming close. "Apart from small animals."

Carlin continued to stare at the building, his eyes drawing close. "Let's check it out."

We took a short stone path that ran from the road to the front porch of the farmhouse. Despite the odd silence, I was looking forward to getting a roof over my head again.

When we drew closer, we could see one of the house windows was broken, and the door was slightly off its hinges.

Carlin pulled a knife from his vest. I released the long-blade from the stick.

Carlin led the way up the porch, stepping quietly. Mic and I followed. The silence grew heavier, as if the house were holding its breath.

When we reached the door, Mic flew through the cracked opening. Carlin looked to me, and I shrugged. At this point, I was confident she could take care of herself.

Carlin started to open the door, but it fell off its hinges with a clatter and sent us sprawling out of the way.

We stood for a moment just outside the doorway. It was dark inside, but Mic returned a moment later, her soft radiance lighting up the interior of a small foyer. From the doorway I could see the floorboards were covered with broken glass and the remains of an umbrella stand.

"You need to look at this," said Mic. "I'm going to cast some more light. Don't worry; there's nothing alive but the rats."

She really lit up then and chased away the rest of the darkness. We stepped inside.

Beyond the foyer was a living room. It, too, was a mess of broken glass and furniture. What looked to be the remains of a grandfather clock was strewn across a ripped couch. The swinging doors that led to the next room were completely off their hinges and tossed in the fireplace. There were deep scratches in the wall paneling.

Mic led us through a door to the right and to the kitchen, which like the foyer was a mess. Copper pots and pans and broken jars of pickled fruits were scattered across the floor, and the giant shelf that once held them was pulled down across a cutting table.

We made our way around the fallen shelving and continued, following Mic. She took us through an open archway, and stopped. This, apparently, was what she wanted us to see.

Like everything else in the house, the room had been

destroyed. Judging from the large blood covered table in the center—the only thing still standing—it had once been the family dining room. The chairs that formerly sat around the table were now just broken bits of kindling on the floor. Glass and pieces of china were littered around a turned over cabinet blocking one side of the room.

The destruction had not ended with the furniture.

A large painting on the wall showed a portrait of a middle-aged couple surrounded by four children. The girls, maybe ten and twelve, were dressed in simple bonnets, corsets and skirts. The boys wore black wool coats with square ties. They were tall and handsome, like their father. It was impossible to say what the mother and girls looked like; their faces had been torn out from the painting.

I heard something squeak, and watched a large rat scurry across the floor. It had been at another puddle of blood near the wall.

Carlin stepped closer to the dining table. I followed him, and Mic came to float above it, casting her light along the surface. The bloodstains sat in a rough outline of a body stretched across the table.

We checked the whole house, and the barn and field.

There was no sign of the family; no bodies, not even a stray tooth or hair. It was as if the blood and destruction had just suddenly appeared out of nowhere.

We left the house, and went back to our original path. Neither of us mentioned stopping for food again, and we walked a long time in silence, each of us lost to our own thoughts.

Eventually the path became a road paved in flat stone. As the light shifted to dawn, I could see the road appeared to end at a small group of hills about a mile away.

"That's our destination," said Carlin, looking at the hills through the glass. He handed the telescope to me.

The hills formed a rough triangle that overlooked a small valley. The bulk of the village was in the valley, crouched inside the protective arms of the hills like an elaborate toy model. A tall wooden fence with a gate spanned the base of the triangle. The center hill was crowned with a large house and winding stairway.

"These friends of yours," I said, handing the glass back to Carlin. "You said we had to go carefully. Why?"

"I'm not sure you'd call all of them friends," he said slowly, "though most are friendly enough with those that understand their way and leave them alone. They are a naturally cautious people, the villagers. They have good reason to be. Most of the First are gone now, but their offspring remember Jack, and the war."

"But they are your friends, right?"

He rolled his whiskers, a faint blush touching his cheeks. "Well, a few."

"Carlin, what are you not telling me?"

"Let's just say, I'm a persona non-grata with some of the local law."

Before I could ask him what that meant, he squared his shoulders and stepped off the road. Apparently, we were taking an indirect, and less visible, route to the village.

When we were about a hundred yards from village gate, we stopped in the last copse of trees before a grassy area that surrounded the fencing. It apparently had been some time since the villagers cut the grass, as it was high enough for a person to hide in if they stayed low. Carlin was studying a man in the top of the gate tower.

"How long has it been since you were last here?" I asked, keeping my voice low.

Carlin shook his head, still looking at the gatekeeper.

"Asleep," he said ruefully. Presumably he was referring to the man slumped against the gatehouse. "Things are going to have to tighten up again, and quick." He bit his lip. "Still, that plays in our favor just now."

He turned to me. "We need to find Hoag."

"Hoag?" I asked.

"The owner of Hoag's Tavern. I call *her* a friend. She's one of the first. If anyone knows about Dun, it will be

Hoag."

He pointed to a small gap between the fence line and the base of the right-hand hill. "That's our way in. We go quietly, avoiding official notice if we can. If we're stopped, I'll do the talking."

"I understand."

He looked to Mic, floating by my shoulder. "I think it's best you not be seen, Mic. You would draw too much attention."

"I can hear and scan things just the same," she said.

I gave her a grateful smile and opened the satchel .

"Keep that stick hidden, too," said Carlin.

I tucked it in a back loop of my belt, well out of sight under the cloak.

Carlin nodded. "Let's go then."

We kept low in the grass, and passed through the fence gap into the village proper. No one shouted for us to stop, or appeared to notice. Security, as Carlin had noted, was a bit lax.

Thinking of Jack, I agreed with Carlin—things would have to change in a hurry.

XVI

The House of Hoag

The sign hanging above the door advertised *Hoag's Tavern and Eatery*. It sat in the heart of a cobbled street, a wooden two-story affair slightly larger than its neighbors to either side, worn and weathered, but solid. Even before we climbed the small front porch I could smell the aroma of food mixed with ale, wine, and smoke. Carlin's face wore the first sign of a smile I'd seen since Lilith's death, and he stepped eagerly through the swinging parlor doors. A young boy in a jerkin was sitting on a stool in the shadows of the entry. As he was asleep, we didn't bother to wake him.

The tavern was warm, dark, and already smoky despite the hour. Light was provided by a wall-to-ceiling fireplace and a few stubborn rays that fought their way through the grime on the windows and the depths of the room. The lanterns hanging from the rafters were already lit. The dozen or so heavy wooden tables scattered haphazardly around the room were full. The fireplace created dancing shadows along the walls and ceiling and was a source of some of the smoke in the room; the rest was provided by the dozen or so pipes hanging from various customer mouths.

I thought the ceiling was unusually low, but as I followed Carlin in, I realized the floor was sunk. I negotiated the steps, almost lost in the flickering shadows of the firelight, and tried not to stare at the patrons. They evidently held no such inhibitions.

I caught up to Carlin, who was leaning against the long bar in the back and talking to a young lady washing out a glass.

Carlin turned as I approached and made introductions,

"Carrie, this is Benjamin Lasak. Lasak, this is Carrie."

Carrie nodded. She was a short brunette with blue eyes and a freckled face. She offered a distracted smile in my direction, but her attention was obviously reserved for Carlin.

"Michael, where have you been all this time?" she asked.

"Busy," he answered, but not gruffly. "How is Hoag?"

"Busy," she returned with a laugh. "I'll get her. Stay here."

I turned with Carlin, and finally took a good look at the room. A half-dozen faces quickly looked away and pretended to focus on their own spaces again.

Some of the patrons were dressed like Carlin and Bell. I saw nineteenth century suits and jackets, a few top hats, and even a cloak or two. The women generally wore dresses, though a few sported trousers and leather jerkins. Judging by the others, however, Jack had not limited himself to the streets of London. Sitting among the waistcoats, smocks, and trousers of the Victorian era were fashions from Asia, the Americas, and several Slavic countries. There were even a few odds and ends that I couldn't place, perhaps a homegrown product. Regardless of their clothing, nearly everyone carried a bladed weapon, stick, or staff of some kind, even the women, and no one made an effort to hide the fact.

Most of the crowd sat in small groups and kept their voices low, their faces lost in the shadows. Only an odd man in the center of the room was holding forth and seemed to enjoy the attention. Plump, with short, thin legs that seemed to belie his rotund figure, he held a glass of wine in one hand and a chicken leg in the other. He had propped two chairs together to form a makeshift bench and stretch his bandy legs. He had no small number of interested listeners, most of which were children. From time to time, he would have one of his youthful listeners fill his glass or fetch something from the kitchen. His voice was a deep baritone and not unpleasant. He reminded of salesman I knew back on Colony I who sold me a suit of clothes that still sit in my apartment back on Earth, never worn.

"As I was saying," The man cast a curious eye in our direction and noted our attention. "We traveled resolutely across the Burgundy…"

"Did you see any pirates?" asked a young girl with a bright bow in her hair.

"My dear Penelope, if you see the metallic Pirates of the Burgundy you don't generally live to tell about it. Fortunately, dear, that's something you don't have to worry about here in the safe confines of the village."

"But we have big snakes," answered Penelope proudly.

"So, you do. So, you do." The big man shifted in his seat. He wore a soft felt hat that tended to slide down the side of his round head. "Now on the other side of the Burgundy, as some of you may know, are the Wild lands. I don't have to tell any of you how dangerous they can be. Few have travelled that distance, and less returned to tell about it. I'm not the first to say that."

He looked for a moment to his young listeners, to check their reaction. Satisfied, he turned to study the ceiling and continued. "It takes a cool head to survive the uncharted regions of that godforsaken land. But as Mother Lamprey, God rest her soul, noted on more than one occasion: *Usil, my boy, you'll never win a foot race, but you'll probably find a way to be first in line to the banquet afterward.* And that, to my understanding, means a clever lad."

He chuckled along with his listeners and took a sip of wine. "Clever is what I needed to be when I left the Wilds and ran into the Baron's men…"

The reaction this drew was obviously anticipated by the speaker and he smiled slightly at the frightened faces of the children around him.

"You *saw* the Baron's men?"

"Where they mostly human, or mostly Graëh?"

"Did they make you a prisoner?"

"How did you get away?"

He raised a fat hand in the air to silence them all.

"I was not made a prisoner. As a matter of fact, I had the privilege of dining with the Baron himself."

I noticed that this announcement had a strange effect on the rest of the Tavern. Up until that point most of the crowd had made a point of ignoring the man. Now an unnatural hush fell across the room, and more than one face turned their attention to the colorful figure.

"Yes, I was a guest of the Baron," said the speaker proudly. "Despite his reputation, the Baron has a fine sensibility, a true gift of discernment I'd say, and he honored me by extending an invitation as soon as he learned I was in the vicinity. A gentleman shows his colors in his treatment of others—I'm not the first to say that."

This drew a scornful chuckle from the shadows, and a man sitting near us whispered something I couldn't hear to his companion. It was obviously not complimentary, judging from his companion's reaction.

The storyteller turned his sausage nose up at the derisive laughter, and carried on with determination.

"As I was saying, the Baron *invited* me." He gave a heated glare in the general direction of the heckler. "Well, I could hardly refuse," he added a moment later, returning his attention to his admirers.

"Weren't you scared?" asked a little boy at his feet.

"No, of course not," answered the fat man, sipping at his wine and ignoring another chortle behind him. "When you have been around the world you see some things, my boy. Some of which are a great deal more frightening than the Graëh Baron. Besides which, as I said, the Baron is a man who knows how to treat a *fellow* gentleman."

This brought a number of catcalls from the room, most in good nature.

Again, the storyteller ignored them.

"It is true," he went on reflectively, "the Baron is a man of peculiar tastes; I'm not the first to say it. And yes,

William, to answer your question, he is mostly Graëh. More Graëh, in fact, than any in his kingdom."

"What would the Baron want of you, Useless Lardpie?" asked a man at the nearby table. He and his companion were dressed in long dark cloaks, their faces hidden in their hoods.

"The name, sir," said the fat man, turning to get a better look at the voice, "Is Usil Lamprey, and I'll thank you not to cast aspersions."

"You'll thank me all right," said the heckler, starting to rise. His companion reached out and grabbed his arm, whispering heatedly. The heckler muttered something under his breath, but sat back down again. He lowered his head and said nothing more.

Usil Lamprey grunted, as if reluctantly accepting an apology. But when he started up again, his voice had lost a little of its confidence and he would occasionally glance toward the heckler's table. Uneasiness settled over the room. Lamprey's youthful audience looked around in confusion, wondering what had happened.

"As I was saying," continued Lamprey around a cough, "the Baron knows a man of worth. We discussed many things, the Baron and I, including the safety of the realm and certain treaties concerning territorial rights..."

"What about them?" called out a woman near the door. She leaned forward to hear better, pulling hard on a short pipe.

Lamprey now had the full of attention of everyone in the room, though it was clear from the blush rising to his cheeks that he wasn't happy about it. "Ah, yes. It seems that the Baron would like to readdress some of the, ah, more stringent domain lines."

"I knew it," said an elderly man at the bar. "The Graëh are rising again."

"The Baron can't do that," worried another. "There are treaties. The Collective Council will not allow it."

"Ah, well," said Lamprey, with another glance at the heckler's table. The two men were sitting close together, their hooded faces turned squarely on Lamprey. "The Collective Council, yes. But the Graëh Baron does not answer to the Council, does he?"

"But the treaties," said the first woman, gesturing with her pipe.

"Treaties, my dear," said Lamprey, "are only as strong as the people and times that make them."

"Enough," snorted the heckler, rising finally, despite his companion efforts. "This fool talks like a woman. He'll have you all soon wetting yourselves over nothing. And you," he turned directly to Lamprey. "I would be careful, Lardpie. The Baron doesn't like loose talkers from what I hear, and I'm not the first to say *that*."

His companion hissed another warning. The hooded man looked around. Everyone was looking at him. He turned abruptly and left in a flurry. His companion threw some coins on the table, and then scrambled after him. There followed an awkward silence as everyone tried to make sense of what had just happened.

"Here!" barked an iron voice near my elbow. "Lamprey, what are you doing chasing out paying customers?"

I turned along with everyone else to see who had spoken. For a moment I wasn't sure I had the right person. Next to me stood an ancient woman, bent with age like a question mark. Her face was the texture of a weathered apple, and her hands shook on the stick she used for support. Only her eyes were unmarked, two sapphires lost in a bed of wrinkled, age-spotted skin. Right now those eyes were measuring Lamprey, and they were not happy.

The storyteller was busily trying to sit up straight in his chair, a thin line of red running up his fat cheeks. His crowd of youthful listeners had disappeared as if by magic.

"Your pardon, Madam Hoag," he stammered. "I did not chase anyone out. The gentlemen left on their own volition."

"Humph," answered Hoag. "Just see you keep your tales to yourself in the future, especially if there likely to upset the guests."

"Of course, Madam Hoag. I was just relating my conversation with the Baron..."

"I heard you," interrupted Hoag. "The whole bloody tavern heard you. You like to hear yourself talk so much the Baron himself probably heard you."

Lamprey's face was now a deep shade of red.

"I think I'll see to my wagon now," he said to no one in particular. "Miss Carrie, the bill, please."

"And if those other two ran out on any of their bill, see that Lamprey makes good the difference," said Hoag. Her iron voice chased the fat man out the door. "I'm sure he's got the money, what with all his friends in high places."

The tension in the room disappeared, forgotten in the laughter, as Lamprey meekly paid his bill and waddled out the door.

I turned back to Hoag, who still stood beside me. She surprised me with a knowing wink.

"Don't worry," she said quietly, "Usil Lamprey will be back for his next meal soon enough, and telling stories bigger than that one, you can be sure. And I'm not the first to say that," she finished with a cackle. She turned to my companion with a smile. "Michael Carlin," she said in a low voice. "What brings you around now, I wonder? Lamprey's worrying folks with tales of the Baron, there are dark rumors from the Forest, and you show up at my door after a long age. Come on then, it's to the back room for something to eat. There you can tell me what it is I don't want to know. Carrie, make yourself useful and bring us some breakfast and drink."

This order delivered, Hoag turned and disappeared behind the bar into a back room. Carlin and I followed. We were soon sitting around a large oak table with four chairs and a bench. The noise and the hum of the tavern were cut off by Hoag closing of the door behind us. She took a long time walking around the table and sitting across from us. When she was settled, she nodded to Carlin.

"Save the news," she said. "Introductions first."

"Madam Hoag," said Carlin. "This is Benjamin Lasak. Lasak is from Earth. He just arrived."

This raised a hoary eyebrow on Hoag, but she didn't interrupt.

"We've come to you, as you guessed, with troubling news. We seek your advice and counsel."

Before Hoag could answer, Carrie entered bringing food and drinks.

"Carrie, fetch Mr. Giersson," said Hoag. "And round up our special guest. He'll have managed his task by now, and want to hear this."

Carrie set the tray on the table and headed back out the door.

"Lars is here?" asked a surprised Carlin.

Hoag nodded, worrying a thin mouth around the few remaining teeth she possessed.

"He's been making the rounds for a month or so now," she said. "Your timing is good, or bad, as the case might be. He's due to be heading back soon. Go on, eat. You're men; you're hungry. I'll talk while you fill your bellies. Like Lamprey, I like a captive audience."

Carrie had brought a pile of eggs, bacon, hash-browns, and a pitcher of light mead, along with wooden forks, plates, and cups. Carlin and I started in without further encouragement.

Hoag let us eat for a time in peace. When she finally spoke, a little of the iron was out of her voice and her eyes grew heavy with reflection. "You've been gone a long time, Michael Carlin. Things have changed, some for the good, some for the bad. The Baron has started making himself known again in these parts. He hasn't openly broken the treaty, but it's no secret the Graëh have been sneaking into the Central Plains."

"Mr. Lasak," she said without looking at me, "as a stranger you might not know what that means, but I tell you it bodes no good. The Baron has always wanted more than what's behind the Wall. A long time before we taught him a hard lesson about going outside his so-called kingdom, but that was a long time ago. We're not so strong or determined as back then, and the Baron's not been idle."

"What about the Forest Enclave, and the Tri-Province Pact?" asked Carlin.

Hoag nodded. "The Forest Enclave is still there, and vigilant. Sarah remains in charge. But they cannot hold off the Baron alone. If he should decide to come out from behind the wall again in force, the Forest will fall first. As to the Pact..." she shook her head. "We have never been able to stop the Baron from sending out spies and troublemakers. It seems some of these have been to see Ming. It is not hard to guess the promises they carried. More territory—Central Plains territory, no doubt—for just a little cooperation. All the Baron needs is the Eastern Territories to stand aside and the Plains will soon follow the Forest in defeat."

"How much of this is speculation?" asked Carlin around his eggs.

"I had it from Ming's own man last year," she answered promptly. "He didn't say it so direct, and he was obviously fishing for information of his own, but I have no reason to believe it is not true. Till now, I think Ming has resisted the idea on principle—the Baron was never kind to the Eastern Territories before. But we've not heard from Ming since that messenger, and I worry he considers that times have changed enough to trust the Baron. I was contemplating sending a special representative to the Eastern Territory, to see just how things stand."

"I can't believe Ming would betray us to the Baron," said Carlin, setting down his fork. "Last I saw him he was more worried about establishing a culture than any expansionism."

"Times and people change," responded Hoag. "I don't think Ming would go to war with the Central Plains directly. But he might rationalize staying out of a fight and picking up some of the pieces afterward. Especially if the Baron should promise not to harm his own territory in the process of destroying ours." She chewed her gums in reflection. "I think, too, Ming is getting some pressure from his own people."

"And the Collective Council?" asked Carlin.

Hoag snorted. "Lamprey had that much right. The Baron doesn't answer to that body, even if all the parties did care to intervene, which they don't. The North might stand with us, but is too far away to act in timely fashion. Sarah and the Forest remain true. I just told you Ming is not so certain. And the Plains itself..."

"The Plains?" interrupted Carlin incredulously. "Surely the Plains..."

"The Collective Council has a new representative from the Central Plains," said Hoag, the iron creeping back in her voice again. "And he doesn't exactly see things like we do."

"Who?" asked Carlin, but I could see he already guessed.

"Your good friend, Lord Edgar," said Hoag.

Carlin's face turned a shade of purple I'd not seen before. "Edgar. How did that happen?"

"Nobody else wanted the job. Or rather, Edgar made sure no one else wanted the job."

"I can't believe you or Carrie couldn't beat him in a vote," said Carlin, his anger mounting. "Things can't have changed that much."

"Oh, but they did," said Hoag with grimace. "A new rule submitted and passed by young Edgar, now Head of the Township Board, states village—excuse me, township—residents may not hold office for more than three turns. That includes Carrie and me." Hoag snorted. "I don't mind so much for me, and there is even some sense to it, new blood and all that. But Carrie could still do some things, if given a chance. Edgar backdated the order to the early days, of course. He's clever, that Edgar."

"New rules," mouthed Carlin with evident distaste. "What is the head of the township board nonsense?"

"Oh, Lord Edgar and his cronies have been quite busy

with new rules and positions since you left," said Hoag. "Ordinances here, by-laws there, decrees everywhere. The village is now officially a township, and has a body to oversee it, the board, headed of course by Lord Edgar." She looked to Carlin, then added softly. "He even made Old Bill's house on the Hill the official manor, and moved himself in."

"He didn't," said Carlin incredulously.

"Something about passed due debt to the *township*," muttered Hoag. "You know Bill, always borrowing against that house of his to improve it. In times past, we turned a blind eye to overdue payments. But not Edgar, not the new Head. Bill was a fool to borrow from him, but there it is. As soon as Edgar saw his chance, he ran Bill out of the house on the hill."

"Wouldn't take money from anyone else either," added Carrie. "It was a crime. A crime done in the name of law."

Carlin looked at them in disbelief. "What happened to Bill and Nancy?"

Hoag sighed. "Bill's not been the same since Nancy left him. Wanders around like a ghost through the town, when he comes around that is. Haven't seen him in some time."

"Nancy is dead?" asked Carlin incredulously.

"Not dead," said Hoag. "Gone. No one knows where. Edgar moved in and she just disappeared. Couldn't take it I imagine. I think it was the final straw with her and Bill."

Carlin was apoplectic, but before he could respond someone knocked quietly on the side door.

Carrie got up and cracked the door a bit to see who it was, then opened it up to let Usil Lamprey in.

"Ah," said Hoag. "Our special guest."

Lamprey nodded once to Hoag, and then found a place at the table. He grabbed a plate and started eating without being asked, his face partly shadowed by his sliding hat.

Before formal introductions could be made, there was another knock, this time at the main door. Carrie crossed the room and let in a tall, craggy faced man with thick hair the color of tarnished silver. He was dressed in a traveled-stained white cloak and light armor, and though his carriage belied the white hair, his enormous hands were red and cracked with exposure and time. His tired expression brightened when he recognized Michael Carlin.

"Carlin," he said in a distinct Scandinavian accent.

"Lars." Carlin stood and offered a warm handshake.

"Carrie," said Hoag, "will you ask Thom to step in a moment, as well."

The ever-accommodating Carrie nodded and disappeared back to the tavern. A moment later an immense troll-like figure with hairy arms and cauliflower ears poked his head through the door.

"Thom," said Hoag, "watch the place for a moment, will you? We're not to be disturbed. That includes the township Head or any of his crew."

Thom nodded, revealing a bald spot on his crown as round and clean as an egg. "Yes'm." His voice was surprisingly soft for his size.

When he withdrew, Carrie came back and took a place by Hoag.

"Now," said Hoag, "more introductions."

She gave a quick look in my direction, as did the stranger in the white cloak, and Lamprey.

"I am Hoag," she said simply, "and this is my daughter, Carrie."

This surprised me. I couldn't see the resemblance. Maybe the eyes....

"We have each served on the Collective Council at one time or the other," continued Hoag, "and we call our home the Central Plains. Usil Lamprey has undoubtedly made himself known to all." She pointed to the colorful man with a smile.

Lamprey waved a fat hand but did not bother to look up from his breakfast.

"Don't be taken in by that little farce outside," said Hoag, turning to me. "Lamprey's brave enough in a pinch, and he's no fool. That show was for the Baron's Graëh men—the loudmouth and his companion. Usil *plays* the fool, and plays it well I might add, but he's as sharp as they come. Otherwise, he couldn't do what he does."

"Which is what, exactly?" asked Carlin.

"Why spying of course," said Hoag with a chuckle.

Carlin sighed. "So, it's come to spying again, has it?"

"Again?" said Hoag in exasperation. "Haven't you been listening, Michael Carlin? I've been trying to tell you. The Baron is rising. Ming is silent. And there are dark rumors everywhere. It's never *stopped* being about spying—and you know that better than any."

Carlin raised a hand in submission.

Hoag then turned to the silver-haired man. "Lars Giersson comes from across the Burgundy Sea. He hails from the Nordic Territories. He, too, brings news."

Taking his cue, Carlin indicated me with a nod. "This is Benjamin Lasak. He's with me. He's a new arrival to our world."

"New?" said Lamprey in surprise.

"Yes. He came in his own ship."

"Which sea?" asked Lars.

"Not that kind of ship," said Hoag, looking at me again with renewed interest.

"So," said Lamprey, setting his fork aside and finally looking up. "After all these years, new blood."

"You mean he's from Earth?" asked Carrie in wonder.

"Yes," I answered, feeling it was about time I took part in the conversation. "I'm a LongPost, a kind of mail carrier. I was traveling to another planet colony when I got...ah, sidetracked and stuck here."

"Michael Carlin speaks for Benjamin Lasak," said Hoag formerly, and looked around the room.

There appeared to be no objections, though I thought Lamprey looked concerned.

"Mr. Lasak," she finished, "you are welcome."

She rested her hands on the table, took a deep breath,

and turned finally to Carlin. "And now, we had best hear your news. I suspect Mr. Lasak's arrival has something to do with why you came down from your nest after all these years."

XVII

Plots, Knots, and Plans

Carlin nodded slowly. "The Baron is not the only one on the rise." He sighed and hung his head. "Jack is loose again."

Someone—Carrie I think—made a start.

Carlin continued, his voice grim, his eyes now fixed on some space in front of him. "He's awakened his henchmen. One of them is on our trail even now. At the very least, everyone in the three Provinces must be warned. Jack is free."

Hoag reached a shaking hand out to Carrie who took it tightly in her own. Giersson's dour expression grew darker. Lamprey stopped eating, set his fork down.

"What's the rest," demanded Hoag.

Carlin hesitated. "Lilith is dead."

This time Carrie buried her head in Hoag's shoulder. Hoag hung her head. The rest looked on in shock.

Carlin then gave an abbreviated account of my arrival, Jack's release, and our flight. He left out the *Trepidation*, Mic, and the stick, simply saying we managed to escape the red daemon. I wondered at this, but I suppose he had his reasons.

"Jack out, and Lilith gone," whispered Hoag, stroking her daughter's head. "To live to see these times again. Oh, sweet Lilith. Carlin!" She reached her other shaky hand across the table toward Carlin. He either did not see it, or couldn't bring himself to take it. He sat instead staring down at the table. Hoag pulled back her hand and wrapped her arms around her daughter.

"I am sorry for your loss, Michael," said Giersson quietly. "Even in the Nordic Territories we know of the Lady Lilith who guards us against the dark—and your love for her."

Carlin raised his head slowly, nodded to Giersson. "It will not be the last loss, I fear."

Giersson drew a deep breath, turned to the table. "My news is also ill, though not maybe as dark as the return of Jack. A new Seer has arisen across the water. She styles herself a priestess of Loki, and calls for the old ways. We have always been able to deal with such uprisings before. But this one is different. The priestess is a true practitioner of the dark arts. I've seen her work myself. She can raise strange forms and manipulate the earth like the Magi of old. Many are flocking to her banner. Such is her power that even the war chiefs have put aside their differences and sought counsel together. It was decided that I would go across the water in hope of succor and advice."

He looked around, but no one spoke. "I have come a great distance and at much peril. But I can see now that any hope for support of our cause must go unanswered. With Jack loose and the Baron active you will be sore pressed to hold your own homes. But I offer a dire warning just the same. I fear the priestess and her followers will soon assume power over the Nordic Territories. The chiefs do not believe they are strong enough to stop her, even if they band together. That is really why they sent me, to seek help in arms." He looked to Hoag, then Carlin. "The Nordic Territory is distant from your lands, but if the priestess gains control, if the chiefs fail, she will not be satisfied with just the North. Prepare yourself."

Hoag shifted in her chair. She released Carrie with a care, and turned to answer Giersson in a voice that had resumed some of its iron quality. "Three enemies on three different doorsteps. Jack, the Baron, and now this Priestess of Loki. But you are wrong in one thing, Lars Giersson. I cannot speak or act for the Collective Council or the village anymore, but you will not go unanswered. We will prepare. As to arms, which is your true need..." She shook her head. "Three enemies, three doorsteps," she repeated. "And Jack is on ours."

Giersson nodded. 'It is as I feared."

"It all starts and ends with Jack," interrupted Carlin vehemently. "The Baron, the Priestess," he glared around the table, "these are just ills rising from the same source. Finish Jack, and the rest will fall in line."

"I'm not so sure about that, Michael Carlin," said Lamprey, breaking his silence. "At least not where the Baron is concerned. He takes no direction from Jack, and he is strong. He'll have to be dealt with on his own, and soon. I suspect the same is true of the Priestess of Loki."

Giersson nodded grimly. "I fear this is true. She does not need or answer to Jack or the Baron, though it is a terrible thought that she might ally with either of those dark powers."

"Aye," said Hoag in a whisper, looking toward the ceiling, "or the three of them together. That is the greatest danger."

"That must not happen," said Lamprey, sitting up. "What with Ming already showing signs of turning…"

"Ming will not turn," insisted Carlin.

"You have been away a long time," noted Lamprey.

"Peace," said Hoag with a sigh. "Yet another task, and not unrelated. Carlin is right there. All of these troubles are connected, however loosely, and we must act in accordance. I see it this way. First, we must secure Ming's allegiance. All enemies of Jack, the Baron, and this new Priestess must unite under the same banner, or there is no hope for any of us. Ming must affirm the pact between East, Forest, and Plains. Lamprey, I fear this mission falls to you. You must go to Ming, convince him of the danger and bring him to our side. You cannot fail in this."

"I will try," said Lamprey simply. "But I still say someone will have to deal with the Baron. Though he tried to hide it, it is clear he has a new army, better and larger than before. And there is more. There is new fervor behind the Wall. The Baron talks of a holy war against the infidels."

Hoag shook her head. "I like this news not. He was

always the manipulator, but he failed in his previous attempts to expand because his troops abandoned him when faced with a real challenge. This religious overtone may serve to strengthen their resolve in ways simple conquest would not."

"He failed, too," said Carrie, "because he was at war with Jack. We must try and stoke that animosity again. Maybe we can enlist the Baron's help against Jack. Surely he would not welcome a challenge from that direction now."

"I would not encourage that thought," said Lamprey. "The Baron would pretend to be our ally in the beginning, only to betray us in our most dire circumstance."

"I agree," said Carlin looking to Lamprey. "Any pact with that man is likely to turn against us."

"We need not go into this blindly," said Carrie. "Two can play the game of deception. If nothing else, we may be able to delay the Baron's preemptive attack with talk of treaty against our mutual enemy Jack."

Lamprey nodded. "It is a dangerous game, but perhaps worth exploring."

"We will get Sarah's take on this," said Hoag. "The Forest Enclave will bear the brunt of the Baron, whatever his action, just as the Plains stands under the foot of Jack."

She turned to Giersson. "In the meantime, it is my counsel you return to your people and warn the chiefs of Jack's release. There is no need to keep the news quiet as your priestess will find out soon enough anyway." She considered her hands on the table, then, "I will send my Thom with you. He may be of some assistance. And we will establish more direct communication lines. The Nordic territories are not so far away that we cannot come to each other's aid should the worse arise."

Giersson nodded graciously. "Any help would be most welcome, Madam Hoag."

Hoag frowned. "That leaves Jack. The Central Plains cannot fight a war with Jack and all his minions alone, even if we could get Edgar and the board to see the truth of the situation and act. We have never been large in numbers, and we have grown soft in our time of peace. We have more farmers and craftsman than warriors now. At best we can resist him for a time here, but will inevitably fail if it comes to open war." She turned to Carlin. "What do you suggest we do?"

"I agree," said Carlin slowly. "The Plains cannot fight a war with Jack alone. But it is clear we cannot count on the Forest Enclave or the Nordic Territories to help either, as they face their own challenges. If Ming is in question…" He looked to Lamprey doubtfully, but sighed and conceded the possibility. "Then anything that must be done will be done by the people in this room. A small group cannot hope to defeat Jack in warfare, but they might be able to address Jack himself, put him back in his cage, or do away with him once and for all. It has always been my belief that without Jack his minions will disband."

"But how can we get to Jack now?" asked Carrie. "Surely he will be building up his defenses."

"Lilith," started Carlin, his face grim with memory. He swallowed, started again. "Lilith suggested we seek out the one called Dun. She believed he might know a way to stop Jack."

"Dun," said Hoag slowly. "That is a name I have not heard in a long time. A legend of a legend." She paused. "Yes, perhaps a legend could help, if he still exists. But the prison is behind the Wall and in the heart of the Baron's kingdom. How will you find him there, Michael Carlin? How will you enter the prison? The Baron is not likely to extend you an invitation." She frowned. "Perhaps Lamprey should take this task."

"As to that," said Lamprey, "the Baron didn't exactly extend me an invitation. I was escorted as soon as I passed the central gates. He has complete control of all the known exits and entrances of the Wall, and he guards them jealously. The only reason I was allowed through and am free today is he believed me a simple merchant. He wanted me to report of his growing power. It is clear he hopes to create fear outside the Wall. Perhaps he hopes we will simply give in to him without the need for war."

"All the *known* exits and entrances," repeated Carlin reflectively. "Are you certain? I found a way through the Wall before, and I may find my way again, and to the prison. As to finding Dun," he turned to Hoag, "I had hoped you might have some information that could help."

Hoag shook her head. "I am sorry. I only know what the legends say. Dun was supposedly created before Ariskant, who you know as well as any. He was said to be that one's equal and a rival, though other tales say Dun was a disappointment to his maker, flawed in some way. Either way, Dun fell out of favor somehow. He was banished or left on his own, depending on the account, and rumored to have traveled to the Baron's kingdom just before the rise of the Wall. After that, the legend dies."

"Then I will seek him there," said Carlin.

Usil Lamprey frowned. "To search for this Dun in the Baron's kingdom is madness. I tell you I only just escaped the Baron because he believed me harmless and wanted me to leave. The place is crawling with checkpoints and spies. Michael Carlin is a name he still remembers, and not with fondness."

"Nevertheless," said Carlin, "there are ways to travel unnoticed, even behind the Wall. What other choice do we have?"

The room grew silent. It was Hoag that finally spoke.

"If you choose this path, Michael Carlin," she said, "than I ask you to stop first at the Forest Province and speak with Sarah. She must be warned of Jack. Tell her, too, Hoag and her people stand ready to work with her—though she may get a different message from our current township leader. I believe she will help you, if she can. She knows the Wall and the Baron better than any. She may even know more of the one called Dun."

"Lady Sarah will only confirm my warning," said

Lamprey, shaking his head. "She will try to stop you. It is no accident that Graëh men were in the tavern tonight—they have grown that bold. If the Baron's patrols find you, at best you will be allowed to take part in his twisted games before you are killed."

"No paths are easy," answered Hoag. "Including your own, Usil Lamprey. Crossing the Blue Dessert to Ming's territory is never an easy feat. Carlin has told us Jack's henchmen are loose again. He will not stand idle while traffic flows uncontested between the Territories. He will try to cut us off from one another. A lone traveler to the Eastern Territories will make a prime target."

"Jack, the Baron, the Priestess," said Carrie. "Any one of which would be ill on their own, but this…"

"We're not without recourses of our own," said Carlin.

"Mr. Lasak's ship?" suggested Lamprey, looking to me hopefully.

"It was never intended for military use," I said. "I don't think it would help us much. Besides, it's stuck in some kind of stasis. Not even Jack could free it."

This raised a bit of alarm around the table, and I had to explain about Jack pretending to be Bill and our initial cooperation, such as it was. But this only raised more questions. Lamprey asked me about the LongPost. Carrie wanted to know about Earth.

Carlin raised a hand to cut them off. "That can wait. The resource I was referring to is with us now." He turned to me. "Show them."

I looked to him for more direction. I had a number of things in my satchel, including Mic and the gun. Did he want them to see everything?

"Jack's stick," he said.

I reached under my cloak, and removed the swagger stick. I put it on the table in front of me.

"Gods above," whispered Giersson, "Is that really Jack's talisman." He looked to me, his eyes growing round. "It is said to be a powerful Magi weapon. Can you use it?"

"Not really," I said. "I'm still learning what it can do. I mean, other than the obvious."

I pulled the hidden blade out, so they could see it. Carrie leaned forward, fascinated, and Giersson asked to hold it. Before I could pass it to him, Hoag slammed her cane on the floor.

"No," she hissed, her face a mask of pain and anger.

The rest of the table looked to floor as Hoag trembled with emotion, her eyes filling with tears. Only Carlin seemed to understand. He put a hand on my arm, signaling for me to put the stick away. I put the blade back in its husk and hid the stick under my cloak again.

"I'm sorry, Benjamin Lasak," said Hoag eventually. "I am not angry with you. You couldn't possibly know. It was another time. That—thing," she indicated the stick in my cloak, "is nothing but evil to me."

She didn't say anymore, and I wondered what further act of horror Jack had caused in the past. Carrie reached out to take her mother's hand in her own.

Carlin broke the silence. "I don't know if we can turn such a weapon against its master without risk, but this was Jack's most prize possession once. It will mean something to him that we have it. I have already seen some of its power." He then described Lilith's re-appearance.

This brought another round of excited questions, but no real directions or answers. No one asked to see the stick again, or demanded I hand it over. They were quite willing to leave it in my possession.

"I have a question," I asked, when the conversation around the stick ground to a halt.

The faces around the table turned to me.

"There seems to be more than a handful of people here," I noted. "So far, I've only counted four—possibly five—of Jack and his cohorts. Even if awakes the whole room full of cloaks, that's only about twenty. I know their tough, but why do you think you're not enough to handle Jack?"

"Jack doesn't fight open wars," said Hoag, "unless he

has to. And he will have learned his lesson from his war with the Baron. He is safe in his sanctuary, where he knows and can guard all the entrances. But he doesn't have to raise an army to regain his power. His way is always through fear, intimidation, and deception. He will send his minions out, like before, to terrorize the Plains, the Forest Enclave, and eventually even the Eastern and Nordic territories. Murder and destruction, that will be the way of it, until the people of the world submit again to his will."

"You say he is safe in his sanctuary," said Lamprey. "But nothing is ever completely safe. Perhaps we should turn the tables on Jack. A small assassination party might succeed where a large one would fail."

"Perhaps it will come to that," agreed Carlin. "Though Lilith cautions against the ending Jack all together. She worries…worried…the world may come apart if Jack is destroyed. It is something we must keep in mind as we make our plans. Killing Jack might not be an option."

The group took this news in silence and bitterness.

The Trepidation, I thought. Someone could take it back to the upper entrance and try to steal back in the way we came out. Was this why Carlin's plan for the ship? If it was, he wasn't sharing, so I kept the notion to myself.

"There is another thing to consider," said Hoag, breaking the silence. "Our numbers may not be as great as we hope. There are many who will choose not to fight Jack. They will try to ride the storm, hoping it may pass them by. And there are others, those who would welcome a return to the days of Jack. Some of these are in our own backyard."

Before anyone could respond to this, there was a knock on the door and Thom stuck his pumpkin-sized head in. "I'm sorry." His face was a beat-red with anger and embarrassment. "But he insists on being let in. Says he'll call the constables if I don't. Want me to toss him on his backside anyway?"

"That would be our new Township Head," said Hoag with a cluck of her tongue. "Apparently he has spies in the tavern. No Thom, we don't need that kind of trouble. Best let him in."

"Just a minute, Thom," said Lamprey, rising quickly to his feet and scuttling to the side door.

"Sorry, Usil," said Hoag. "Thom, give us just a minute. Tell his Lordship he is welcome, but take your time."

Lamprey checked outside the side door, then turned to give Hoag a nod. "I'm off." He caught Carlin's eye. "It may be that we will be traveling the same road for some time if you plan on taking the main pass. My wagon is just behind the village hills. You are welcome to ride along."

Carlin nodded gratefully. "We may take you up on that. What time do you leave?"

Lamprey did some quick calculating. "Tomorrow night. Send word if you want to come. Use Carrie."

"Thank you," said Carlin.

Lamprey waved a fat hand at the rest of us and then disappeared out the door.

"Lamprey's involvement is not something we want Edgar or the Township Board to know about," said Hoag with a meaningful look at everyone. We nodded our understanding.

A moment later and the main door opened. In walked a trio of men, led by a figure dressed in split tails and a top hat. He stood at the head of the table as if he belonged there, as his companions retreated to the shadows behind him. The man at the table looked around the table, pulling his white gloves off one finger at a time and removing his top hat, handing both back to one of his men in the shadows. He turned with a flourish back to us and lifted his head slightly, his thin mouth curling slightly at the corner.

"Well, well, well," he said in a slight lisp. "I appear to be late for the meeting."

XVIII

Lord Edgar Holds Court

"You can't be late," said Hoag. "If you were never invited. Pray, Edgar, what can we do for you?"

Edgar frowned slightly at this, but ignored her. He was a slight man with curly black hair. He looked around the table, his eyes settling on me. He stared for a moment at something near my hip. I pulled my cloak closer, covering up the handle of the stick.

"It has come to my attention," he said, turning back to Hoag, "that we have visitors. As you know, Madam Hoag, all new callers to the Township must have approval from the board." He looked pointedly around the table, stopping at me and Carlin.

"I knew no such thing," said Hoag. "Another midnight ordinance?"

Edgar's nostrils flared slightly. "This has been on the books for some time. Passed openly by the board, under my direction, for the protection and well-being of the Township. Guest are supposed to present themselves at the gate for official documentation and approval. It seems these two have bypassed that regulation." He turned to Carlin and me. "I am well within my rights to have them arrested..."

There was a stir around the table at this, which Edgar stilled with a raised hand. "But as these are *special* guests, I thought I see to the matter myself."

He turned directly to me. "I do not believe we have met before, sir."

"Edgar, this is..." started Hoag.

"Lord Edgar, if you please, Madam Hoag," he interrupted superciliously. "We must adhere to the niceties whenever we can."

Hoag cackled again. "Aye your highness, mustn't forget the niceties. *Lord* Edgar, let me introduce Benjamin Lasak. Michael Carlin, I believe you know already."

"Edgar," said Carlin pointedly.

Edgar's nose twitched, but he didn't correct Carlin. "Michael Carlin. What a surprise to see you again."

I didn't think Edgar looked surprised.

"No doubt you bring more dire tidings and world calamities," he added with a smirk to the men behind him.

"Are you the man to see about dire tidings?" asked Carlin with open skepticism.

Edgar lost his smirk and looked purposely at Carlin. "I have the privilege of being the new Head of the Township and representative for the Central Plains Province. I don't believe that was the case last time you were here. And it is *Lord* Edgar, sir."

Carlin pulled out his pipe and took his time filling it. All eyes were on him. He leaned forward and considered the new Head. "Last time I was around there was none of this township head business, and the Collective Council representative was an elected position, not a peerage. Just what are you lord of, Edgar?"

"Still the same old arrogant Carlin, I see. I'll not waste my time bantering with you." Edgar turned to Hoag. "Back to the matter at hand, Madam Hoag. I assume you speak for these men."

Hoag eyes narrowed. "I do."

"Then I must ask why you are sheltering them against regulation. At the very least, they should have been reported to the chief constable or brought to my attention at the Manor."

"Oh, is that what you're calling it now?" interrupted Carlin, clearly itching for a fight. "Last time I was around, the *Manor* was just Old Bill's Place. What happened to Bill, Edgar?"

Edgar continued to ignore Carlin. "Well?" he said,

staring at Hoag. "I am waiting for an answer, Madam."

"Carlin is no stranger," she said. "You said so yourself."

"That does not explain Mr. Lasak's presence," said Edgar. "Regulations demand..."

"Damn your regulations, Edgar," said Carlin, pulling the pipe from his mouth in exasperation. He stood up. "Jack is free. What are you going to do about it?"

Edgar's reaction was slow in coming. There was the slightest twitch around his eyes, followed by a furtive look to his men. But when he spoke, it was with measured calm. "So, you say."

He looked around the table, obviously in no hurry to deal with the matter of Jack. "It appears you are missing somebody," he said, pointing at Lamprey's plate. "Who was sitting there?"

"Did you hear me, fool," hissed Carlin. "Jack's loose. Call the village elders and send messages to the other provinces. We must prepare."

Edgar raised an eyebrow and looked to his fingertips. "Yes, yes. Alarms and Alerts. Jack is free. Jack is coming to get us all. Michael Carlin has come down from his haven to deliver the news and save us all. Dire news, indeed."

"What the hell does that mean?" snarled Carlin. "Do you think I'm making this up?"

Edgar smiled at Carlin. In the pause that followed, I heard soft scratches rising from one of the shadowed corners. That's when I notice one of Edgar's men was busily taking notes. I suspected he'd been writing for some time.

"We need to warn the people," said Carrie. "The farmers in the outlying areas need to be called in. Surely you agree, Edgar...Lord Edgar."

"Thank you, Miss Carrie. I think I know what to do." Edgar ignored Carlin's scoff, and addressed Hoag again. "If Jack is actually loose...."

"You son of a..." started Carlin.

"*If* it is true," continued Edgar, speaking over the protest, "then how did it happen?" He finally turned back to

Carlin. "I thought you were watching him?"

The sound of writing grew ominously loud in the sudden silence. Carlin glared at Edgar, his face turning a dark shade of red, but he didn't answer.

Edgar blinked in slow, comfortable arrogance. "Do you mean to tell us you let Jack out?"

"You go too far, Lord Edgar," said Giersson quietly.

Carrie was blushing as brightly as Carlin now. Hoag was glaring with open contempt at Edgar.

"I suppose if anyone's to blame it is me," I said, breaking the silence. "In my defense, it was an accident."

Edgar turned slowly in my direction. "Ah, we hear from Mr. Lasak. An accident, you say? Just how did that happen?"

"I don't know," I answered. "That's part of it being an accident."

This answer drew a grim line along Edgar's mouth. "Who exactly are you, Mr. Lasak?"

"Benjamin Lasak," I answered. "LongPost."

"And where are you from?"

"Originally from Chicago."

"I am not familiar with that Territory," said Edgar with a quick glance to one of the men in the corner. The man shook his head.

"I'm not from here," I answered. "I came on a ship."

"A ship?" said Edgar, raising an eyebrow. "From the Territory of Chicago."

One of his men leaned forward and whispered something in his ear.

"He's from Earth, you idiot," said Carlin, sitting down again. "And he's stranded here like us."

There was a brief silence at this remark, followed by the quick resumption of the note taker.

"Michael Carlin," said Edgar, "you seem to think you are in charge here. Let me correct you of that assumption, sir. I will decide what needs to be known. I govern here, not you."

"You mean the board will decide," said Carrie, staring at

Edgar. "And it is the Council that governs the provinces."

Edgar waved the point off. "Yes, of course, the Council governs the provinces. But as Head of the Township Board, I have the authority to conduct investigations as I see fit. This certainly seems to warrant one."

He turned to me again. "So, tell me, Mr. Lasak, why did you let Jack out?"

"He told you," said Carlin. "It was an accident. Jack's vault…"

"A vault you were supposed to be guarding," noted Edgar quickly.

"The point, Edgar, is Jack is free."

"Is that the point, Carlin?" asked Edgar. "How do we know it was an accident? How do we know Lasak didn't do this on purpose? How do we know he is not working with Jack? If he is free," he added quietly with a meaningful look to the transcriber.

Carlin was dumbfounded. It had obviously never occurred to him that anyone would doubt his news of Jack's release, or my involvement. I felt a measure of sympathy and compassion for his evident trust in me, but I noticed Giersson was looking uncomfortably at the table and avoiding my gaze. Apparently, the question *had* occurred to him, as well. Even Hoag was looking at me again, though it was impossible to read her expression.

"It was an accident," I repeated. "I've never seen this place or met any of you before, including Jack."

"So, you say," said Edgar.

Carlin stood up again, his eyes now threatening violence. I put a hand out and restrained him.

"I know this man better than anyone here," said Carlin in a tight voice, staring straight at Edgar. "I tell you, Edgar, I trust him. Lilith trusted him." He looked around the room as if that were proof enough. Then he turned back to Edgar. "You, on the other hand, I do not trust."

The two men glared across the table, Edgar's mouth pressed in a tight line of hatred to match Carlin's.

"I think you have caused enough trouble for now, Edgar," said Hoag. "You should go. This is still my house and no one—not even the Head of the Township—can come and go in it as they please. Thom!"

The door opened, and Thom walked in, his head nearly touching the low ceiling and his massive arms, like logs, crossing themselves purposely over his barrel-sized chest. The pen stopped its scratching.

Edgar glanced at Thom, some of his certainty retreating. He gathered himself together, and when he spoke it was with the aggrieved air of a mistreated public servant. "I had hoped to handle this matter peacefully among friends. Alas, it appears that is not possible. The matter must come before the Board. In the meantime, I order all of you to remain within the confines of the Township until further notice." He looked pointedly at Carlin and me.

"Lord Edgar," started Giersson. "I cannot see how you...."

"Of course, this does not apply to you, Ambassador Giersson," said Edgar. "You may return to your lands any time you wish. I ask only that you use discretion regarding what has been said here—until we have determined the truth of the matter."

Giersson hesitated, then nodded slightly.

"The village must be told of Jack's release," said Carrie. "You must send carriers to the provinces."

"Until the matter is fully investigated," said Edgar, "the board will not participate in unfounded rumor and fear-mongering."

"You can't mean to do nothing?" asked Carrie incredulously.

"Madam Carrie," said Edgar, gesturing for his hat and gloves. "I assure you I intend to say a great deal on this matter, immediately. Good day."

He turned to leave, stopping purposely in front of Thom who blocked the doorway. Thom glanced at Hoag who waved a weary hand. The big man stepped aside. Edgar walked out the door without looking back, his men following in his wake.

XIX

Night Work

Carlin sat back down with a thump, rubbed his eyes.

"That went well," said Carrie dryly.

"I'm sorry everyone," said Carlin behind his hands. "That man brings out the worse in me."

"Edgar tends to do that," said Hoag.

Carlin dropped his hands. "Who else is on this Township Board?" he asked quietly.

"Tully the Barber, and Mrs. Jenkins, wife of the Chief Constable," answered Carrie.

"I don't know them; or don't remember them. What about this constable?"

"The Chief Constable is a reasonable man," said Hoag. "But he doesn't sit on the board. His wife, on the other hand, tends to follow Edgar's direction blindly. Star-struck, that one. Tully is levelheaded enough, but he's not the most vocal man when it comes to challenging the Lord Edgar. I think he's just waiting until his time is up to quit."

"Tully and Jenkins are exactly what Edgar wanted," said Carrie. "He knew we wouldn't let him put his cronies on the board, but he didn't want any challenges to his new directives either. Tully and Jenkins were the compromise."

"Edgar should have been dealt with long ago," muttered Carlin. "His kind always causes trouble. It's not too late to for a coup, I suppose? A bloody one, I think."

The others grew quiet and looked at him with various levels of concern and embarrassment. It occurred to me that the village and Carlin saw the matter differently. Carlin looked up at the sudden silence and seemed to recognize his faux pas.

"Sorry," he said again. "I'm just tired. Of course, we can't do that—even to Edgar."

"You've had a rough time of it," said Hoag. "It is understandable."

Carlin buried his chin in his chest, avoiding everyone's eyes, his face grim.

"So, what next?" asked Giersson, looking from Carlin to the rest of the table.

"First," said Hoag, "Lamprey will have to be told what transpired. He must start right away, as Edgar will try to retain him, if only to cause more mischief. Michael, you and Mr. Lasak had best be off with him soon. There's no telling what Edgar's cooking up."

"I'll tell Usil," volunteered Giersson, getting up from the table. "I can use some of my so-called diplomatic status to smooth out any difficulties."

"Be as discreet as possible. Edgar will have his spies watching. You should return to your home as soon as possible, as well. He couldn't order you to stay, given your status, but he may find a way to retain you just the same."

"We have to warn the people," said Carrie, "regardless of what Edgar says. Especially the ones in the outlying areas."

"We will," said Hoag. "I'll see to that. Mr. Lasak, you'll be safe here until you leave."

"Where is Bill?" interrupted Carlin, looking up suddenly. "You said Edgar moved him out?"

"He tends to wander around now," said Hoag slowly. "He's taken to sleeping in the miller's loft on occasion."

"I must see him before I leave," said Carlin, standing.

"He's not the same man you knew," warned Hoag. "The loss of his wife broke something in him."

"All the more reason," countered Carlin. He started to the door.

"Hold a moment, Michael," said Hoag, some of the iron coming back in her voice. "This is not the time for you to be poking around the village. Edgar is certain to have you and

Mr. Lasak watched."

Carlin hesitated.

"You said you walked all night," continued Hoag. "Let Carrie show you to your rooms. Things will be clearer with a little rest, and we'll think of a way for you to see Bill."

Carlin seemed to weigh this, then nodded.

The meeting broke up with that, each going off to his appointed tasks. Carrie took us to our rooms, dropping Michael Carlin off first. He hardly said a word to Carrie or me, his expression fixed in a scowl.

Carrie showed me my room, coming in briefly to point things out. It didn't take long. The room was small, with a twin-sized mattress, no head board, a rocking chair under a window overlooking the nearby hill, and an empty chest at the foot of the bed. The bed looked to be a bit on the lumpy side, but appeared to be free of bugs.

Carrie retreated back to the door.

"Maybe we can have a drink some time, Mr. Lasak," she said. "I'm sure you have lots of questions, and I doubt Michael has been much company."

"That would be nice. Please, call me Ben."

She smiled, closing the door behind her.

If the bed was lumpy I didn't notice. I was out the moment my feet left the floor.

I woke to someone poking me in the shoulder. I opened my eyes to find Carlin standing over me.

"Come on," he said. "We've got some things to do."

I sat up. It was growing dark outside the window.

Carlin tossed a small loaf of bread next to me. "I told Carrie I'd bring you dinner, and that we needed more sleep."

"What's up?"

He looked me over. "Are you in this thing with me all the way?"

"I told you I was."

"I want to look into this matter of Bill."

I met his eyes briefly. "Are you sure?"

"Yes. Hoag and Carrie can handle the village, but I don't want to leave without knowing what happened to Bill."

I had misgivings, but I'd already committed. "Okay," I said, putting on my boots and grabbing a bite of bread. I stood and reached for my satchel.

"Leave that," said Carlin. "I assume Mic is still in the satchel."

"She is."

"Leave the stick and your gun," he said. "They'll be safer here than with us. No one gets in the tavern without Hoag's say-so, and we can lock the door after us."

I opened the satchel. "Did you get that?"

Mic flew out. "Yes, but I would prefer to go with you."

"Too much attention," said Carlin. "Sorry," he added a moment later.

"Can I at least fly free in the room? I'm very good at hiding quickly."

"She avoided Jack," I pointed out.

"Fine," said Carlin. He hesitated, looked to Mic as if he owed her an explanation. "I would take you with us, but we need someone to keep an eye on that stick. Can you do that?"

"I think so."

I wondered what Mic would do if someone tried to take the stick, but I didn't ask.

Carlin led the way out the side door into the back of the tavern. He was wearing a hooded cloak, and he pulled the hood down to hide his face. I followed his example, and we made our way through the alleys behind the stores. Carlin kept us in the shadows and out of open spaces whenever possible, and stopped twice to see if we were being followed.

The heart of the village was made up of two rows of buildings facing each other across a cobbled thoroughfare. Houses and shops were built side-by-side on both sides of the street. Generally, they were two stories high, the stores marked by timber facades and the houses tending to be of an early Victorian architecture. Some of the statelier were bricked and terraced with gables and peaked roofs.

As we neared the thoroughfare I saw a bowler-hatted lamplighter making his rounds, lifting his long pole and wick to the basket lamps fronting the walkway that ran the entire length of the street. He stopped to chat with a black man in checkered pants and red vest walking a bulldog on a leash.

Carlin walked us quickly but deliberately across the main street. A couple dressed in frock coat and bonnet were talking to a policeman in a tall round hat and blue wool coat. They stood in front of a two-story house. The man in the hat glanced in our direction, but we ducked in another alley before the patrolman, as I assumed him to be, could head in our direction.

Carlin immediately took us to the right and out of sight of the tower guard on the hill. This one was awake, but he was looking out of the village for trouble, not in it. We used the cover of the scattered tree line to similarly avoid a blacksmith's hut and the small cottage beside it. Lit candles were already appearing in the window of the cottage, and the smith was obviously working late, the lonely toll of his anvil clear in the deepening dusk.

Our path soon took us to a stream, which was broad, fast and black, and a moment later I saw the waterwheel revolving slowly next to the mill. Carlin glanced to the hill tower, then rushed to the entrance.

The top half of the mill's stable door was opened, and inside I could see a complex interworking of shafts and grindstones. A large man in an apron was working by lamplight over a workbench filled with wooden cogs and gears. The air was filled with heavy dust motes, and I had to fight back a sneeze as Carlin opened the bottom half of the door and we slipped inside. The man at the worktable did not notice us; no one could hear much above the constant grind and noise of the mill.

"Hugh," called Carlin, loud enough to be heard over the grinding gears.

The man at the work table turned. Hugh was shirtless under the apron, and his arms and shoulders were covered in fine black hair that glistened with sweat in the yellow lighting.

"Michael Carlin," said Hugh, setting his hammer aside and brushing his hands down his leather apron. He walked across and shook Carlin's hand.

"I'm looking for Bill, Hugh," said Carlin.

Hugh nodded. "He stays in the loft from time to time." He looked to the ceiling. "But he's not here now."

Carlin frowned. "Did he say where he'd be?"

Hugh shrugged. "Bill comes and goes as he pleases, and he doesn't say much when he's here." He frowned. "Though, sometimes at night I've heard him talking to himself."

"Can I take a look?" Carlin glanced upstairs.

"Sure," Hugh looked curiously to me.

"Sorry, Hugh. This is Benjamin Lasak. He's new to the village. Lasak, Hugh White."

"Mr. Lasak." Hugh nodded.

Carlin was already heading upstairs.

The second floor was a smaller and less cluttered version of the first. Carlin kept going. The top floor was a low-ceilinged loft with exposed beams and one darkened dormer window. There was a crumbled blanket on a cot near one wall, and a wooden barrel beside it to serve as a night table. On the barrel was a framed black and white photograph of a woman with long wavy hair, and a brass sexton. Under the cot was a brass bedpan.

Carlin examined the sexton and the photograph. "These are Bill's." He said. "That's Nancy."

He walked over to a small table against the wall. On the table was a short-clay pipe, a small mirror, and a straight-edge razor. He picked up the straight-edge. It was stained along the blade. He set it down again with a frown; it was a big stain.

We searched around the rest of the room for a time, but found nothing to help us.

"Let's go," said Carlin with a sigh, leading the way down the stairway again.

Hugh was waiting for us.

"When's the last time you saw him," asked Carlin.

Hugh scratched his head with a thick finger. "About four days ago. But he might've come in when I was out."

"Any idea where he might go when he's not here?"

"Sometimes he walks the village. Nick Smith saw him out near his field's once." Hugh crossed his arms across his massive chest with a sigh. "He's not right in the head, Michael."

"What happened?"

"He took it real hard when he lost his house." Hugh hesitated. "Especially when Nancy left him."

"Nancy left him?" Carlin seemed to find this hard to believe.

"So, I gathered."

"Where did she go?"

"Don't know. It was a bad affair, in the end. Edgar's men had to drag Bill out of the house and down the hill. He kept yelling for Nancy, but no one saw her. Edgar said she left Bill when she found out he'd lost his house. If she did, she didn't stop to say goodbye to anyone."

Carlin took this in, thanked Hugh, and we left.

I wasn't surprised when we started for the back hill and the manor.

The lamplighter had completed his rounds, and the village glowed in soft yellow candlelight. It would have been picturesque, if it weren't for my recent memory of the bloodstained razor blade.

There was still enough shadow for us to draw close to the hill and the stairs without being observed, but there we had to stop.

Two enormous lamps stood to either side of the start of the long hill stairway. These were replicated at every landing. A group of men stood around the bottom of the stairs. A big fellow in a vest and rolled up sleeves seemed to be in charge. He was smoking a cigar and watching the shadows around the hill. The men were dressed in civilian clothes, but they all carried small clubs.

"Those aren't bobbies," said Carlin in a low whisper.

We were standing just behind the last house of the village. Between us and the stairway was nothing but well-lit empty space.

Carlin looked to the shadows around the hill. I thought it looked a bit steep. We might stay outside the light of the stairway, but the climb would be difficult. There was also a fence to contend with around the manor itself. It ran around the top of the hill and looked high, maybe twice the height of man, and something glittered in the torch light along the top—glass, or bits of wire?

"What do you want to do?" I asked Carlin.

"I want to get in that house," he answered, without turning around.

I counted maybe a dozen men at various places along the stairs.

"Should we go around to the back?" I suggested.

"Edgar's sure to have that watched, as well," said Carlin. "Did you notice something strange around the manor?"

I looked to the long house, just beyond the fencing. It was dark, with just one lonely light in a bedroom window, but otherwise looked like any other house.

"The men," prompted Carlin. "There's no one there."

I looked again. He was right. There were two men outside the fence gate, but otherwise the house appeared free of patrols.

"I guess Edgar likes his privacy," I offered.

Carlin stared a bit longer at the men on the stairwell, then turned to consider me. I guess I didn't inspire confidence, judging from the frown that set the bristles on his chin wrinkling. He turned for one more look at the manor, and shook his head.

"There's got to be a way," he said. But then he shook his head. "Let's go."

We made our way back down the street and were soon

back in the tavern.

"Get some sleep," he said to me outside my room. "We're not leaving tonight. I'll tell Hoag."

He left me then without another word. I don't how exactly, but I felt I'd let him down somehow.

Mic came out from under the bed when I stepped in the room.

It had been quiet on her end, she said. I told her about our excursions, including the number of men guarding the manor, and Carlin's apparent determination to get in anyway.

"Maybe I should take a run up there," she suggested.

"I think you would have a better chance than the two of us," I agreed. "Though, I don't like risking your discovery. Let's see what Carlin has to say tomorrow. If he's still dead-set on the idea, then we'll bring it up."

She agreed.

I left her out, but told her to hide if someone knocked. Then I went to bed—for the second time that night.

It was a little more difficult to sleep this time. I stared at the ceiling, thinking of different ways to get in the manor, or better yet, put Carlin off of the idea altogether. Visions of red-tipped cigars and bloody razors kept getting in the way.

Somewhere late in the night, I drifted off again.

XX

Carrie On...

Carrie found me the next morning—well, afternoon—and took be by the arm. Michael was nowhere around.

"Let's find a nice quiet space away from the crowd," she suggested.

"All right."

We took a table tucked away in the corner. A boy soon brought us two pewter mugs of brown beer. Most of the breakfast crowd had thinned out. A few regulars sat at the bar, dressed in homespun with their cudgels leaning against the rail beside them. Two men dressed in fine silk hats sat near the fire sipping wine, and a young couple was busy holding hands in the shadows of the far wall. The silk hats gave us a bored once over; the young couple had eyes only for each other.

Carrie took a long pull from her beer. I sipped at mine. I was tired from my restless night and feared I'd soon have my head on the table if I followed her lead.

I wondered about Carlin. He wasn't around and hadn't left me any instructions. Still, I wasn't too disappointed with my present company.

I gave Carrie a more detailed account of my adventures since arriving, including the Solarium underground and Lilith's demise.

"Poor Lilith," she said.

"Did you know Lilith?"

"Only from what Michael Carlin and parents told me."

"Hoag's your mother?"

She smiled, and I guessed she heard my disbelief. "She is."

"And your father?"

"He died some time ago." She lost her smile.

"I'm sorry."

"It was a really long time ago. I hardly remember him. He was one of the First, like my mother and Michael Carlin"

"The First?"

"Those brought to this world from Earth."

Then it struck me what this meant about Carrie. Though Carlin and Jack had indicated as much earlier, I hadn't made the connection to everyone else. "Carrie, how old are you?"

The smile returned. It was a nice smile. "That's not a question a gentleman asks."

"Sorry."

"Oh, it's okay. Mom says it's not the same back on Earth. I imagine everything here is a bit strange to you." She took another pull from her beer. "I quit counting after a hundred years. I'm pretty sure I doubled that by now. My mother and father had me when they were a bit older—she must be close to 300 years or more now."

"How do you measure a year here?"

"We have seasons, though the change is mild. I'm told the stars revolve slowly from one end to the other. Somebody tried to figure out the conversion once. I think it's a little more than an Earth year, maybe 500 or so days."

I was too tired to check the math on that one. I wish I had brought Mic along.

She cocked her head to the side. "Thom's actually my older brother."

"Hoag is Thom's mother?"

She nodded, watching me with a humorous expression. "We have different fathers." She lost the smile and looked down. "We don't talk about that. Maybe he'll tell you, or mother might. It's a dark tale."

"Sorry again," I said.

She waved it off and took another sip from her beer.

"Carlin was one of the First," I said slowly. "But your mother, she looks much older." I stopped, realizing I was committing yet another faux pas.

Carrie chuckled. "Carlin has aged very well, hasn't he?"

"Not just well," I said. "He's preserved, where Hoag at least shows some sign of her age."

Carrie leaned a little closer. I noticed she had very even teeth and small freckles across her nose.

"Carlin doesn't come down from the sanctuary," she said, "for a number of reasons. Lilith was one, of course; and Carlin didn't like to leave Jack alone for long. But I suspect another reason is the aging. It is clear something keeps Carlin from growing old like the rest of us. We don't know if it is where he resides, or if it is just something unique to Carlin. No one else has been in the sanctuary long enough to find out." She gave me a quick glance. "There were strictures set down long ago against anyone entering the sanctuary without Carlin's permission. He doesn't want people going up there, poking around, in case…" She shrugged, looked down at her beer.

"In case somebody accidentally let you-know-who out," I finished with a grim smile.

She reached out and patted my hand. "You didn't know."

We sipped our beers. I felt the touch of her hand along the back of mine for a long time.

"Some of the village," she continued, "like Edgar, are beginning to take an interest in the upper regions. They wonder about its reputation, why it is off-limits. We know the history of Jack, of course, but many were born after his imprisonment—and that was a long time ago. The fear of Jack is not as deep in the younger generations. Some even suggest what Carlin's guarding is not dangerous, but just the opposite. They point to his apparent enhanced preservation and say we all should enjoy it. I suspect Edgar and his crew are behind that."

She looked down to the mug between her hands. "Most ignore the talk. We live long enough, and the world takes care of us. But many of Carlin's former supporters are gone now, or out of power. He never was one to make new friends. I'm about the only one of the new generations who he talks to." She looked away. "He was very close to Bill for a time, and my mother, but…" She shrugged. "Time changes everything."

I nodded.

She took a deep breath. "You should know that something happened a few years back to turn some of the village against Carlin. He recruited a few of the younger men, and took them with him to a small island on the far side of Burgundy. He needed their help, he said, in an important task. I think it was to find something for Lilith, something to make her whole. Only Carlin returned."

She shook her head. "That was a bad time, for Carlin and the village. He felt terrible of course, though it was clear from his tale it was not his fault. It was around this time that Edgar started challenging the strictures against the upper regions and casting aspersions on Carlin. Carlin can be stubborn and very insistent in his ways. He put Edgar and his cause down, hard—Edgar didn't enjoy the power he does now. It's been a sore spot between them ever since, and Edgar hasn't let the matter die. Now, every time Carlin does return—looking unchanged—he only adds fuel to the fire of those who suspect he holds a secret. If it wasn't for my mother and Old Bill, I think Edgar would have thrown the strictures out long ago concerning the upper regions. What that would mean to Carlin…" She shrugged.

"Carlin is his own man," I said.

"Exactly."

The conversation drifted then to less immediate subjects. She wanted to know about Earth, and traveling through space. She was just as surprised to learn my age as I was hers. I explained about the cryo-traveling, and our own advances in medicine and genetics.

"You must have powerful Magi," she said.

"It's not magic," I said. "Is that what you call it here?"

"Some call it magic," she answered slowly. "Some say it

is just manipulation of this world's power—the same power that keeps us young, gives us light, stars, earth and water, makes the creatures, and all the rest. There are not many who can work with the power. There's Jack, of course. And Lilith, to some extent."

She grew reflective. "They say there is a Magi still at the Forest Enclave, but I've never been there to see. Most are gone now; and good riddance. If this Priestess in the North is really a Magi, that's ill news. Everyone, even the younger generations, remembers K'an Issus." She lowered her head close to mine and whispered, "They say he was a son of Jack's."

So, Jack could procreate. Great. But why was she blushing? Then I it struck me—Thom. Was this the nature of Hoag's anger? Was Jack the father of Thom?

Carrie was frowning down at her beer. Clearly, now was not the time to pursue the manner.

"Do you have family?" she asked.

"I have an older sister."

"Are you close?"

I bit my lip. "We were. We try to keep in touch when I'm home or at a Colony, but it's difficult. It's odd. She keeps changing, and I don't."

She nodded. "That happens here sometimes, too."

She considered me for a time over the top of her hands. "You're a brave man, Mr. Lasak, traveling all that way alone, cut off from everyone."

"I can always cryo if it gets lonely. And, I have Mic. Don't know about brave."

I considered telling her my sister's theory, the one I'd shared with the Lady in the woods, but I couldn't bring myself to tell her I was lazy.

"A Romantic then," she said, "in search of adventure."

"I suppose. I certainly found it here." I looked to my cup. "What about you? What was it like growing up in this world?"

"Oh, it wasn't so bad," she answered. "I missed most of

the terrible years, when Jack was still loose. It was peaceful, I suppose, growing up in the village. Later, I had my own children, and grandchildren—and great grandchildren. There was always something around here to do, to build, or see, or survive."

"Are you married?"

She laughed lightly, her frown and sadness lifting again just like that. "Marriage is not so popular here. I understand it is back on Earth. My mother says in the beginning there were more marriages with the First. But we we're so small in number and so many families were ripped apart in those early days..." She grew reflective again. "After a time, it was clear we were living much longer. It just made more sense I guess not to worry about lifetime commitments, especially when that could mean hundreds of years."

Her freckles danced as she winked. "I'm sorry, that makes it sound so crass. It wasn't, really. If someone loved someone they stayed with them for as long as they liked. Like Michael Carlin and Lilith. There were no ceremonies or paper work. My mother and father had such a marriage. And I understand many of Ming's people still marry. Ming's big on ceremony."

She took another swig. "I didn't answer your question, did I? No, I am not married. Not now. You?"

"No," I answered. "No children, no wife. Close once on the wife, but I guess it wasn't meant to be."

"Who broke whose heart?"

"I guess you could say I broke her heart," I admitted. "Couldn't have been too damaged, though. Last I heard, she was married with three grandchildren."

She nodded. "It was the same with me and my first. It doesn't always take."

"No," I agreed.

I finished my ale, and tried to stifle a sudden yawn.

"You're tired," she said.

"Sorry, late night."

"How's that?" she asked with a curious expression.

I didn't like lying to her, but I suspected Carlin didn't want our nightly excursions advertised, even if it was Carrie. "Just had trouble sleeping."

The freckles wrinkled again, and she considered me for a time, but let it go.

"Why don't you go rest," she said. "I'll let Michael know where you're at if he comes looking for you. I imagine he'll spend most of the day seeing old friends."

"Thanks. That sounds good." I raised my mug. "A toast."

"To what?" she asked.

"To new friends."

She titled her head and gave me a wry, appraising look. I was too tired to be sure what it meant, or act on it if I did. She raised her mug. "New friends."

"And women wise beyond their years," I added with a grin.

She made a tsking noise. "I told you, never discuss a woman's age. Next time, I want to hear more about Earth."

"Agreed."

As I stood to get up, a young man in a constable uniform entered the tavern. He looked around, and then walked directly to our table.

"Miss Carrie," he said, touching the brim of his round hat.

"Conner," she answered.

"The chief wondered if he might have a word with the gentleman here."

"About what?" she asked.

"He didn't say."

She looked to me. I shrugged.

"Carlin's out," she said, turning back to the constable.

"Yes, ma'am."

I looked to Carrie. "I guess I'll go then."

"I'll tell Carlin," she said, looking a bit worried.

I followed the constable out the door as the rest of the room watched us leave.

Carlin, it turned out, was already with the chief. He was sitting in a wooden chair across a simple desk, looking impatiently to the large figure in a blue wool coat on the other side. The only other person in the room was a thin man in a short coat and spectacles. He was holding a small scratch pad and ink bottle in one hand and a quill in the other. I recognized him from the other day. He was one of Edgar's clerks.

The constable dropped me off with a salute and left us alone, closing the door behind him.

Chief Constable Jenkins rolled forward in his chair and put two massive hands on the desk. His blue coat had shiny brass buttons along the front but was otherwise unadorned. He was going bald on the top, and his heavy jowl sported the start of a double chin. But he looked purposeful enough, and he filled the jacket out well. There was power in those big fingers tapping the desk top.

"Mr. Lasak," he said in a deep rich voice. He didn't say anything else.

The man with the quill looked on impatiently.

The chief didn't appear to care. He rolled back again in his chair, scratched at his ear lobe.

"There has been a question of your status, sir," he said. "And, Mr. Carlin's."

"Specifically," said the clerk, stepping forward, "ordinance number twenty-three: failure to document presence with the local authorities."

The chief looked to the clerk, who pushed his glasses back with his quill hand and cleared his throat.

"Yes," said the laconic chief, turning back to us. "Ordinance twenty-three."

"Lord Edgar insists these men be held under guard and their assets brought immediately to the manor," said the clerk.

Talk of commandeering assets drew a deep frown from Carlin.

The chief waited patiently for the clerk to finish, which involved more eyewear adjustment and throat noises. He then turned to Michael Carlin.

"I know you, Mr. Carlin. My father talked about you quite a bit when I was young."

Carlin looked to the man across the desk, his eyes drawing close in concentration. "You're Ted Jenkins boy?"

"Yes, sir."

Some of Carlin's impatience retreated. "He was a good man. We fought together in the war."

"Chief Constable," interrupted the clerk. "I hardly see what this has to do with the matter."

The chief turned slowly back in his direction. "Well, Winston, it does, whether you see it or not. I know Mr. Carlin by reputation. I judge him to be no immediate threat to the township. What's more, he has been here before. I'd say that ordinance twenty-three doesn't apply to him."

Winston blinked a few times behind his glasses. "Mr. Carlin's reputation does not apply in this matter, sir. And frankly, I'm not sure what reputation you are referring to."

"Are you calling my father a liar?" asked the chief. His voice and expression remained placid, but there was a noticeable tension in the air now.

"No," stammered Winston.

"Good," said the chief. "I wouldn't like that."

The clerk looked nervously to his pad. I saw Carlin's lip twitch at a smile. The chief remained as passive as ever.

Winston finally regained himself and looked up again. "But there's Mr. Lasak."

"I vouch for Mr. Lasak," said Carlin.

The chief turned to Carlin, and then back to Winston, raised his hands. "So, there we are."

Winston turned a deep red. "Chief, I think you are making a grave mistake. When the Lord Edgar and the board hear you've let these men…"

"They'll accept it," finished the chief flatly. "Ordinance thirty-six gives me final authority on all issues of township security. That includes who can come and go."

"Thirty-six," said Winston, looking to his pad in confusion.

"Thirty-six," said the chief. "You can go now, Winston. Tell Edgar, I've got the matter in hand." He raised his voice slightly. "Conner."

Conner opened the door.

"See Mr. Winston out, please," said the chief.

"I…I have to go and report this matter," said Winston.

"You do that, Winston."

The clerk turned on his heel and shot out the door. Conner followed him, closing the door behind him.

The chief drummed his fingers on the desk a bit, looking at the closed door. Then he turned to us. "They didn't think I could read," he said.

Carlin was grinning broadly now. "I'm surprised Edgar allowed ordinance thirty-six."

The chief caught his eye. "Part of the conditions of my appointment." He pursed his lips. "And, maybe Margaret slipped it in when Edgar missed a meeting."

"Margaret Jenkins," said Carlin. "Your wife. She's on the board."

The chief nodded. He leaned back in his chair, making it creak. He folded his hands across his belly.

"I like to keep Edgar out of this kind of thing," he said. "But, I would have called you both in anyway. I have some questions of my own."

Carlin lost his grin. "Go ahead."

The chief rubbed his ear, looking at the top of his desk. "I know you by reputation, Mr. Carlin; my father spoked very highly of you. That's why I didn't take Edgar's demands too seriously. And your support of Mr. Lasak carries some weight, too, at least with me."

"I appreciate that, Chief," said Carlin. Obviously, he wanted the chief to get to the point.

But the chief appeared to be in no hurry. "Things are pretty peaceful around here now, Mr. Carlin. Many of us worked hard to get it that way." He looked to his hands pressed against the table. "I like the peace that we've carved out, though maybe you think we've grown a little lax, too bureaucratic. I wouldn't disagree."

"On that score," said Carlin, "things are going to have to change. Did Edgar tell you why we are here?"

"He did not. But don't blame Edgar for that," he added, seeing the expression on Carlin's face. "I was away most of the night and this morning. That's another reason why I wanted to talk to you, and Mr. Lasak—alone."

Carlin and I exchanged a look. The chief watched us carefully. Despite his blank expression, I felt a sudden empathy with Winston.

"Where were you two were last night?" he asked.

"Here, in the village," answered Carlin.

"Both of you?"

"Yes," I answered.

"And the night before that? Mr. Lasak, please," added the chief, raising a hand to Carlin.

"Traveling to the village," I said.

"See anything unusual along the way?"

I immediately thought of the bloody farmhouse. I looked again to Carlin. His lips were pressed in a tight line.

The chief leaned forward. "It would be better if we had an understanding, gentlemen."

"We came across a farmhouse," said Carlin, his voice as tight as his expression. "It was torn up, and there was blood. We looked, but we didn't find any bodies."

The chief measured him for a moment, and then leaned back. "Nick and Molly Ferguson's place," he said. "They had two children. I didn't find them either." He looked from Carlin to me.

"It happened before we got there," said Carlin. "I'd say no later than a day, or day and a half."

The chief studied his desk for a long time, and then turned back to Carlin. "I can't believe the man my father talked about would have anything to do with it, or be seen with someone who did."

"You would be right," said Carlin.

The chief nodded. "I believe you, but that won't matter if Edgar learns of this and gets his hands on you. I'm in charge of security, not justice. It's the Township Board that passes judgement on guilt."

"Your wife is on that board," said Carlin slowly. "And another, Tully, the barber."

The chief nodded again. "They are. But don't let that comfort you. My wife is very proud of her position and believes in Edgar. Tully..." He shrugged. "He doesn't say much."

Carlin shook his head. "We have no time for delays, Chief. This is just the start. You'll hear about it soon enough, but you have the right to know now. Jack is loose."

There was twitch along the chief's jowl as he stared back at Carlin.

"I thought it might have been Bill did the Fergusons," he muttered after a time.

"Bill?" asked Carlin incredulously.

The chief nodded. "Bill's missing, and he's not the same man you knew, Mr. Carlin."

It was clear from Carlin's expression that he didn't believe anything could change Bill that much.

The chief stood and started pacing, the first sign of emotion I'd seen since we entered the office.

"Jack, free," he said slowly. "We're not ready for this."

"No one ever is," said Carlin.

The chief stopped his pacing and turned to us, looking again to me. "I'd ask you both to stay at the tavern until I can settle the Ferguson matter. As a courtesy," he added, seeing Carlin stir.

Carlin retreated slightly, shook his head. "Chief, we can't stay. This was just a temporary stop to warn the village. We have to go."

The two men considered each other, each waiting for the other to blink.

"Okay," said Carlin, reluctantly. "For a little time. I have some things I want to take care of here. But I can't promise we will stay long, and nobody—Edgar, or otherwise—is going to keep us here when we decide to go. This is much bigger than the village."

I thought this was a bit strong, considering.

"Fair enough," said the chief, with much better grace than Carlin. "In the meantime, I would recommend you remain out of sight. Nothing about the Ferguson's, right?"

"Right," said Carlin.

I followed Carlin out, looking back to find the chief watching me closely. He nodded as our eyes met.

"He seems all right," I said, as we crossed the street to the tavern. "The chief."

"Hmm?" said Carlin, not looking at me. "A lot of nonsense about Bill," he said distractedly. A moment later he added, "Don't forget his wife is on Edgar's side."

I let the matter drop.

We reached the tavern.

"I'm going out," he said, leaving me at the entrance. "I'll see you later."

"You sure you don't want company?"

He glanced in my direction, shook his head. "I have to do this alone."

Back in my room, I checked on Mic, who reported nothing unusual. I filled her in on the day so far, deciding I could use a nap.

"The thing is," I said, pulling my boots off and lying down. "I'm not sure Carlin really cares about anything but getting Jack. He's not making many friends."

Mic floated over. "He's still very hurt."

"Yes. I suppose that might be it."

"What's wrong, Ben?" she asked.

"I don't know, partner. I just have this bad feeling. I wish Carlin would trust me more."

She flashed a quick green pulse—which I took to mean

everything would be all right—and went back to whatever AI existential musings she was currently wrestling with.

I lay back on the bed. It had been a long night and a morning already. Sleep came eventually, despite my misgivings. I remember thinking of freckles and smiling eyes, and then the world went away for a time.

XXI

Frontier Justice

It felt like I had just drifted off to sleep, when someone began shaking me by the shoulder. I looked up to find the withered face of Hoag looking down at me.

"Up, Mr. Lasak," she ordered. "I'm afraid trouble has found us sooner than expected."

I began pulling on my boots. "What's happened?"

"They have Carlin and my Thom," she said. "And we can't find the chief."

"What?" I was still muddled from lack of sleep. I couldn't imagine anyone "having" Carlin, much less Thom.

She didn't answer but waddled to the door. "I'll wait out in the hall while you get ready. Hurry."

"Just a minute. You said the chief is missing?"

"It's Edgar's men who have them," said Hoag.

My brain was starting to catch up. I looked to my satchel. "My stuff?"

Hoag frowned, then seemed to do some fast thinking of her own. "Better take it with you. With Thom not here, I wouldn't put it passed Edgar to send someone in."

"Okay. Just a second."

She stepped out.

I opened the satchel, and Mic flew out.

"You heard?" I asked.

"Yes."

"I don't like this news about the chief."

"Do you want me to go looking for him?"

"Can you do it quietly?"

"Of course."

"Start with the farm we passed, the one with the bodies."

I put my earpiece in. "Contact me if you find anything, and keep your ears open."

"I will, but remember the interference."

"Okay. Rendezvous back here in an hour no matter what. Agreed?"

"Agreed."

"Good luck."

She raced out the window.

I put on my cloak, tucked the stick in the pocket, and threw the satchel over my shoulder.

"I'm very sorry you are being pulled into this mess, Mr. Lasak," said Hoag, as I stepped in the hall. "I suspect your association with us is about to become very uncomfortable."

Was she testing my resolve? "I'm with Carlin, Madam Hoag, and those who stand by him. I want to help."

Her wrinkled eyes studied me for a time, then she led me down the steps and out of the tavern, her cane tapping the floorboards in quick, angry clacks.

Outside, just a few yards down from the tavern, we found Lord Edgar and six of his men surrounding Thom and Carlin. A small crowd was gathered around. Thom had a giant welt above his eye, and Carlin's left sleeve was ripped. Both men had their hands tied behind their backs, Thom's with an especially large number of ropes. Two constables wearing dark blue jackets and tall bobby hats with silver badges stood between Edgar's group and the crowd. Another three were approaching from across the street. The bobbies gathered around the first two for a quick conference, looking from Edgar to the crowd.

"I bet it took all of them to get my Thom down," muttered Hoag by my side.

We were in the back of the crowd and moving forward. As we drew closer, I recognized the man from the other night outside Edgar's manor, the one who appeared to be in charge. He had lost his cigar and gained a sling, which held his left arm across his chest. He, like most of Edgar's men, looked like they had the worse of the recent brawl.

Most of the crowd looked simply curious at this point. The next building down must have been a school because there were a number of young faces crowded against the windows watching the proceedings with an equally curious teacher just behind them making half-hearted gestures to call them back. I saw Carrie, then. She was standing with her arms folded across her chest, blocking Edgar's path, her face red with anger.

"Carrie caught wind of Edgar's doings and called the constables," said Hoag in a whisper. "That wouldn't have stopped Edgar long, but fortunately a crowd gathered quickly."

Standing next to Edgar was man in a white smock. He had slick black hair and a polished moustache. He was a bit shorter than the middle-aged woman in a frilly hat beside him.

"That's Tully and Mrs. Jenkins," said Hoag, nodding to the dark-haired man and the woman in the hat. "They got here quick enough."

Edgar noted our arrival and turned to say something to one of his men. The underling stepped briefly in the light. It was Winston. He listened carefully to Edgar's whispered instructions, then nodded and made his way to the constables. He passed along the message in another whisper, and both men turned to look at Hoag and me. The constable gestured to one of the others, who immediately left the group and circled around the crowd to stand behind it.

"My good people this is official township business," said Edgar, "and I'll thank you to return to your homes." He started forward with a nod to one of the constables.

But Carrie was having none of that. She planted herself in front of the constable, ignoring his extended baton and addressed Edgar directly.

"What are you doing with Thom and Michael Carlin?" she called out, loud enough for everyone to hear.

The crowd looked expectantly to Edgar for a response.

Edgar turned to Carrie, but his voice, too, carried over

the crowd. "They are being taken in for questioning."

"Questioning for what?" asked Carrie.

"Trespassing and assault," said Edgar. "That one," he pointed at Thom, "has left my man Hastings crippled."

"His name is Thom, as you well know, Edgar," said Carrie. "And Thom would not hurt a fly—unless there was cause."

Some of the crowd nodded at this, but others looked doubtfully to the immense figure of Thom straining at his ropes. I could understand their hesitation. Thom could certainly hurt a fly, and probably bust a shoulder, with or without cause.

"I have many witnesses," continued Edgar, "who saw Thom and Michael Carlin assault my personal staff while trespassing on private property. They unfortunately fled before they could be apprehended at the manor, but we have them now. I have asked the other board members to attend an emergency hearing, which is where we were going before this unfortunate interference." He frowned at Carrie.

"I don't know what you're talking about," said Carlin, his sideburns bristling. "We meant no harm. We just wanted to see Bill. Is this how the village treats its guests and friends? Used to be a man knew his friends around here."

There was some more murmuring from the crowd at this. A few of the older ones looked to Carlin with recognition and a little shame. The crowd pushed closer.

"Ignorance of the law is no excuse," said Edgar dismissively. Mrs. Jenkins nodded emphatically beside him. "And you certainly did harm Hastings. Is that the action of a friend, sir?"

"Edgar, this is a waste of time," said Carlin in exasperation. "We can settle our differences later. What's important is that we warn the people."

"What's he talking about, Lord Edgar?"

I turned to see Hugh the miller standing nearby.

Edgar waved his hands for silence. He looked to Tully and Jenkins beside him, then continued in calm, patient tones. "I'd hope to spare you all from unnecessary hysteria. At the very least, I wanted to inform the board first. However, I can see there is no other way but to address it now. Michael Carlin has come to our town again, after all these years," he looked to his man in the sling, "and once again he seeks to stir us up with wild tales of doom. Before we proceed, I'll remind you of what Carlin's tales and demands have cost us in the past. Just ask the men and women who have lost their sons and daughters to his vain-glorious schemes."

Carlin's cheeks turned a deep red over his whiskers, but he said nothing. I saw more than one pair of eyes turn in his direction with hurt and anger. Carrie noted it as well. Beside me, Hoag was twisting her cane, her eyes drawn to fine lines of disquiet. The crowd waited impatiently for Edgar to continue.

He let them wait for a time, then turned to Carlin. "Tell us, Michael Carlin, what tale of doom do you bring us this time? Or do you need more talismans for your Lady?"

It was the wrong thing to say; or just exactly the right one.

"Damn your eyes, Edgar," said Carlin, his face a bright red as he pushed against his captors. "This is no time for games."

"I do not think the loss of innocent township lives is a game," said Edgar, matching his anger and turning to the crowd for support.

Carlin, breathing heavy and looking more and more like the trouble-maker Edgar made him out to be, also turned to address the crowd.

"Jack is loose," he said. "We must prepare ourselves."

This had an interesting effect on the gathered township. Some of the younger ones, following Edgar's lead, looked to one another and Carlin with sarcastic doubt. Most of the rest, however, stood in stunned silence.

"No less than the infamous Jack," said Edgar. He raised his hands for silence at the laughter and cat-calls this caused among the ones already on his side. "So, this is the latest message of fear Carlin and his friends would have you believe, believe without question of course, for it is the great Michael Carlin."

"But what if it's true?" asked a gray-haired woman in homespun standing next to Hoag.

"Truth, madam?" said Edgar, standing straighter. "Yes, that is what concerns us now. What is the truth of this matter? The real truth?"

"What are you talking about?" asked Carrie.

Edgar looked down on Carrie. "I'm talking about hundreds and hundreds of years of deception."

Carrie's mouth fell open in disbelief.

"I'm talking," insisted Edgar, "about a falsehood so ingrained in our culture that we have never looked at it closely, never considered its authenticity. I'm talking about the lie Michael Carlin and his associates have perpetrated on the central plains and the world, a lie to protect him and his precious secrets."

A deep, angry grunt made the crowd turn in my direction. Those standing next to us stepped back as Hoag raised her cane to shake it at Edgar.

"You fool," she said. "You have no idea what you are doing."

Edgar returned Hoag's glare, his features composed but determined.

"Michael Carlin fought with us in the Disruption Wars," said Hugh the Miller, coming to Hoag's side. "He helped establish the Village. You weren't there, Lord Edgar. You don't know."

"No, I was not there," admitted Edgar carefully. "But that can be said of most of our new township. I did however, like many here, grow up with the legends of Michael Carlin and the notorious Jack. I learned, as we all did, that it was Michael Carlin—and only Michael Carlin—who was to be Jack's keeper. I believed those legends. I was impressed when the actual man came down to see us. I listened trustingly as he spoke of this or that danger, this or that pressing need. I, too, did my part to support him. After all, our most respected elders encouraged us to do so."

He looked to Hoag, as did most of the crowd.

"But in time," he continued, "I—and others like me—began to wonder why Michael Carlin so jealously guarded the upper regions. Why could others not help in this most serious matter? And I began to wonder, too, as the years went by, why he and he alone *did not age*."

This raised another cry from some of the youths in front of the crowd. They were dressed in striped pants and split tails, with frills on their cuffs and high button shoes. I began to suspect some of these were plants as they kept looking to Edgar for direction. Maybe this street confrontation was not as spontaneous as it first appeared.

"Some of you will recall," continued Edgar, "that I asked Carlin about his remarkable appearance when he was last here, some years ago. I even volunteered to return with him to his sanctuary to see for myself the dangers. You will recall that Michael Carlin grew very angry at the suggestion, and that others," he looked significantly to Carrie and Hoag, "also spoke against the idea. I lost that argument. Now, I think I know why."

Edgar stepped to the edge of the planked walkway, his voice growing more strident with each statement. "Michael Carlin has good reason to return from time to time to our Township, to keep us in fear, to keep us from asking too many questions or to seek answers in places he would have us not go. He wants to keep us ignorant of the truth. But this time, this time he is not the only one to return. This time another has arrived from the upper regions, and he tells a much different story."

There was an eruption of wonder at this announcement. Even Hoag looked taken aback.

"I had hoped to show the truth of this matter to all of you in good time and in the proper manner," cautioned Edgar. "Again, I thought the Board had the right to know first."

Tully glanced nervously at the crowd as it turned its attention to him. The other board member, Mrs. Jenkins, raised her head proudly.

"What the hell are you talking about?" asked Carlin. "What other person?"

"An ambassador, sir," said Edgar. "An ambassador from the upper regions, one who speaks of criminal imprisonment and lifetimes of cruel deception. An ambassador who offers peace and freedom from the long years of fear you and your fellow conspirators have held us under."

"Upper regions? Ambassador?" asked Carlin incredulously. "Edgar, what are you talking about?" A sudden suspicion drained the color from his face. "My god, Edgar, what have you done?"

"I did what any official would do," said Edgar. "I heard him out. I am glad I did so, sir. I know now why you sneak into our homes in the dead of night. I know why you always speak of fear and forbid the rest of us from enjoying the obvious benefits you reserve only for yourself. I know what secrets you hold, Michael Carlin, and I say to you, sir, your deception is at an end."

"Enough!" yelled Hoag beside me, her body shaking with anger. "Enough, I say."

She pushed her way through the crowd. Carrie turned to help her up the steps. Mother and daughter stood defiantly across from Edgar and his men.

"Edgar, you have always been an ass," said Hoag. "But this time you go too far. If you think to rewrite history and hide the truth over some petty squabble with Carlin, I will not stand for it. Jack is free, Edgar! Do you understand? No one is safe."

This brought another mixed reaction from the crowd. Edgar's chief supporters—the four young men in tails near the front of the crowd—tried at first to shout Hoag down, but more called for silence and the youths soon backed off. I heard a few worried "Jacks" mumbled among the back, and saw more than one anxious look directed to Edgar.

"Madam Hoag," said Edgar carefully, sensing the tenuous nature of the crowd. "Everyone knows of your service and sacrifice to the central plains. I do not like to think that you were a willing victim to the lies of Carlin..."

"He does not lie," interrupted Carrie. "And how dare you accuse my mother."

This brought another, stronger reaction from the elders of the crowd. Tully's moustache twisted in a worried frown. Mrs. Jenkins looked doubtfully from Edgar to the gathered township.

"A moment," said Edgar. "I do not speak lightly." He turned slowly to Hoag. "Madam Hoag, do you deny that Carlin has hidden life-preserving effects of the upper regions from us?"

Hoag took a deep, angry breath but said nothing. Carrie turned a dark red and looked quickly to Carlin.

Edgar, too, looked at Carlin. "Or you, Michael Carlin?" he asked. "Do you deny it?"

Carlin started to speak, hesitated, and finally shook his head unhappily. "It is true," he said quietly. "Jack's domain appears to preserve life longer than elsewhere. But this is beside the point, Edgar."

"So, you admit it is true," said Edgar triumphantly.

"That isn't fair!" shouted one of the youths up front. "Carlin keeping a gift like that for himself."

A few of the elders, old men and women in coattails and dresses, looked to one another, some of the recent support for Hoag and Carlin retreating. They turned glumly to Carlin as if to confirm the evidence of his deception with their own eyes.

"Indeed," said Edgar. "Look well. Look at the unchanged Carlin and compare that to the lines on your face or the ache in your joints. Think of the ones we have lost."

Many of the elderly in the crowd appeared to be doing just that, and even the younger ones were staring at Carlin thoughtfully with new suspicion.

"No, it is not fair," said Edgar, "and this deception makes the rest of his lies all the clearer."

"Stop," interrupted Hoag. She looked to the crowd, her ancient face red with disgust and anger. "I will remind you all, Carlin guards us all against the Butcher, at great risk to himself and at great personal loss. He does this selflessly, for you, for me, for all of us. You, young ones," she pointed to the youths in front, "you do not know, cannot know what it was like. We were herded and kept like cattle for his twisted amusements. There was no village, no safe homes or happiness, no freedom of any kind to speak of. We lived in terror of what would come next."

She turned to the others, the elders. "And you, have you already forgotten what it was like under Jack, what it cost us all? If not for Carlin, we would still be under his knife."

For a moment, no one spoke. I saw some of the elders starting to nod grimly in memory.

"So, we have heard, countless times," said Edgar, breaking the spell. "But the days of Jack are long gone, and now we have peace. We are no longer the fledgling village of yesterday, dependent on the few. It is time we free ourselves of the last remnants of that terrible history. It is time we remove the blinds from our eyes and enjoy all that this world has to give. It is time Carlin came down from his mountain of secrets and lift the strictures."

"Shut up fool," barked Hoag. "Carlin does not stay there for personal gain. He stays for us, and I tell you he has paid in blood." She looked to Carlin, her ancient eyes brimming with tears. "If you must blame someone for the strictures, you need look no further. It was I who insisted the sanctuary be off-limits. I did so for all our good. We could not afford to have people running around like children inside that hell house. The risk was too great."

"So, Madam Hoag," said Edgar carefully. "You admit to being part of the deception."

Hoag looked ready to bite Edgar's head off, but like Carlin, did not try to deny the accusation.

"If Carlin tells us that Jack is out now," she said finally, trying to control the tremors in her voice, "no amount of denial or nonsense from you Edgar will keep him at bay."

"You do me wrong, Madam," said Edgar, turning from her and talking to the crowd again. "I am merely pointing out that Carlin has been a source of deception, a lie that has cost our Township a great gift." He paused. "The matter of Jack must be addressed, however, regardless of its source."

This brought an immediate silence to the crowd. Even Edgar's stoolies looked to each other in concern.

Hoag stopped, stunned by the apparent concession. "But, if you admit Jack is free…?"

"Just a moment, Madam," said Edgar. "I did not say that. I said that we must address the matter of Jack."

He turned to signal someone in the back of the crowd, and two strong hands grabbed me by the arms and marched me forward.

"Michael Carlin arrives in the dead of night to tell us Jack is free," said Edgar. "But he does not come alone. Who is this man, this stranger that walks now among us?"

I suddenly found myself the object of the crowd's attention. It was not a pleasant experience. The man holding me was a constable. He was young, and gripped my arms as if I could launch myself at the crowd at any moment. Indeed, Mrs. Jenkins shrank from my presence with a shudder. Edgar's youths looked to me with open contempt. Even Hugh the Miller looked to me curiously.

"That is Benjamin Lasak," said Carrie. She turned from Edgar to the crowd. "He is a friend of Michael's."

It was the wrong thing to say if she wanted to assuage suspicion. She seemed to recognize that as she saw the reaction of the crowd.

"I have spoken with him myself," she insisted. "He is perfectly harmless."

"That will be determined shortly," said Edgar.

Carlin was turning a bright red again. "Edgar, you have no idea what you are playing at. This is just the kind of thing

Jack wants. To turn us against each other while he works to regain power."

"Mr. Carlin," said Edgar, "if you continue to interrupt the proceedings I will have the constables remove you—and anyone else who tries to interfere."

Carlin made a visible effort to control himself, obviously not wanting to miss any of the proceedings.

"Where is the chief constable?" asked Carrie, turning to Mrs. Jenkins. "He should be here if there's any questioning to be done."

"My husband is attending other matters," said Mrs. Jenkins, with a slight raise of her chin. "In such cases, Lord Edgar is acting authority." She looked to Edgar, who bowed slightly.

Where was the chief, and Mic? I tried to raise her with a whisper, but the earpiece remained silent.

"Let us proceed," said Edgar. He turned to me. "We met this morning did we not, sir?" He spoke loudly, so everyone in the crowd could hear him.

"We did," I answered.

"Louder please," he insisted.

"We did."

Edgar turned directly to the crowd. "It was not by his choice, ladies and gentlemen, I assure you. I can reveal now that I had been warned of this man and Michael Carlin's imminent arrival. I also learned of a secret meeting being held in our own township. I found this man there yesterday." He looked again to Hoag and Carrie.

This raised a few derisive calls from Edgar's men toward Hoag and Carrie. Edgar made a show of calming them down.

"Winston," he continued, "please read out the names of those found in the secret meeting held yesterday in Madam Hoag's tavern."

Winston stepped from the shadows and read out the list, including Hoag, Thom, Giersson, myself, and Carlin.

"Bear that in mind," said Edgar pointedly, "as we

proceed." He turned to me again. "Are these—your collaborators—your only evidence of who you say you are?"

I shrugged, which was difficult as I was still being held by the arms. "I have some ID, but it's back on the ship."

"The ship?" said Edgar, turning theatrically again to the crowd. "What ship is that, pray?"

"The *Pelagius*," I answered.

"And where is this ship, this *Pelagius*?"

"Back in what you call the upper regions."

Edgar shot another look at the crowd.

"But I'm not from the upper regions," I added hastily.

Edgar raised an eyebrow. "No? Pray then, where are you from?"

I sighed, seeing where this was going at last. "I'm from Earth."

"From Earth," repeated Edgar over the murmurs of the crowd. He, at least, did not seem surprised. "Do you mean you are one of the First?"

"No," I answered. "I came on a space ship a few days ago."

This drew a clamor of questions from the street. Edgar waved them silent again. "You arrived from Earth a few days ago, traveling through the stars on a…space ship. A fantastic story, to say the least. How is that you became involved with Michael Carlin?"

I described my arrival and the struggle at the vault. Edgar stopped me at the point of Jack's release.

"Are you saying, sir," he asked, his voice rising, "that you are responsible?"

"It was an accident."

"Can you prove this?"

"Carlin…" I started.

But Edgar waved that off with a roll of his eyes, and his stoolies in tails drove the point home with derisive laughter.

"Yes," said Edgar. "Carlin supports your story."

"But it *was* Jack I freed from the vault," I insisted.

Edgar pursed his lips as if considering this possibility.

"How do you know this man was the notorious Jack? Did Carlin tell you?"

"Yes."

Edgar threw up his hands.

"But I saw proof of it later," I said, raising my voice above the rising mutter of the crowd.

"I see," said Edgar, looking slightly put off by this declaration.

I sensed this was not an answer he'd expected.

"This proof," he continued carefully, "can you present it?"

"No. It's not that kind of proof."

"Ah," he said, growing confident again. He gave the crowd another knowing look.

"I saw the man butcher a woman in his private amphitheater," I said flatly.

This stilled the crowd again.

"You saw him?" asked Edgar.

"It was a hologram of sorts."

"Hologram?"

"A moving picture."

"I see," said Edgar. "Like an illusion."

"It was no illusion."

"Well, we have no way of knowing that, do we?" he countered. Then, before I could answer, "Let us turn to another matter. This man, he was the same man you say you accidentally freed?"

"Yes. He called himself Bell."

"You talked to this man?"

"I did."

"And did he identify himself as Jack?"

"No. I told you, he said his name was Bell."

"He denied being Jack?"

"Well, yes. But as I say, I saw with my own eyes later..."

Edgar stopped me again. "Proof, unfortunately, that you cannot provide."

"No," I admitted.

"So, it is possible that this man is not Jack," said Edgar, "But Bell, as he claims to be."

I started to protest again, but Edgar talked over me. "Tell me, sir. That cloak, where did you get it?"

I felt my stomach drop. It was clear that Edgar had planned events very carefully, including my cross-examination. I looked to Carlin. He was glaring at Edgar, his expression one of muted anger and frustration.

"The cloak is Jack's," I answered, seeing no point in delaying the revelation.

The crowd, predictably, grew more animated. Edgar was careful to smile only with his eyes. He gave a quick nod to one of the men holding me. They opened my cloak and found the stick. Edgar took the swagger stick from him and held it in the air for the crowd to see.

"And what," he asked, "is this?"

"It's Jack's stick," I said with a sigh.

Edgar waited again for the noise of the crowd to subside.

"He wears Jack's cloak," said Edgar. "He has Jack's stick. And Carlin comes in the dead of night to tell us Jack is loose…"

He didn't have to say anything more.

XXII

Hole Cards

"There's a reasonable explanation," I said, but my words were drowned by the nervous clamor of the crowd. A good thing too, when I thought about it. I'm not sure how my dream-vision would play just now, but it certainly bent the definition of reasonable.

"Oh, this is really too much, Edgar," said Carrie, coming to my rescue. "You've made a big mistake. Why would Carlin travel with Jack? And you forget, my mother and others know Jack. She's seen him. If that was Jack, she would have said so long ago."

"Lasak is not Jack," agreed Hoag. "What's more, Edgar knows it."

This took some of the fire out of the crowd. They looked to Edgar.

"I beg your pardon, Madam Hoag," he answered, "I don't know that he is not Jack. I have never seen Jack. He could be Jack for all I know. He certainly seems to dress as Jack. He bears Jack's tools of horror. What does that leave us?" He turned to the crowd. "He says he is not Jack. Madam Hoag says he is not Jack. Carlin, I'm sure, says he is not. A very interesting assortment of support. The same people, I believe, who have misled us all these years about the upper regions and who sat at the table in that secret meeting."

Edgar checked the crowd to see how they reacted to his further implications. Support for Hoag was not so easily lost and many of the crowd looked uncomfortable at this last implication.

Hoag apparently sensed this as well. She stepped forward again. "What are you playing at now, Edgar? Will you have me and my daughter hanging from a tree?"

This was greeted by a short yell of support by the youths, which was immediately stilled by an angry hiss from the rest of the crowd and a quick gesture by Edgar.

"My dear Hoag," said Edgar. "I am not playing at anything. I take this matter very seriously. At best, this man represents a dangerous unknown. He accompanies Michael Carlin, a man now revealed to be a liar. He admits to being responsible for the release of one he claims to be Jack. Yet, he comes bearing the attire and weapons of a legendary killer. Why are you so quick to defend him?"

He glanced to Hoag, Carlin and Thom, but the crowd remained stubbornly silent, still unwilling to believe Hoag and the others would purposely aid Jack in any way.

"These are, I admit," said Edgar, picking his words carefully, "unusual circumstances. No one, least of all me, wants to believe Madam Hoag and the others are involved in this ugly affair. Perhaps they have been misled by the clever lies of Michael Carlin."

This went over a little better with the Township. A misled Hoag was something they would consider, at least. I began to see why Edgar was using a public forum. His inquisition was little more than a series of unsupported accusations and circumstantial evidence. He wasn't trying to win a case, he was just trying to create enough bad blood against Carlin and me to get what he wanted. The pressing question for us was, what did he want?

"If the truth is so complicated," continued Edgar "where can we turn for answers?"

"Your so-called ambassador," said Carlin, stealing Edgar's thunder.

"Yes," said Edgar, obviously not pleased by the interruption. "The ambassador."

He stood straighter and turned again to the crowd, his polished persona once more in place. "Ambassador Bell offers a much different version of recent events. There *was* a person recently released from prison, but it was not Jack. It was George Bell, and he has finally escaped to tell his tale."

Carlin and I looked to one another as Edgar confirmed the source of his information: Jack, once more pretending to be Bell. He must have guessed our destination and gone directly to the village, perhaps traveling on the same balloon with the red daemon we'd seen from the grove. Somehow he contrived to meet Edgar, secure his loyalty, and set up this kangaroo court. It was not hard to imagine the lies and promises he used to sway Edgar to his cause. I didn't think he'd have to work too hard. He might even have something to do with the chief constable's absence.

The crowd was more curious than convinced, but clearly wanted to hear more.

"Here me," continued Edgar, waving them down again. "I can assure you George Bell is a noble man of good character. I have met with him at length. I remind you, too, that it was the ambassador who warned me of Carlin and this man's imminent arrival, something that they tried to hide. It was also the ambassador who recognized the stick and cloak, which I saw at the secret meeting in the tavern."

"There's a good reason he recognized them," said Carlin.

The crowd looked to Edgar, some of them catching Carlin's inference.

"Yes," said Edgar. "There is. The same reason you and Madam Hoag recognize it. Ambassador Bell is one of the First."

Carlin scoffed, but Edgar had the crowd.

"Bell's story is a sad tale," he continued. "One not uncommon to many of us. He was separated from his home and loved ones and kept by Jack for his terrible purposes. I will not go into all of his history, I can say, the ambassador was there when Jack was finally overthrown. But he, at least, did not receive the support or accolades Michael Carlin enjoyed—for the simple fact that no one knew of his involvement. Michael Carlin made of that."

Edgar paused. "You see, Ambassador Bell knew the

truth of the upper regions and its amazing power to prevent *all* aging and disease. That was his undoing. In those early days, just after Jack was imprisoned, he tried to persuade Carlin to make the area available to everyone. Oh, how our history might have changed." Edgar shook his head. "But Carlin would not share, and instead imprisoned the ambassador. And thus, Carlin has been able to keep his precious secret these many years. Until now."

Edgar turned dramatically to Carlin. "But now we know at last, we see the real reason at last for Carlin's return. He feared that Ambassador Bell would find us, and expose his secrets—and his worse fear has come true."

The crowd looked to the fuming Carlin.

"Hang them both and be done with it," yelled one of Edgar's plants.

This was not shouted down with the rigor of before.

"Friends," said Edgar, clearly happy with the way things were going. "I would not have that stain, however justified, on our heads. We have always strived for peace and security in our township, and we will not abandon it even now."

He nodded to Tully and Mrs. Jenkins. "There is, fortunately, a better solution. Ambassador Bell has graciously invited members of the board to visit him in the upper regions, to establish a new partnership between the central plains and his land."

"His land," muttered Carlin sardonically.

"In return," continued Edgar, ignoring Carlin. "We merely have to show our good faith by handing over these two men, along with the tools of Jack's wickedness. The ambassador does not want them ever again to fall into evil hands, something we can all understand. He assures me he will destroy them immediately. As to Carlin and Lasak, they will occupy the same cell Carlin once kept Bell in, a fitting and just punishment I think, and one that keeps the stain of blood from our own hands."

This set the crowd to discussion again. Edgar had cleverly dropped Hoag's involvement and given them a quick and painless solution, one that even granted them potential access to the upper regions. There were still a few, a precious few, who did not seem completely convinced, but they looked to the others and kept still.

"I'm not Jack," I said, struggling to be heard. "He hasn't proven anything."

The crowd either did not hear me, or did not care to. But Edgar did. He signaled to his men to remove me. They started to march me away. Carrie and Hoag both protested, but this time Edgar's men stepped in and formed a wall around them.

"Is this central plain's justice?" yelled Carlin. "Is this all we've learned from the past? Will we not be given a chance to be heard?"

"We have already heard enough of your lies," said Mrs. Jenkins, stepping forward. "We stand with Lord Edgar in whatever he decides fit."

Edgar nodded graciously to her. "As Mrs. Jenkins has pointed out we have already heard enough to pass sentence on both this man and you, Carlin. Protesting your innocence will not serve you at this point, and I warned you...." He nodded to the men holding Carlin. "Gag him."

"Well, pardon Lord Edgar, Mrs. Jenkins," said a tiny voice from the shadows.

The crowd quickly grew still, struggling to hear this latest development.

Stunned, Edgar turned to look at Tully. The men pulling me along stopped as well.

"I mean to say," continued the barber, blushing furiously under Edgar's glare, "we really haven't heard his side—that is his side," he nodded to me. "You've only asked him questions."

"Yes," said Carrie. "Where is it written that a man can't defend himself?"

"Nowhere," answered Tully. "At least, I'm not aware of any laws to such. He has a right to speak, I think."

Edgar was so surprised by the unexpected challenge that

he could only stare in disbelief at Tully.

"Really, Tully," said Mrs. Jenkins in exasperation. "Where's your loyalty?"

"Only trying to be proper, Margaret," said Tully defiantly. But he looked timidly to Edgar.

Edgar licked his upper lip, his color growing dark. "Mr. Tully..."

"I mean," persisted the barber guilelessly, "you're always reminding us to pay attention to the particulars. Isn't he, Margaret?"

"Yes," said Carrie. "Shouldn't we know both sides of the story?"

"C'mon, Edgar," said Hugh, "no harm in hearing some more."

Edgar, with a glare at Tully, took a moment to collect himself before turning back to the crowd. "Very well, if it will please the board member, though I see no point in the exercise. We stand to lose a great deal with our new friend the ambassador if this should get out of hand."

"The village doesn't answer to this new friend of yours," said Hoag. This brought about a number of nods from the elder members of the crowd.

Edgar took this in with a frown and then turned to me. "Well, what do you have to say for yourself?"

I stood a little straighter, my mouth suddenly dry. I searched for something to say that would prove my innocence and not sound like a madman or liar. I looked to Carlin for help. He nodded encouragingly, his eyes holding fire.

The silence grew.

"He has nothing to say," said Edgar quickly, turning again to his men.

Then a voice spoke in my ear. "We're almost there, Ben. I heard a bit of this coming in. I have his proof."

"Mic," I said with feeling.

"What?" asked Edgar, turning back to me. "What did you say?"

For the first time, Carlin smiled. "He said, Mic."

"I do have something to say." I turned to the crowd, dragging my two guards with me.

"Out with it then," said Edgar brusquely, watching me carefully.

"First, of all," I said. "I don't think much of your so-called proceedings or its idea of fair play."

"Bah!" said Edgar. "Who is this stranger to tell us...?"

"Let him speak," said Carlin. His voice fell like a thunder clap over the crowd and Edgar. Despite his bound, disheveled appearance and the recent attacks to his character the crowd, even Edgar's youths held their tongue. This, I thought, was the Carlin of old, the Ripper's keeper. Edgar turned back in his direction, noticeably agitated, a blush running up his thin neck.

"I told you to gag that man."

"Let him speak, Edgar," said Hugh White. "You've said enough."

This brought a few chuckles from the crowd.

Edgar looked down his nose at Hugh, then waved me on churlishly. The man with the handkerchief retreated.

"As I was saying," I continued. "I am not Jack. I'll give you proof of that in a minute, much more proof than you were ready to condemn me for. But before I do, I want to ask you a question, Edgar. Where is this Bell, this ambassador?"

Edgar's eyes betrayed him, sliding for just a moment to the manor on the hill. Everyone saw the glance and knew its meaning.

"He's in the manor," I said, making myself heard to the back of the crowd.

Edgar nodded once, tersely.

"Well, why isn't here, making his own case?"

Carlin's laugh was short, brutal. "Yes, Edgar, why don't you bring the ambassador down and let us meet our accuser face to face."

The crowd looked expectantly to the manor, then Edgar.

"This is exactly what I feared," said Edgar. He pointed

the stick at me. "This man means only to distract you from his own guilt, to undermine my efforts with the ambassador and any chance we have of seeing finally the upper regions…"

"Look!" someone shouted from the back of the crowd.

We all turned as one to look down the street.

Riding on what looked like a wooden bicycle, was the chief constable. He was laboring at the pedals, having just passed through the gate. For a brief second, I thought I saw a white orb at his shoulder, but it took off just as the chief reached the first row of street houses.

I turned back in time to see Edgar frown in frustration, glancing from the chief to the crowd to the men holding me.

"Looks like the chief is back," I said, before he could act. "I think I'll wait for him, if that's all right with the Board."

Tully was already nodding. Mrs. Jenkins, with a guilty glance at Edgar, said nothing. Edgar looked from his men to the constables, all of which were looking expectantly to their approaching chief. The man holding me turned to Edgar, obviously wanting orders. Edgar looked to Hastings. The latter shook his head. With a snarl, Edgar waved his men down.

The chief, his coat stained with sweat, came to a stop behind the crowd. He climbed down from a bucket seat, and let the bike rest against a walkway railing. He took a moment to wipe his brow with a handkerchief, and only then turned to the group on the walkway, his expression as placid as ever.

He nodded to his wife and Mr. Tully, glanced at Edgar's men and his own constables, and then the bound Carlin and Thom. He ignored Edgar.

"What's going on here, Perkins?"

One of the constables, a young man with fiery hair, stepped forward. "Bit of brush up, sir, with the Lord Edgar and these two." He pointed to Carlin and Thom.

"Chief Constable," started Edgar, "these men are very

dangerous and should not be allowed to move about freely. But I have—that is the board has—matters well in hand. We are taking these three with us to the manor."

The chief looked to me. "Why?"

"It is too complicated to explain here, sir," said Edgar, before I could answer. "I will send you a complete report as soon as possible."

"He thinks that man is Jack," said Tully.

Edgar went white with anger.

"Jack?" asked the chief, turning to me. "I thought your name was, Lasak?"

"It is," I answered.

"We have already established this man is a liar, Chief," said Edgar.

"Pardon, Lord Edgar," said Tully, "but it was Mr. Carlin you were making out to be a liar. This man was still being questioned."

"*Thank you, Mr. Tully.*" Edgar turned on his fellow board member in such a fury, Tully took a step back.

But he recovered himself a moment later, turning back again to the chief with a smile. "Mr. Tully is quite right. We are taking this man to the manor to determine his status." He gestured to his men, who started to move me along with Carlin and Thom.

But the chief nodded to Constable Perkins who immediately blocked their way.

"Chief Jenkins," said Edgar, a slight twitch playing along his forehead. "You are interfering with board business. Will you please tell your men to get out of the way?"

"Why?" repeated the chief.

"Excuse me?" asked Edgar.

"I want to know why you're taking these men to the manor?" asked the chief. "If it is a question of the law, then they should be brought before the township court for processing."

Edgar stared at the chief.

"It is not a matter of law," said Edgar carefully. "Not

exactly."

"You were accusing me and Thom of trespassing and assault," said Carlin.

"And we will pursue that charge, I assure you," said Edgar with another twitch. "But just now we have a delicate...political matter that must be addressed." He looked to the chief. "You may take Carlin and Thom to the courthouse, if you must. I only need this man." He pointed to me.

The chief nodded, as if thinking about this. He wiped his forehead, and then turned back to me. "Is that all right with you, Mr. Lasak?"

"I think I'd rather just talk here or the courthouse, chief," I said. "Lord Edgar has made some pretty serious accusations against me, and I'd like the chance to address the matter publicly."

"Sounds only fair, Edgar," said the chief. "If you've been talking in public already—and there are no formal charges. No *new* charges," he added before Edgar could speak. "I've already addressed the issue of their presence in the Township—as you know."

"I am the Head of the Board and Council representative of the Township," stammered Edgar.

But he had lost the crowd and the round, and he never had the chief. The latter nodded to his men to release me.

"Okay, Mic," I said. "Are you ready?"

"I am."

Mic sped around the corner, drawing excited gasps and a short scream from the assembly.

"What devilry is this?" shouted an old man clutching his wife to his side.

"I told you this man is dangerous," howled Edgar. Strike it down, Constables."

"Take it easy, Edgar," said the chief. He turned to the crowd and his men, many of who were holding their batons up as if to strike. "Nothing to worry about here. Everything is safe."

"How can you possibly know that?" asked Edgar.

"Because I've talked with her," said the chief with a knowing glance to Edgar. "And she has some very interesting things to say."

"You know this thing?" Edgar looked from Mic to the chief incredulously. "You...you talked to her?"

Mic was now burning a righteous red and sailing over the small crowd. "I am not a thing," she said. "Though, to be fair, I'm not a human person either."

"This is Mic," I said. "She is my good friend and traveling companion. Among other things she is a recording device. Mic, the good people of the township seemed set on hanging me for the Lord Edgar."

Some of the quicker ones in the crowd actually had the grace to look guilty, but most just stood in wonder, staring up at Mic. Carlin was grinning from ear to ear. Edgar didn't appear as surprised as the rest. I wondered if Jack had told him about Mic as well.

"Benjamin Lasak is a LongPost runner of lengthy and laudable service," said Mic, turning back to her traditional white. "He was born in Chicago on the planet Earth. Here is a copy of his official identification, on file at LongPost Central, Earth."

She projected a copy of my ID for all to see in hologram. "He is certainly not the notorious Jack the Ripper."

"A trick," said Edgar. "A clever illusion. Chief, I'm beginning to wonder at your involvement..."

"Edgar!" Mrs. Jenkins turned to Edgar in shock. "What are you saying? This is my husband."

Edgar started to reply, but a look at Mrs. Jenkins face and the crowd convinced him he would have no success in this line of attack either. He retreated a step, his mouth grim with bitter frustration.

"Go on, Mr. Lasak," said the chief. "You and your friend were saying?"

"Mic," I said. She dutifully flew to my side. "Show Lord

Edgar and the good people the ship and our arrival."

Mic turned slightly and projected a tour de force hologram of our adventures since arriving, including the white room and our short exploration of the control room after Jack left. The images were projected above the crowd on the street in three-dimensional detail and large enough for everyone to see.

I studied the crowd carefully. After their initial shock, they grew curious and watched the unfolding events intensely. Even Edgar seemed temporarily captivated. Then Mic's projections moved on to the more recent scenes of Jack and his henchman. This was from Mic's perspective as she watched them secretly outside the control room door. There was an audible gasp as the crowd saw Jack/Bell standing with Ariskant and his red cloaked monsters. Above the sudden gasps rose a single confused voice.

"But that's Ambassador Bell," said Edgar, the blood draining from his face.

"That's Jack, you ass," said Carlin. "And if you don't recognize the monsters by his side, then you are either delusional or in league with him. The red daemons answer to no one but Jack."

"It's an artifice, a clever tool to confuse us," stammered Edgar. He looked to the board and then the crowd. Most were staring at the holograms, the red daemons in particular, and drawing a different conclusion.

"Bell said he was trying to stop you…" he started again, his voice breaking.

"*Jack* was trying to stop them," answered Hoag. "We told you."

Mic was now showing her flight from the strange creature Pesanta. There was certainly more than a seed of doubt now in the court of public opinion. Even Mrs. Jenkins looked doubtfully to Edgar.

"Chief," said Carlin, breaking the spell, "if he really is up in that manor, we have to move quickly."

"But he's not," said a voice from the alley.

Jack stepped out the shadows, followed by two of his red cloaked demons. "He's here."

XXIII

Cards on the Table

Jack, dressed in a dark cloak similar to the one I wore, stood with his hands on his hips. He looked over the crowd with measured disdain, as his monsters swayed in their red mantles, towering over their master like dogs waiting to be released.

I heard Carlin whisper heatedly at the constable beside him.

"Mic," I whispered. "Get out of sight."

The hologram image immediately stopped. Mic dropped and flew along the walkway to the corner of the nearest building.

"Ambassador Bell," started Edgar.

"Don't be a fool, Edgar," warned Carlin.

"Ah but he *is* a fool, Carlin," said Jack, "I'd hoped to use him a little longer, but sadly he's already made a hash of things." Jack sighed and turned to me. He seemed perfectly at ease. "I didn't know that silly little flying contraption could record. Where did it go by the way, Mr. Lasak?" He looked around for a moment, and then turned to the group of us on the walkway. His eyes narrowed as they focused on Edgar again. "Give me that," he pointed to the stick in Edgar's hands.

"Don't do it, Edgar," said Carlin.

Licking his lips, Edgar looked from Jack to the red-cloaked monsters beside him. I stepped in front of Edgar, and met his eyes. I held my hand out for the stick. He gave me a desperate, foul look, as all of his frustrations suddenly found a focus and he raised the stick to strike me.

But Edgar was no fighter, and I saw the attack coming a

long way off. I caught the stick before he could bring it down, and then struck him with a hard right cross his chin. He went down on his back with a cry.

I now held the stick. Edgar's men finally woke up and hurried to help him to his feet. Edgar pushed them off with a snarl.

"You will pay for that, sir," he hissed, glaring at me.

We all turned back to the sound of Jack clapping.

"A whole town of fools," he laughed. "Bring me the stick, Mr. Lasak."

I shook my head.

He turned then to the chief. "You. You seem to be in charge. I would suggest you bring me my stick. I value loyalty. You will find it far better to serve me than to make an enemy of me."

Before the chief could act, Carlin stepped down and moved to the front of the crowd. Thom soon followed. Both men had their hands free again. He took a club from one of the crowd, who offered it up without protest.

"Chief," said Carlin, staring all the while at Jack, "get the women inside."

The chief glanced at Carlin, then me and the stick, and then finally Jack and his henchmen.

"Chief Constable," said Edgar from the shadows of the walkway. "Listen to me. Hand over that stick. You heard the man. We can avoid unnecessary bloodshed. Give him his stick, and let us be done with the matter."

The chief did not answer him.

Jack crossed his arms over his chest, a long stickpin flashed along the lapel of his coat. It was in the shape of a dagger.

"Chief, is it?" he said. "I take it you represent what law there is to the village. Very well. Edgar is a fool, but in this matter, he is right. I will give you one chance. Obey me in this now, and you will be well rewarded. Deny me, even in the slightest, and you and yours will know true pain."

Mrs. Jenkins, still standing next to Tully, was wringing

her hands and staring white-faced at the red daemons. "Bryan," she whispered into the pregnant stillness.

"Constable Perkins," said the chief, his voice as slow and laconic as ever. "Women inside, now. The rest of you form up, front and center."

The constables immediately formed a line across the cobbled street, cutting off Jack and the red daemons from the crowd. Hugh White and a number of the crowd filled in behind them, joining Carlin and Thom. The miller was carrying a heavy hammer now. I left the walkway and joined them as well. Tully the Barber pulled a straight razor and came to stand by my side. We were joined a moment later by Constable Perkins.

I saw Edgar say something to the man in the sling, Hastings, and move with his clerks in the direction of the livery. Hastings stared after him, his eyes drawn in a tight line, a frown on his face. Carrie and a few of the older men took position in front of the closed livery doors. Carrie now carried a pitchfork, and she planted it squarely across the entrance as Edgar approached.

"Shouldn't you be out there?" she asked.

"Move aside, woman," he said. "The government must be preserved."

Carrie shook her head but let them by.

The rest of Edgar's men stood on the walkway with Hastings. They didn't join us in the street, but they didn't follow Edgar in the livery either.

Jack, who had been watching all of this with the same amused detachment, laughed. "So, the village has found its backbone?"

"Times have changed, Jack," said Carlin, bringing Jack's attention back around. "You'll not have your way so easily this time."

Jack looked at the small crowd aligned against him, and raised his hands in feigned worry. I could see his point. They were simple men, old and young, with pitchforks, clubs, and swords, dressed in bobby uniforms, split-tails, and homespun.

"Oh, times have changed indeed, Michael," said Jack. "For one thing, I am free again to enjoy such farces."

He looked to the chief. "You've made a mistake. You will pay for this with your life, as will the rest of the fools behind you." He then turned with a sudden fury to Carlin and me. "But you, Michael and Mr. Lasak; I want you to survive this. Yours will not be as easy as mere death." He looked to the red daemons to either side of him. "You understand?"

There was an unnatural grunt from one of the hoods of the monsters, followed by a series of loud, short broken squeals, as if it were calling to someone or something.

"Ben," said Mic in my ear.

I didn't know where she was hiding, but I was glad she remained out of sight.

"Two more red-daemons are coming up the other side of the road."

"Michael," I said quietly, "behind us; two more henchmen."

"Did you get that, Chief?" asked Carlin, also keeping his voice low.

"Perkins, Conner, Thom," muttered the chief. "Look to the rear."

Constables Perkins and Conner and Thom moved to the back of the crowd.

"I see your clever little friend is still causing trouble, Mr. Lasak," said Jack, frowning at the movement. His eyes danced a bit as he considered the stick in my hand. "Do you know how to use it?"

"Come find out," I answered.

"Perhaps I spoke too quickly," said Jack. "You are a newcomer and have fallen under the spell of Carlin. It is not too late to recognize your error. Give me that stick and I will forego your punishment."

"I saw what you did to that girl, Jack," I answered. "Down in your torture chamber."

"You know my work," he said, his lips twitching in

pride. "Then you should welcome the chance to avoid similar treatment."

"He's stalling," said Carlin, still whispering.

"But why?" asked the chief.

"He's mad," I said, loud enough for Jack to hear me and meeting his fevered eyes. "This is all part of the pleasure for him."

The chief gave me a sidelong look.

"Perhaps, Mr. Lasak," said Jack, smiling. "Last chance. Will you return my stick?"

"Why don't you leave these people alone, Jack?"

"People?" asked Jack. "These are not people, Mr. Lasak. They're property, stock to do with as I please."

"Mic," I said under my breath, "how close are those other two?"

There was no answer.

"Mic?" Still no answer. "Carlin, something's wrong with Mic."

Carlin glanced to the livery, then up. "Pest."

I turned to look in the same direction.

The creature called Pesanta was on the roof of the livery struggling to hold something in its hands, something roughly the shape of a bowling ball. Pesanta suddenly curled in a ball around the object, and rolled off the roof.

"Mic!" I yelled.

"So much for your little friend," said Jack. "But enough games."

He gestured to his henchmen. "Bring me the stick."

Carlin stepped in front of me. "Chief, the stick must not fall in Jack's hands."

"Right," said the chief, his voice rising in authority. "Around, Mr. Lasak."

I suddenly found myself encircled by constables and the rest of the men.

"Stay where you are, Mr. Lasak," said the chief.

I glanced to the livery. Carrie and her group closed ranks before the livery doors, a small group of old men with sticks and one woman with a pitchfork. Mic and Pesanta were nowhere to be seen.

"Here they come," called someone from the back.

I turned with the others to see two more red daemons running down the street from the other direction. Another corrupted wail turned me around again.

And then all hell broke: the monsters charged.

I watched in rising guilt and fear as Carlin, Chief Jenkins, Tully and a young farmer with a scythe met one head on, while Hugh White and three of the constables took on the other. Both monsters seemed determined to reach me and the stick regardless of what stood in their way. Two elderly men in split-tails and vests and a pair of constables dropped back to box me in. The elderly men bore thick swagger sticks like my own.

Carlin was now dancing like a sailor, hacking at one of the red-daemon's massive arms, while the chief, Tully, and the young farmer looked for opportunities to help without interfering or hurting the others. Hugh White and the three constables were fairing less well but holding their own. One of the constables was writhing on the ground, his hands grasping his recently crushed throat. I saw the miller score a heavy blow with his hammer to the monster's right arm. It roared, and the arm dangled uselessly by its side for a moment. It turned in the same instant and reached for White with its other hand. The constables and one of my elderly guards closed in to interfere. I could do nothing but stand there hopelessly, the town fighters constantly shifting to place themselves between me and the enemy.

Turning in frustration, I found Thom wrestling one of the daemons behind me. He was losing. The monster had lifted Thom in a bear hug, its clawed hand drawing blood from Thom's sides. Two men with swords were stabbing the red-cloaked monster daemon, but were having little effect. Just beyond them the last red daemon held a man in each hand, its massive claws encircling their throats and using their flailing limbs like whips to fend off attackers.

The men around me closed ranks as the human swinging daemon started in my direction. Feeling a sudden press of weight at my back, I turned again as the body of a constable, his face crushed like a rotten tomato, slid to the cobblestones at my feet. I stepped back in horror, only to be pushed back again as one of my rear guards fell into me to avoid the other daemon. More men rushed in to fill the gaps, and for a moment I found myself in the eye of the storm.

It was clear to me that despite our numbers, Jack and his daemons were too much for the village. People were going to die protecting the stick, protecting me.

I took a knee, pulled my satchel off, and drew out the gun. Courage, freckled lady? I'm not sure I can claim that, even now. I just wanted to stop Jack.

The daemons pressed from all sides as I stood up. I held Jack's stick in one hand and the gun in the other, but my living shield worked against me now. Every red daemon was engaged by several village men. I couldn't take a shot without the risk of hitting someone.

Then the swarm of struggling forms shifted again, creating a small opening to my left. I stepped through the space and toward the monster choking Thom. A man with a goatee and small sword followed me.

Thom had freed himself from the bear hug, but was bleeding. He staggered and fell to one knee. The daemon pounced, its hood falling back as it climbed on Thom and started to choke the life out of him. A farmer with a pitchfork stabbed at the daemon's back from the other side.

The goateed man started to move around me, but I held him back. I stepped to the daemon's side and struck it with the tip of Jack's stick at the back of its pulpy head.

The stick shook like before, and the electric shock was nearly instantaneous. The daemon let out a strange, unearthly cry and let go of Thom. It struggled to its feet and stood for a moment in shock. I aimed my pistol at the twisting organ in the middle of its head, and fired. An explosion of viscous green gore brought another scream, and the daemon crumbled to its knees. It raised its arms to its head and the raw hole where the organ had been, and collapsed to the street.

I didn't have time to see if it was dead. The red daemon swinging the constables like clubs let out an answering wail, dropped the lifeless constables, and charged in my direction. My gentlemen protector imposed himself between us before I could react. He raised his sword but was sent sprawling by a vicious backhand of the daemon, his body crumpling against the stones like a bag of broken sticks.

Someone yelled. It might have been me. I raised the stick, but the daemon struck me head on like a battering ram, sending me falling against the cobblestones like my protector. I climbed slowly to my knees, struggling for breath, feeling like I'd been hit by a truck. I still held the stick, but the pistol was lost somewhere in the melee. I turned at a passing shadow. The daemon stood over me, his clawed hand raised to strike.

Before it could act, a figure in blue jumped on the daemon's back and one of my protectors stepped around to thrust a pitchfork into the shadowed hood. The daemon let out a squeal and turned, the fork remaining stuck inside the hood. That's when I recognized young Constable Perkins clinging to the daemon's neck.

The daemon ignored Perkins and knocked the pitchfork from its face. He closed with my other rescuer, grabbing him by the arms. The man was vaguely familiar, but I couldn't recognize him with his back to me.

With a terrible scream, the daemon lifted my rescuer up, then pulled him in two as if he were a child's doll. A bloody sling fell to the street in front of me, and then I knew.

I tried to climb to my feet. The daemon reached behind him and lifted the struggling Perkins from his back, then drove its fist into Perkin's face with a sickening crunching sound. He tossed Perkins aside as casually as the others. Two more men jumped in to fill the gap.

I hung my head as blood poured from my nose, then

climbed shakily to my feet, staggering in the direction of the fallen pistol and away from the daemon. Bodies were scattered all around the street, and blood ran along the cobbles.

"The talisman!" shouted Jack over the chaos. "Bring me my stick."

A daemon dropped the broken body of an old man, and turned in my direction. It bunched as if to spring. I lifted the stick between us. The few standing townsmen moved to encircle me.

Everything stopped as a shot rang out. A moment later, the sudden silence was split by a cry. We all turned as one, including the daemons, to the source of the shot.

Carlin stood on the walkway, the pistol in his hand, the direction of the gun pointed at the fallen form of Jack lying across the cobbles. There was a brief silence, and then the daemons raised a chorus of wails, some running to their master, the others falling on those around them with renewed fury.

From the corner of my eye I saw a mass of whipping red cloth fall, then one of those terrible appendages dug its claws in my shoulder, sending me sprawling again with a powerful pull. I smacked the street, feeling something give in my shoulder. The stick flew from my hands and landed in the middle of the road.

The red daemon ignored me and bent to pick up the talisman. It lifted the stick with a triumphant squeal, but stopped a moment later at the mournful call from one of its companions.

Through my blurry vision I could just make out one of the red daemons holding the figure of Jack, his body limp and lifeless across those massive arms. Another daemon, shaking off a trio of attackers, soon joined the first and they both raised a despondent wail.

The one nearest me answered in kind.

"The stick," I said, reaching out hopelessly in the direction of the daemon.

But my voice was little more than a whisper; no one could hear me above the red daemons wails.

Carlin fired again, and I saw one of the red daemons around Jack flinch. I turned my head in the direction of Carlin, wanting to warn him about the stick.

"Carlin..."

"I'm coming, Ben," said a familiar voice in my ear.

"Mic."

My vision blurred again.

Then someone threw a ball of white fire down the hood of the stick-caring daemon. It stumbled back with a scream, reeling like a drunk man in my direction.

The skyline grew dark with blood, and the world crashed around me. Everything went away.

XXIV

Picking Up the Discards

I woke in a strange bed, the fragments of a bad dream racing away. Disoriented, I looked to a plastered ceiling. Then the pain hit. I looked down to find my shoulder bound in a sling, felt my nose and head on fire.

"Easy," said a voice at the end of the bed. "Take your time."

Carlin was sitting in a hard chair, puffing like a steam engine on his pipe, an old carpetbag at his feet. His face looked like a well-tenderized piece of meat and his head was wrapped in a bandage.

He gave me a careful once over. "Do you remember where you are?"

"Michael," I said, my voice as rough as my head.

He nodded. "You've been in and out for a day now. I think you struck your head on the street when daemon fell on you."

I tried to sit up. Carlin stood and helped me, putting his pipe down to pour me a cup of water from a pitcher on the bedtable. He held the cup to my lips while I sipped.

"The battle? Jack?" I asked, when I'd quenched my thirst. "What happened?"

He sat again in his chair, puffed away for a time on his pipe. When he pulled it from his mouth, he met my eye. "You stepped up nicely, Mr. Lasak. I confess, I didn't know you had it in you."

I looked down. I was shirtless under the sheet, my body a mass of bruises and abrasions. It felt odd to have Carlin address me this way. I hadn't planned any of my actions in the fight. I wasn't sure I deserved the compliment.

"You got him," I said, raising my eyes again. "You got Jack."

Carlin shook his head. "No, I don't think so. I hit him, yes—and that was a lucky shot; I was aiming for the daemon next to him. But I don't think Jack is dead."

He sighed, waved the smoke from his head. "Maybe that's for the best. The world's still in place."

I started to nod, then stopped at the pain. "I suppose there's that."

I watched Carlin tap the ash out of his pipe, reload it. He seemed different now, more tempered.

"Mic?" I asked quietly, holding my breath. "Is she…?"

"I'm here, Ben," said a voice from the corner of the room. She flew over to settle by my head. She seemed somehow smaller, almost fragile, her coloration speckled like a bird.

"She's been keeping watch," said Carlin.

"That was you," I asked. "The ball of fire at the end?"

"You were in trouble. I assumed my most intense form."

"How did you get free of Pesanta?" I asked, looking to Mic.

"Carrie found us behind the livery and drove it off with a pitchfork. It got away in the confusion though."

The speckles burned briefly against the soft eggshell blue background. There was something about the slight hesitation in her revolutions.

"I'm glad you are all right."

The revolutions accelerated a beat, the speckles briefly retreating.

I turned back to Carlin.

"What," I asked slowly, "was the damage? Who did we lose?"

A bit of the old glum Carlin returned, and he looked away. "Too many."

"Thom, Carrie, Hoag…the chief?" I asked.

"Thom's recovering in the room next door," answered Carlin, "as much from the shock at meeting something bigger than him as the beating he took. Carrie came out of this without a scratch, as did everyone in the livery. Hoag is okay, too. The chief's got a nasty cut on his arm but he's already up and about and seeing over the defenses. We had a long talk," added Carlin with a grim smile.

I turned to Mic. "I'm glad you found him. Was he at the farm?"

"Yes," she said. "Someone had told him where the bodies might be, suggested he look there."

"Someone?" I asked.

"Mrs. Tully," said Carlin, scowling. "On directions from Edgar. As I said, the chief and I had a long talk."

"What will happen to her?"

He shrugged. "That's their business."

"I suppose that's the end of *Lord* Edgar, at least."

Carlin snorted. "Hardly. He's off licking his wounds, but he's not beaten, yet."

"What can he do?"

"Edgar's still technically the Council Head."

"But he supported Jack. He hid in the livery."

"He's having his people put it about that Jack tricked him," said Carlin. "He says he used his men in the battle—a sacrifice he calls it. If I know Edgar, he'll wait until enough time has passed, then waltz back into the thick of things."

I remembered the bloody sling on the cobblestones. "They weren't all bad."

"No," said Carlin thoughtfully. "That Hastings was all right. I'd like to have had a few words with him outside Edgar's control. Shame."

"At least the chief sees through Edgar now," I said.

Carlin nodded. "That's true. He's fortifying the front gate, and closing the gaps as we speak. The village and plains can't fight an open battle with Jack for long, but they'll not be caught off guard again." He leaned back, tucked a thumb in his vest pocket. "There is some more good news in that direction. Hoag and Carrie have been appointed Defense Councilors, with full authority over the village defenses. Edgar is completely out of it."

"Good for them," I said.

"Yes." He leaned back in his chair, and waved his pipe stem between us. "What's more, we are now, officially, friends of the village."

He seemed slightly amused by the idea.

"So, what now?"

"We go on with the plan. Giersson is on his way to warn his people. Lamprey will seek out Ming. Jack won't catch anyone by surprise."

"No, I mean for us. What's next?"

He looked to my arm. "You rest."

"And you?"

He tapped his pipe out on his boot again. "Hoag and Carrie have asked me to stay a day or two, to help with the defenses. I will, because I still want to find out what happened to Bill. I don't like that Jack was staying in that house. He was smart enough to keep the daemons hidden from Edgar, but that wouldn't stop him from doing harm."

"Won't Edgar be up there now?"

"Then I'll have the pleasure of running Edgar out."

"I don't imagine he'll just let you do that."

He shrugged. "It's Bill's home," he repeated stubbornly. "Ordinances and boards and Lords can go to hell."

I didn't point out this might affect our *friends of the village* status. I liked this new, more temperate Carlin and didn't want to chase away it with sobering practicalities. Instead, I returned to my original concern.

"And after Bill?" I asked.

"We find Dun."

I shifted carefully. "Okay. When do we travel?"

Carlin gave me a long look around his pipe. "You've

done your part, Ben, as has Mic."

"That's not what I asked."

"If it is a fight you want," he answered, looking down, "there will be plenty of it here soon enough. Carrie and Hoag could use both of you. Jack was wounded, and one of his henchmen—two if you count the one who fell from the *Trepidation*—are dead. He couldn't have expected that. He's lost the first round and the element of surprise, and he knows the village doesn't fear him. My guess, he will marshal his forces for a time and when he comes again it will be all out war. And don't forget Edgar. Someone has to keep him in check, as well."

I met his eyes. "I was standing beside you that day, Michael. Lilith told us both to seek out Dun. I'm going with you."

"And I'm with, Ben," said Mic, moving to Carlin.

Carlin looked to us both. "Are you certain?

"I am."

"We are," corrected Mic.

He took a deep breath, and broke into a smile. The biggest I'd seen yet. "Good. Then we'll leave as soon as you're well enough to travel."

I sank back in the bed, relieved. "And you won't try to sneak away without us? Like you did with Thom for the manor?"

"I won't," he said, blushing slightly. "In truth, I'm happy to have you with me. I only asked because Hoag offered to give you a place here if you wanted."

He looked to me again, and I shook my head.

"That's settled then," he said.

"It's dead then, the daemon I shot?" I asked.

He nodded. "I don't think anyone has ever killed a daemon before."

"The head," I said. "You have to hit that organ on its head."

He caught my eye as he lit his pipe again. "Good to know."

"What happened to the rest?"

"They dragged Jack off and retreated for the plains."

We spent a few moments talking of our plans, until Carlin caught me yawning, and brought things to a close.

"One more thing," I said, before he could leave. It had been on my mind since I awoke, but I'd put it off as long as I could.

"Perkins," I said. "What happened to him?"

Carlin's face fell. He shook his head.

Young Constable Perkins.... He didn't know me from Adam, but he had jumped on that monster's back without a second thought. I thought of the old man in tails, the bloody sling. I didn't ask about the others. I didn't want to hear the answers. It was enough for now; too much.

"Get some rest," said Carlin quietly, watching me closely. "You need it."

"What I need, is a shot of something aged..." I sat up quickly, despite the pain, the blood draining from my face. "Michael. Jack's stick. I lost it."

Carlin waved me down again. He pulled the stick from the carpet bag. "The daemon dropped it. We can thank Mic for that, as well."

I looked to Mic, who came to hover near my hand. I opened it up and she settled in my palm, warm and alive like a newly fallen star.

Carlin handed the stick to me. "This belongs to you now. Let's find another name for it."

Here ends Book I

The adventures of Lasak, Carlin and Mic continue in *My Ripper's Keeper: Book Two of the LongPost Chronicles.*

Made in the USA
Middletown, DE
29 September 2021